80AD
The Hammer of Thor

(Book 2)

Aiki Flinthart

ISBN-13: 978-0-9945660-3-4
Computing Advantages & Training P/L

Discover other titles by Aiki Flinthart at: http://aikiflinthart.weebly.com/

Cover Art by : Jason Seabaugh

Review:
"This story is very unique. The premise is immensely entertaining. It's a great story!".......Chilli Tween Reads October 31st 2011

NOTE: this series is written with the young adult agegroup in mind. Having said that, thousands of adults have read and enjoyed them as well. Please bear this in mind when reading and leaving feedback.

80AD

Level Two

The Hammer of Thor

LONG BAIYU

Curled in shadow and huddled against pain, Long Baiyu waited. Where once he had waited in fear; without hope or strength; now he had hope, at least. Hope that his meagre efforts had been rewarded; hope that deliverance was on its way; hope that the reign of terror and power held by his nemesis would soon be over.

Sometimes, however, a little hope can be almost as painful as none at all.

The door to his cell flew open, crashing against grey stone. Silhouetted there was the man Baiyu least wished to see: his captor; his enemy; his oldest friend, Feng Zhudai. Raising a heavy head, Baiyu blinked in the feeble candlelight. His gaoler knew better than to bring anything brighter.

"What do you want?" Baiyu's voice was hoarse from lack of use; his throat dry; lips cracked with cold.

For several moments Zhudai simply stood in the doorway, his face hidden in shadow. Candlelight gleamed off rich gold embroidery on his silken robes. The sound of his harsh breathing echoed in the cold stone chamber. Finally, he took a hasty step into the room and lifted the candle. His skin was taut with anger, cheeks hollow, dark eyes fiery with glittering intelligence and barely-hidden rage.

"What have you done?" Anger snapped through his voice, lashing at his prisoner.

Baiyu flinched, blinked again but said nothing. Zhudai made a noise of frustration and stepped closer. Hope surged in Baiyu. He gathered his strength. Did he have enough to defeat his enemy and escape? Only let him come a few paces nearer. Even if he died trying, it would be better than this endless imprisonment. Death would ensure the end of his captor's plans. Zhudai needed him alive.

That flicker of hope must have shown in his eyes. His keeper stopped and glared at him before backing away again.

"Oh no, old friend," he said more calmly, "you won't trick me that easily. I have just come to tell you that your little scheme will not work."

"What scheme is that?" Baiyu tried hard to sound indifferent but disappointment tightened his throat.

"I felt your pitiful attempt at magic." Zhudai sneered. "Felt it and tracked it down. You tried to draw help from another realm but you failed. They have been destroyed. You are still my prisoner and you will not escape. In time, you will be the instrument of my success – whether you agree or not."

Baiyu fought his own internal battle. His long incarceration had drained much from him. It was too easy to believe his last strength had failed and the help he had sought was not coming. The dark hole of despair beckoned.

No. A small part of him fought back.

He had felt their success.

His masters' words returned to him: he who speaks, does not know; he who knows, does not speak. If Zhudai had killed them then he would not have bothered to ask what Baiyu had done; would not have been so enraged. No, they lived.

Realising this, Baiyu was tempted to gloat; to throw the logic back in his blood brother's face but that would be stupid. He who knows, does not speak... Let Zhudai think he had broken his prisoner at last. Let him become careless in his arrogance. Perhaps that would allow the rescuers he had drawn into this world a chance to succeed again.

CHAPTER ONE

Jade opened her eyes to an uneasy world of greys and blacks; of unidentifiable shapes and soft, sighing sounds. She lay on her stomach, awkwardly sprawled on something cold, slippery and hard. Her right knee ached like she'd knocked it and her right hand stung.

"Hello?" Her voice seemed muffled. Something cold and wet feathered across her cheek. She touched her face with numb fingers and shivered. "Phoenix?"

The darkness eased somewhat. Perhaps her eyes were adjusting. Around her patches of light and shadow shifted and swam. It was difficult to tell where the ground ended and the rest of the world began.

She gathered her feet beneath her and staggered upright. Shaking, she pulled the hood of her cloak up and tucked half-frozen fingers into her armpits to warm them. Her backpack slipped off her shoulder, dragging at her arm. As she took an uncertain step, her foot kicked something long and wooden: her quarterstaff. Snatching it up, she tried to feel more secure.

Was she alone here? Wherever this was, it certainly wasn't home. She tried to hold back a rising sense of betrayal. She'd been so certain that finishing Level One would catapult her home again. It hadn't. This wasn't her England. In fact, it probably wasn't England at all.

A wolf howled: distant; mournful; eerie.

Definitely not England.

Sharp, fitful breezes stung her eyes. Jade blinked and scrubbed a hand over her face, trying to hold back bitter tears of disappointment. She just wanted to go home.

For the hundredth time in the last five days, she wished

she'd never turned her father's computer on; never been drawn into this bizarre digital world; wished that she was home again in her warm house with her six annoying sisters. She missed her father; her own, warm, comfortable bed - and hot showers!

Roaming the 80AD world sounded awesome - when she was watching her avatar on a flat screen from the comfort of her father's study. Living it was a whole different thing. Her scared thirteen year old mind was trapped inside the digital body and memories of a seventeen year old half-elf in a strange time and place. She'd been nuts to think living the adventures she'd always read about in books would be romantic and exciting. Right now, the most awesome thing she could think of to see would be the giant golden arches of a MacDonalds restaurant - or her very own bathroom.

The ground crunched as she stamped her feet to warm them. More cold, fluffy stuff fell on her face and Jade at last realised what it was: snow. A wolf howled again, closer; a primeval sound that echoed strangely and made the hairs on the back of her neck rise up. Dark forms around her resolved into trees. She was in a snowy, dark forest somewhere. Well, that didn't help much. How could it be snowing at night when it had been a clear spring dawn in the ancient Britain they had just left?

The last thing she remembered was jumping through the portal from Stonehenge in a desperate attempt to escape a horde of Roman soldiers and their ambitious governor, Agricola. She'd thought the portal was going to get her home but it must have brought her to Level Two of the game, instead. If that was right then home was still a long way off – four more Levels, in fact.

So, if she was on Level Two, where were Phoenix and the others?

A low moan to her left sent her in that direction, feeling her way carefully. A dark lump in the snow moaned again. Her hands touched leather and steel.

"Phoenix?"

He moaned again.

"Phoenix!"

She dropped to her knees. He lay face down in the snow, his skin cold, pulse a bare thread. She ran her hands over him, using her Spellweaver skills to try and sense injuries. He had fought the Romans until the last to give the rest a chance to get through the portal. Had he been wounded?

Her seeking fingers touched wood. She gasped. Two arrows protruded from his back, very close to his heart by the feel of them. Her instinct was to yank them out but she took her hand away. She had fought the Romans with as much magic as she could. If she pulled them out now, she didn't have the strength to Heal such deep wounds quickly. He would die. His only chance was if they could find shelter and warmth. She needed food and her herbs to replenish enough strength to save him.

She needed help.   Where were the others?

"Oh, my head!" A voice behind made her turn.

"Marcus!" She hurried over, slipping in the deepening snow. Strong hands grasped hers. Jade sobbed in relief, clutching at them like a lifeline. "Are you ok?"

"Yes - just a headache bad enough to kill a god. Where are we?" The Roman boy sounded pained.

Another, smaller figure joined them. "Somewhere dark, wet and way too cold," it said, helpfully.

"Brynn!" She hugged him, feeling how thin and small he was beneath his patched clothes. "Where's Truda?"

"I'm here," the young redheaded girl piped up. "It's awful cold here."

She wrapped her too-big druid cloak tighter about herself. A flurry of wind and snow snatched the hood off her face. In the gloom, her big blue eyes were dark holes in a white oval.

Jade grabbed Marcus' hand and hauled him upright. "Phoenix has been hurt. We need to find shelter or he's going to die."

"Show me," Marcus ordered.

She led them to their fallen friend. Marcus felt his pulse for a long moment.

He shook his head, barely visible in the dim light. "It's too late, Jade. His heart has stopped. He's gone. Phoenix is dead."

"No!" Shoving him aside she dropped to the cold ground.

Her hands shook with fear and cold as she felt Phoenix's jugular. Nothing. Leaning down, she placed her ear against his back, listening hard for breath or heart sounds. Still nothing.

"No," she whispered again.

Yanking the arrows out, she put her fingertips to the wounds. There was no bleeding.

Marcus was right. His heart had stopped.

She shoved Phoenix over onto his back, trying to remember her CPR classes from school. Laying her hands over his heart, she pushed down as hard as she could, over and over, counting aloud. One, two three. One two three. Tears dripped down her cheeks and froze into little icicles on her chin. Every once in awhile, she stopped to force a breath into his cold lips or to feel for a pulse. The others stood around in awkward, breathless silence; not really understanding her actions.

Pump; pump; pump.

Nothing.

Again.

Still nothing.

"Live, you idiot! Breathe!" she yelled, thumping his chest in frustration. "You can't die on me now, Phoenix! You can't leave me here alone!"

A warm hand covered hers. She looked blearily into

Marcus' grim face.

"He's gone, Jade," the Roman murmured, his eyes dark with pain. "Even if you started his heart again, he would just bleed to death if you can't heal him. Can you?"

Numbly, she shook her head.

She slumped, covering her face, unable to believe it. "He can't be dead, Marcus. He can't be. What am I going to do? If he's gone then I can't go home, either. I…I…" She ran out of words as her throat closed up with tears and disbelief.

Marcus drew her to her feet and held her. Brynn and Truda gathered close, adding their small bodies to the warmth and shared sorrow.

"He died a warrior's death. It will be alright," Marcus said at last, stroking her hair.

Jade blinked, brushing freezing tears from her cheeks. How could he say that? A warrior's death? What was the use of that? Dead was dead. It wouldn't be alright. He didn't understand. Phoenix was a real person, like her. What had happened to his body in the real world? What would happen to her now? Her only connection to her world was gone. She would be stuck here forever. It wasn't supposed to be like that. She was already supposed to be home. What was she going to do? How could she survive this place on her own? What about her real life? What about her family and Phoenix's?

With Phoenix gone there was no way she could stop Feng Zhudai and save both worlds. This world and her own would be destroyed if Zhudai succeeded in his ultimate plan. They had been drawn here together. They were supposed to stop Zhudai – together. It wasn't supposed to be like this!

Fresh tears burned her cold cheeks. She turned from Marcus to stare blindly into the dark forest, feeling helpless and very young. Without Phoenix, it just couldn't be done. Zhudai would win. She would die here too and never see her father again.

"Jade," Marcus spoke again, gently. "I know this is tough but we need your help. If we don't get out of this cold we'll all die. The wind and snow is picking up. We need to get into shelter. Can you see any nearby?"

Taking a long, slow breath, she tried to get hold of herself. Here, it wasn't possible to curl up in a ball of misery and hide like she did at home. People depended on her here. Marcus was right, she couldn't let them down. They were all she had now. Pushing aside grief for later, she extended her half-Elven senses to penetrate the gloom.

"There." She pointed off to the left. "I think there's a little hut through the trees."

Brynn looked toward it, shoulders hunched and face turned from the freshening winds. "I'll go check it out."

A wolf called. Its desolate cry was answered by another, somewhere very close. Truda pressed herself into Jade's leg.

"I don't like wolves," she whispered.

Jade closed her eyes, listening to the shadowy forest. "They're closing in on us; a pack of ten. They're starving and desperate or they'd never come near humans. Marcus, we have to get to that hut fast." She looked at him then down at Phoenix's still form. "But Phoenix… we…we can't leave him here. Help me lift him. Brynn, stay with us."

Marcus handed Phoenix's sword to Brynn. The boy grasped it gingerly, struggling to hold its weight up. Marcus sheathed his own weapon and bent down. With a grunt of effort, he picked Phoenix's body up in a fireman's carry over his shoulders.

"Let's go. I can't carry him far." He groaned. "He must weigh three hundred libra!"

Jade snatched up Phoenix's backpack and slung it over her shoulder, staring into the darkness around them. She pushed Truda in front of her. Brynn lead the way, sword raised as high as he could lift it.

A low-pitched, snarling rose from the shadows to their right, making the hairs on the back of Jade's neck tingle. Truda whimpered. Another snarl came from the left. A ghostly, grey shape drifted through the trees, pacing, watching. A second appeared; a third. They slipped closer, ever closer.

"Faster, Marcus," Jade urged.

"Which way?"

"A bit to your left," she said. "About another twenty or so paces."

From the corner of her eye, she saw movement. A huge she-wolf sprang from behind. With a cry of warning Jade spun, swinging her quarterstaff in a defensive arc. The tip connected solidly with exposed canine ribs. The wolf yelped, twisted in midair to snap at the staff then landed and backed away with a snarl.

Another wolf rushed, snapping at her heels. She jabbed backwards, catching it across the sensitive nose. It yipped and retreated. Snarling and biting at each other the dogs closed ranks, keeping apace with the humans as they ran.

Jade reached within herself, searching for reserves of magic she could use against them to buy some time. There were none. She had exhausted herself escaping from the Romans and helping the druids at Stonehenge. It was a miracle she even stayed on her feet.

"Almost there!" Brynn called, catching hold of Truda's hand as the child stumbled in the snow.

Marcus staggered to the door of the hut and pushed at it with a foot. It was locked.

"I'll have to break it down."

"Then we won't be able to close it again. Move over." Brynn shouldered the Roman, completely failing to shift him.

Marcus stepped aside, lowering Phoenix to the cold

ground.

The boy-thief crouched down, peering closely at the door. "Give me a little time and I'll get this open."

"Marcus!" Jade tried to watch all the wolves at once as they slowly closed in on their intended victims.

Together, she and Marcus faced the hungry canines with nothing more than a staff and a sword between them. Jade handed Truda her knife and shoved her behind.

"Watch over Phoenix and protect Brynn."

Trembling, the girl nodded, edging backward until she almost stumbled over Phoenix's prone form.

The wolfpack sidled nearer.

Jade stood shoulder to shoulder with Marcus and faced the animals with frozen fingers and a racing heart. Was this it? Would they all die here in the freezing snow, torn to pieces by wild animals?

Behind the main pack a single, huge male wolf sat back on its haunches and watched. Jade's gaze was inexplicably drawn to the animal. There was something intelligent, almost regal, about its bearing. In a jet black pelt its eyes were a startling clear, pale grey. It turned them on her. Its jaw dropped, pink tongue lolling out and, just for a second, she had the strangest feeling it laughed at her.

The wind picked up, wailing like a banshee through the treetops. It flung snow in their faces, blinding and cold. The temperature dropped. Jade blinked away the snowflakes and the sense of connection with the black wolf dissipated.

Growling, a closer animal launched itself. She brought her staff around, cracking it across the muzzle. With a yip of pain, it landed awkwardly and scampered backward. Three more crept in, heads down, muscular shoulders rippling as they looked for a way past the weapons. Marcus jabbed at one, wounding it on the shoulder; it paused then kept coming.

"Any time now, Brynn!" Jade whacked another toothy

muzzle.

"This isn't easy!" the boy returned tartly, sawing at the door latch. "The leather is frozen solid. I'm almost through."

A huge, silvery animal slunk forward, lips pulled back in a tooth-bearing snarl. It darted around, catching Truda's druid cloak in its fangs. It dragged her, trying to separate the smallest, weakest member from the rest of the group. She screamed.

Marcus swore. He struck at the wolf's neck. A single blow severed its spine. The black wolf howled, raising its muzzle to the night. Truda burst into tears.

"Got it!" Brynn yelled.

He shoved the stiff door open and yanked Truda to her feet. Together, they dragged Phoenix's body inside. Moments later, Jade and Marcus followed, slamming the door shut and leaning against it. Outside, a horrifying snarling, snapping, growling ruckus told them exactly what happened to the wounded animals they'd left behind.

For several long moments the four simply stood, shaking in the darkness. At last the sickening sounds stopped. The wolfpack moved noiselessly off into the worsening storm. Truda's tears calmed to occasional sniffs.

Someone groaned.

The dark-silence suddenly became tense again.

"Was that you, Brynn?" Jade asked reluctantly. It hadn't sounded like him, or Marcus.

"No," the boy whispered.

Truda pressed herself up against Jade, shivering.

Another groan cut through the apprehensive stillness.

"Is someone here?" Jade called, unable to suppress a faint tremor in her voice.

There was no answer. The room waited, shadowed and still.

She heard someone fumbling in their clothing. Brynn

struck a small flame with his flint and tinder. It illuminated the space for long enough to reveal a central hearth, already laid with tinder and wood. There were no other people. He lit a fragment of straw and held it beneath the dry firewood. It caught. Very soon a cheerful, warm fire cast dancing golden light onto rough, thatch-and-timber walls and a dirt floor. It wasn't much but it was better than being outside.

Once more a faint groan sounded. Stunned, the four companions looked down. The noises came from Phoenix's body.

Jade dropped beside her friend and felt for a pulse. It was ridiculous, of course. They were imagining things. Phoenix was dead. There was no way both she and Marcus could be mistaken…..

Thump-thump…thump-thump…..thump-thump.

A heartbeat.

An unmistakable pulse in his throat.

Phoenix lived.

CHAPTER TWO

"He's alive!" Jade looked up at Marcus, stunned.

With a grunt of effort, she rolled Phoenix over and felt for the arrow-wounds in his back. They were gone: nothing but hard little bumps of scartissue through holes in his jerkin and shirt. Dumbfounded, she rolled him back and stared at him for a moment. He moaned again and opened vague blue eyes. Hope jumped in her heart. He really was alive. It was impossible and incredible but true.

"Jade?" His words were slurred and slow. "Where the heck are we?"

"Uh…" She glanced around the little room. "I have no idea – not home, anyway." She couldn't stop grinning like an idiot.

Phoenix pushed himself up from the hard floor, holding his head with one hand. "Why are you grinning like an idiot and why do I feel like a hit and run victim?"

"I…I'm pretty sure you were…um…dead," she replied at last, touching his shoulder to assure herself he was actually real – well, as real as it got in this world, anyway.

"Huh?" He blinked at her then looked at Marcus for confirmation.

The young soldier nodded solemnly. "Two Roman arrows through your back."

Phoenix twisted his arm awkwardly up behind himself, feeling for the scars and holes. He rotated his shoulders then stared at the backs of his hands as though surprised to see them.

"I was…dead?" He shivered, lapsing into confused silence.

"Let's all get warm." Jade gave him a gentle shove toward the fire.

It was a bedraggled, damp and exhausted little group that huddled around the cheery fire. They stared at the flames in silence for a long time. At last, Truda stirred, yawned and gave them a grateful smile.

"I'm glad you're alive, Phoenix," she said earnestly. "And I'm glad the wolves didn't eat me. And I'm really glad you came and got me. The druids were nice and all," she waggled her plump fingers toward the heat, "but I'm looking forward to getting home. I miss my Pa."

"Uh huh," Jade replied automatically.

She wasn't really listening, being more focussed on warming her numbed hands and casting sidelong glances at Phoenix. How could he be alive? What did it mean?

"Yep," Truda said, "my Pa'll be so glad to see me. So will Ullr and Ma but," she turned thoughtful, "I don't know about Magni or Modi – they can be mean sometimes - but Grandpa Odinn'll be real glad. He's nice."

"Uh huh," Jade repeated, scooting closer to the fire.

The pointed tips of her ears were frozen and she couldn't feel her toes. She was relieved to be out of the wind. It sounded like a regular blizzard rising outside. The wolves howled again, further away now.

Inspecting the room again, she spotted a pile of furs and skins in one shadowed corner. Scrambling up, she pulled several closer to the fire. Wrapping a thick fur around the still-chattering girl, she handed some to Brynn, who snuggled into them, extending his bare toes almost into the fire. She heaved a huge bearskin to Phoenix, who held it in his hand for several seconds before apparently realising what he was supposed to do with it.

She stared at him again, gratitude mixing with incredulity. He was alive! Even with magic, she'd felt no trace of life before. One arrow had gone right into his heart. How could he possibly be alive?

He turned his head to look at her, blue eyes darkened by remembered pain.

"I was really dead?"

She nodded at him. He shivered, pulled the fur around his shoulders and resumed staring at the fire.

"I tried to kill your father, Marcus," he murmured. "Sorry."

Jade gasped and glanced at their friend, worried. Brynn and Truda stared at Phoenix, eyes wide, mouths agape.

The Roman glanced up, his expression arrested. "Don't be. I would have done the same, given a chance," he finally admitted, extending his hands toward the flame. "Did you succeed?"

Phoenix shrugged. "Don't think so. Pilum through the shoulder should slow him down for awhile, though."

Marcus shook his head. "Zhudai will heal him."

Phoenix grunted and lapsed back into silence. A short while later he turned his back, curled up under the fur and appeared to fall asleep.

Eventually, Jade roused herself enough to bring out the Hyllion Bagia. She spread the magic bag on the floor and dipped a hand into its black maw. Muttering a request, she drew out the remains of the enormous meal that had been provided, two days before, by the dryad Queen, Lady Aurfanon. There wasn't much left but it was enough for the four conscious companions to each have something with a little left over for Phoenix. A small, logical part of her mind noted that it was still perfectly fresh. Perhaps something in the magic of the Bag kept it that way.

"Will he be ok?" Brynn asked, putting a small pot of water on to heat over the fire.

Jade cast Phoenix a worried glance then nodded with more assurance than she felt.

"I think so. He's sleeping. The arrow wounds are just tiny scars. I guess he just lost some blood and is tired."

She sighed and sat down, extending her hands toward the fire. "I think we're all worn-out."

The others agreed wholeheartedly.

"We should be celebrating," Marcus murmured, chewing on a piece of unleavened bread. "Phoenix is alive. We succeeded in our first Quest." He waved the bread at Truda. "We have the Jewel of Asgard and we're one step closer to killing Feng Zhudai."

"Yes, I suppose so." Jade scrubbed at her face, yawning. "It's just a bit hard to get all excited when we haven't really rested for five days. I'm so tired my brain feels like it's stuffed with cloth. Plus, I have no idea where we are or what we're supposed to do next."

She clenched her fingers and jaw against a wave of fear and worry. She'd never thought they'd have to face the second level at all. She'd be so certain that just finishing Level one would be enough to get her home. It wasn't and now she had no idea what to do. At least, with Phoenix back, she wouldn't have to do it alone.

"I know what you have to do," Truda piped up. The others looked at her expectantly. "You have to take me home." She spread her hands and smiled, blinking her big eyes at them.

Jade grimaced. "We know that," she tried to be patient, "but we don't have a clue where your home is from here. Do you know?"

"Oh yes," the little girl replied with bright assurance. "It's Bilskirnir."

"What's a Bilskinor?" Brynn cut in.

"It's my pa's house and it's Bilskirnir," Truda corrected, her small face serious. "The Druids never could say it right, either. They couldn't even say my name right. It's more like: 'Throoder'." She said it with a sort of sing-song inflexion and almost swallowed the last sound. She smiled at their blank looks. "But I like Truda, so you can keep calling me that."

"Wait," Jade held up a hand, "we're getting off track. You are the thing we had to get to complete our first quest: you are the Jewel of Asgard. I thought Asgard was the place you were from but this Bil...whatever...that's your home? A house somewhere?"

Truda nodded, red braids bouncing. "That's where Pa and Ma and my half-brothers are. I've been gone an awful long time. Weeks and weeks, I think. So long I've almost missed my birthday. Uncle Loki stealed me from my bed one night and took me to stay with the Druids. He plays silly jokes on us all the time but this one was a bit mean. I'm not happy with him at all!" She pouted at the fire.

The others stared at the girl, dumbfounded.

"Your uncle stole you as a joke?" Jade managed at last. "He took you away from your family for months as some sort of prank?"

Truda nodded, apparently not fazed by the situation at all.   "Uncle Loki is fun but sometimes he can be misch...misshhev... mischiv.."

"Mischievous?" Jade prompted.

"That's it!" the girl exclaimed, beaming. "Loki's not my real uncle but that's what we all call him."

There was a pause. Jade looked thoughtfully at her. "Um....is this kind of behaviour normal in your family?"

"Oh yes, we're always getting into fights and playing tricks an' stuff," Truda replied, poking the fire with a handy stick. "Once my Pa dressed up as a bride so he could get back his favourite hammer from Thrym – he was the big meanie giant who stole it."

"A bride?" Brynn giggled. "With the flowers and dress and everything? Just to get his hammer back?" When Truda nodded and looked mildly offended, he howled with laughter, apparently finding it highly amusing that a man would dress up as a girl just to get a tool back.

"It's Mjölnir," Truda muttered.   "It's a special hammer."

Jade shook her head irritably. Somewhere in her brain, a small part was trying very hard to get her attention. Something about Truda was important. Something her conscious brain was trying to make sense of, much to the annoyance of her subconscious, which had already worked it out. At last, several things clicked into place. With a sinking feeling in the pit of her stomach, Jade asked the inevitable questions.

"Truda," she interrupted the girl's chatter, "did I hear you say something about Grandpa Odinn before?" Truda nodded, her bottom lip sticking out; eyes huge. Jade sighed and dropped her head into her hands. "Am I right in thinking that your Pa would be Thor then?"

"Uh huh," Truda confirmed, obviously worried that she'd done something wrong. "Is that bad?"

Jade glanced up, not sure whether to laugh or cry. She sent a resigned look at Marcus and Brynn, both of whom stared back at her in confusion.

"It's not bad," she sighed. "I should have realised, really, when I heard she was the Jewel of Asgard."

"Would you mind explaining exactly what you should have realised?" Brynn said.

"Remember what our next task is?" Jade reminded him. "We have to return the Jewel of Asgard," she pointed at Truda, "to its owner in Asgard. Asgard is the home of the Norse gods. It turns out that Truda is the Jewel and her father, her 'owner', is Thor. Thor," she finished with a tired, slightly hysterical laugh, "is none other than the Norse God of Thunder and War."

Quite appropriately, there was a sudden increase in the ferocity of the wind outside, followed by a distant rumble of thunder.

Truda looked up, her face alight with excitement. "Pa!"

She jumped up and raced toward the door. Marcus was quicker and barred her way. Jade followed. She still had trouble believing that, in this realm, the Norse Gods – and their powers - were actually real, not just exciting stories she'd read. It was pretty daunting.

"Oh no." Marcus grabbed Truda's arms and held her still. "You can't go outside in this storm. You'd freeze in ten seconds - and remember the wolves?"

"But it's my Pa up there," she wailed, pointing to the ceiling. "Right now, he's up in his chariot, throwing Mjölnir to make the thunder and lightning." She stomped one slippered foot and looked mutinous. "I want to see my Pa."

"C'mon," Jade tried to be reasonable, "if you did go out now, he wouldn't be able to see you or hear you in all this snow and wind anyway."

Truda looked doubtful for a moment then her expression firmed again into determination. "He might." She scowled, folding her arms.

Abruptly, Jade had had enough. She was too tired to cope with a tantrum-throwing kid at the moment – godsdaughter or not. She jerked her head at Marcus and together they moved aside.

"Fine," she said coolly. "Go out and yell your head off. I don't care. In fact, if he does hear you, it makes our job much easier but," she warned when Truda's face lit up, "don't blame me if your yelling attracts the wolves. Right now we're in no position to fight any battles for you." She stood back and folded her arms too, watching the precocious child.

Truda flounced to the door and grabbed the wooden doorlatch. She opened it a fraction. Wind and flurries of snow slipped in, making the fire flicker and jump. She shivered but opened it a little wider and peered up into the heavy, blue-dark sky. Cupping a hand around her mouth, she shrieked into the wind:

"Pa! Pa! Come 'n get me, Pa!"

Somewhere in the distance, a wolf howled its wild,

weird call. Its packmates answered with a hair-raising, disharmonious chorus. Some were still quite close by the hut. Truda slammed the door shut and pressed her back to it, eyes wide. She straightened up with a quirky, apologetic sort of grin at Jade and Marcus.

"Maybe I'll just wait until we get to Bilskirnir then."

"Wise move." Jade exchanged ironic, laughing glances with Marcus.

She ushered Truda back to the fire, where the girl-child snuggled under the furs with a dispirited sigh. Brynn produced his little wooden whistle and twiddled a few tunes until Truda complained it was too shrill. They huddled together beneath the furs, looking very young and very sleepy.

Jade watched. Someone had to be responsible for them. True, Brynn was a tough kid. He'd looked after himself for months after his parents were killed by Roman soldiers on orders from Feng Zhudai. Truda, however, might be the daughter of a god and as tall as Brynn but she was really very young.

Jade looked away, tears filling her eyes. This was stupid. Her, responsible for two kids? In her world she was hardly more than a kid herself. She missed her own father fiercely. Taking Truda back to Thor seemed like an impossible task. Instead of being safely back home, as she'd hoped, she was stuck trying to save both this world and her own from Feng Zhudai's schemes.

Somehow, they had to stay out of Zhudai's clutches and find Thor; but where? She had no idea. She'd read a little bit of Norse mythology back home but not enough to remember where Thor hung out. A vague recollection that all the Norse gods lived in Asgard didn't really help much. How did they get to Asgard? How long would it take?

Then it occurred to Jade that Zhudai would still be hunting for them, even though they'd left ancient Britain. She shivered and clutched the furs closer. If the warnings of the Druids and the strange woman in gray were true then Zhudai wanted Truda for some power she had. He wasn't likely to give up easily if she had something that would let him control or destroy the world. Arch-villains were like that: tenacious, ruthless.

They had to find a way to get the girl home – quickly.

"Jade?" Truda's sleepy voice interrupted her thoughts.

"Mmmm?" She scrubbed a hand over her face and added a little wood to the fire, trying to push aside her fears.

Marcus, nearby, paused in the act of sharpening his sword to listen.

"It is almost my birthday, y'know," the young girl murmured, her eyes drooping.

"That's nice," Jade replied, watching sparks fly up from the fire.

"I've sorta lost track but I think it's only about five or six days away. I'll be seven and I really do have to be home by my birthday." She lay down, pillowing her head on a fur and dragged another over her bare legs.

"We'll do our best." Jade sighed. Marcus smiled at her.

Truda yawned. "No, I mean I really have to be home. If I'm not then Spring won't come. Winter will stay and people will die everywhere. It'll be the worst winter ever. Then'll come the fires; then wars between the gods and giants. It'd be the beginning of Ragnarok – the end of all the nine worlds. So I really…have…to…" She fell asleep in mid sentence.

CHAPTER THREE

Phoenix curled under the furs, staring at the rough timber wall. He heard the low murmur of voices as Jade and the others talked about where to go next but none of it had really registered. One thought possessed his mind: I'm alive.

He'd been dead. Dead; gone; finito; over; finished; kaput. He knew it. Every cell in his body somehow knew it. It had only been for a few minutes but he'd never forget it.

There'd been no "near death" experience; no white light to stay away from; no seeing his body from outside; just...nothing – and that scared him more than anything. Was it only nothing because this was a digital world, so his death hadn't been real? That old woman in the gray limbo land had said this world was as real as their own. Dying had certainly felt real.

Without really wanting to, he relived it.

In some ways, death had come as a relief. The blinding agony of those two Roman arrows in his back was unbelievable. Drawing a breath became impossible. He'd felt his body shutting down and almost welcomed it. Pain vanished; fear slipped away along with his consciousness.

Coming back to life was the shock. At the time, Phoenix only registered he was numbingly cold and wet. He slipped in an out of awareness as the others carried him towards the hut. He barely remembered the wolf attack – just the cold, weakness, pain.

Now inside the hut, he was content to lie in the furs in order to just think for awhile. Sleep wasn't yet an option.

It seemed too much like the nothingness of death.

Instead, he revelled in the sensations that told him he lived: the sound of his own breath; his heart; the rush of blood surging through his veins; even felt the fuzz on his unbrushed teeth. It was hard to believe that this was only a digital body, not a real one. The complexity of a software program which could make everything so very real was unimaginable. He felt real. Death had felt real. Too real. Coming back to life was impossible but then, so was being magically transported into an adult body in a different world. Maybe the old lady who'd told them this world was real was right. Maybe it was.

He was so used to this warrior's form now that it was hard to remember living in his gawky thirteen year old body at all. After being killed once, he now had a very strong desire to keep this body healthy.

Most of all, the overwhelming idea that he had actually died, kept hijacking his brain; derailing every attempt at focusing on the future. All he could think about was the past.

For three years he had been angry at his father for dying in a car accident in the real world. For three long years he'd blamed his father for giving up and leaving his family when they needed him. At the scene of the accident, the paramedics told his mother that her husband had just lost too much blood and had too many injuries to be saved. Phoenix hadn't believed them. He'd always thought that his dad could have lived – if he'd really wanted to. He thought it just showed his dad didn't care enough about his family to stay around.

Now, finally, Phoenix had a dim insight into what his father must have been through. His body had sustained far fewer injuries but he'd been glad to let go when the pain got too much. All thoughts of Jade and getting both of them back home had become irrelevant. He hadn't even tried to hang on.

Somewhere, deep inside, an old knot of pain dissolved forever. For the first time in years, Phoenix thought about his father with love and regret, rather than anger and hurt. For the first time, he painlessly remembered all the great, fun things they'd done as a family; how hard his dad had worked to support them; how he'd never missed any of Phoenix's Aikido gradings or school functions.

Phoenix struggled to come to terms with how he felt. It was like he'd somehow let his father down by not appreciating their time together; and by being so angry with him when he died.   His throat closed as he fought back long-suppressed tears.

Voices intruded on his thoughts. Someone, maybe Truda, said something about the end of the world. A somewhat stunned silence followed.   Phoenix drifted slowly up from his own memories and resurfaced in this reality to glance around. Jade was staring at him, frowning and nibbling on her lower lip as she did when she was really worried.

He rubbed a hand through his long hair and sat up. Time to rejoin the land of the living mentally, as well as physically.

"What?" he prompted her.

"You ok?" She cast an anxious look at the sleeping girl as though she wanted to ask him something else but felt obliged to check his health first.

He shrugged. "Guess so. I was dead. Now I'm not. I'll get used to it, I suppose.

"But how...?" Jade began, apparently distracted by his words.

"The daggers, remember?" Phoenix tapped the hilt of his iron dagger where it sat on his hip. He pulled it out, turning it so six of the seven rubies embedded in the handle glowed blood-red in the firelight. One jewel was cracked; dulled into an ugly, dirty dark pink.

She sat up straight, pulling out her own bronze blade.

He watched as understanding sank in: they each had seven lives in this game-world. They'd guessed these might be represented by the seven rubies in their respective daggers but they hadn't been certain. Now they were. The gems in her knife hilt were unsullied for she had lost no lives.

He saw fear dawn as she realised he had only six lives left. It looked like there really were still four levels of the game to complete before they could hope to get home to the real world. Each level would be more challenging than the last. Half-a-dozen lives might not be enough. He grimaced at her look of horrified comprehension. They would just have to be enough. It was just a game, after all. He'd played enough to know how it worked. If he kept his wits about him, he could pull them through. Besides, it was still kinda fun – apart from the dying bits, anyway. He'd just have to avoid doing that as much as possible.

"I don't understand," Marcus interrupted. "What has your dagger got to do with not dying? I thought the druid's Spring Equinox rites must have healed you the way they did me." He turned his bare leg to show a thin, healed sword-wound. Phoenix knew it had been inflicted only a short time before, by Roman soldiers.

Phoenix saw Jade open her mouth. Before she could say anything, he touched her on the arm and shook his head.

"I think Marcus has proved we can trust him, Jade. I vote we tell him everything now. We can bring Brynn up to speed later, when he wakes up."

Jade shut her lips, gave a reluctant nod and stayed quiet while he did his best to explain without resorting to techno-babble about computers. That would be magic in this world, anyway.

Marcus glanced between them. "You're saying that the two of you have come from another world to this one by magic?" he said evenly. "You have more than one life and the magic is somehow linked to your knives and those two amulets you wear?"

Jade drew out the necklace she wore tucked under her clothes. Phoenix lifted his off his chest. Side by side, it could be seen that the amulets fitted together neatly – two curved teardrop shapes; one in pearly silver, one in gold and each with a dot of the other colour in it. It was the ancient Chinese Yin-Yang symbol, indicating Balance and Harmony.

"Why don't you just use magic to make the amulets take you home again?" Marcus seemed almost angry. "Why do we have to go through this?" He waved a hand around, indicating the hardships they had already encountered and were certain to meet ahead.

"We tried," Jade assured him, "but it didn't work."

"I'm pretty sure now," Phoenix cast a sidelong glance at Jade, who sighed and nodded, "that we have to complete all five quests in order to save both our worlds from Zhudai and get back to ours. We also," he added as an afterthought, "have to make sure our amulets stay out of Zhudai's hands. Evidently they would give him some sort of extra power."

Marcus shuddered. For several tense moments, he stared hard at them both, his face an unreadable mask. Was he annoyed with them; or even afraid of them? Both would be understandable. As they watched, the tension drained from his shoulders and the Roman sat down cross-legged before them.

"And this new quest?" Marcus seemed to accept the situation, even if he didn't understand it.

Jade brought Phoenix up to date on what they knew of Truda and Thor.

"O...K...," Phoenix mused, "so the question remains: where are we and what do we do next?" He eyed Jade. "What was it Truda said before? Something about the end of the world?"

Jade shivered and wrapped her arms around herself.

"She said if we don't get her back to Thor and her home by her birthday in five or six days, winter won't end; then there'll be wars between gods, followed by the end of the world – they call it Ragnarok."

He looked at her for awhile, trying to process the information. He looked at Marcus, who seemed unfazed as he resumed rhythmically sharpening his sword. He looked at the sleeping Truda, innocent-seeming instigator of another adventure.

"Is that the end of the world five days or so from today," he asked, "or from tomorrow?"

"Phoenix!" Jade seemed shocked at his cavalier attitude. "Don't you get it? We've only got five days to get her home to Bilskinor before all hell breaks loose."

He held up his hands for peace. "I get it. I get it. I just don't know what we're supposed to do about it right now. It's the middle of the night, in a storm, in a god-knows-where forest, and we're surrounded by wolves. What do you want me to do?"

"He has a point," Marcus put in. "We're best off getting some sleep while we can. If the storm has died down in the morning, we can work out where we are."

Jade flung off her furs, stood up and strode to the door and back several times before finding the words to express her obvious agitation. "But what if the storm goes on for days? What if we do get out but the wolves come back? What if we can't find Bilskinor? What if we can't find where we are? What if Zhudai tracks us down again; or Agricola follows us? We can't let them get our amulets or Truda, remember?"

"Agricola is Governor of Britain by the wishes of Titus, Emperor of Rome," Marcus reminded her. "My father can't leave his post just to chase us around the world. We're safely away from him."

"And what about Zhudai?" she shot back.

Marcus twisted his mouth up in a grimace. "Now

that's another thing altogether. Is that illusion spell you put on me still working?"

Jade sucked a quick breath. Phoenix glanced at her in surprise. Had she forgotten her own handiwork? In Britain, Zhudai had been able to use his magical abilities to track Marcus by Farseeing because he knew the son of the Governor by sight. Once they'd realised it, she had placed a spell on Marcus to deflect Zhudai's Sight.

Tilting her head, Jade narrowed her eyes at Marcus. Her gaze unfocussed and she didn't blink for so long that Phoenix's own eyes began to water in sympathy. Finally, she nodded and he saw relief flicker across Marcus' face.

"And he's never seen the rest of you, so Zhudai can't know where we are," the Roman noted. "If he can't find us, he can't send anyone after us."

Jade sank back down, some of the worry easing from her expression. "So how do *we* find out where we are and where we have to go to get Truda home then?"

Phoenix shrugged. "In the morning we climb a mountain or a tree and find the nearest village and ask them how to get to Bilskinor. We know we have to return the Jewel – Truda – to Thor, so we can probably assume we're somewhere in one of the countries that follow the Norse gods. Don't forget the second half of our quest," he reminded them, "we're also supposed to get hold of Thor's hammer, Mjölnir. We need it for the third quest."

Jade groaned. "Stealing things from Gods is always hazardous to your health."

Marcus expelled a short breath and nodded.

Phoenix scrubbed a hand across his hair. Dust flew out. "I guess we'll cross that bridge when we come to it. The first thing is to find out where we are and how to get to Bilskinor."

"So, do either of you know anything about these Norse lands?" Jade said.

Marcus shook his head. "My sister's husband, Tacitus,

has travelled the Germanic countries somewhat but I confess I never read his journals. He mentioned barbaric, petty kingdoms spread across many lands and separated by a narrow sea – the Suebian Sea, I think. That's all I remember," he admitted. "His writings make dull reading."

"I never paid much attention in geography," Phoenix admitted. He eyed Jade expectantly. She was the book-worm.

She dropped her chin into her hand and gazed into the fire. "I'm pretty sure that the countries we call Norway, Denmark, Sweden, Poland and Germany wer…are all Norse people in our world. I just can't remember what we call the sea that's in the middle of them all. It joins the North Sea." She huffed, clearly frustrated that the name eluded her. "For goodness sake! I could tell you exactly what plants grow there." Sitting up, she stretched and twisted her back with a grimace. "We'll have to ask someone. We'll look pretty stupid saying 'hey, what country are we in?', though."

"The Baltic Sea!" Phoenix exclaimed, recalling a documentary he thought he'd successfully ignored in history class. "That's what we call the Suebian Sea."

Jade glared, visibly irritated he had remembered it before she had. "Helpful," she scoffed. "Now all we need to know is…oh, wait," she said in mock surprise, "where we are and where to go."

"Hey!" Phoenix glared right back at her, stung. "Bit harsh."

She flushed and turned away. "We're not going to get anywhere tonight. I'm going to sleep." Jerking the furs up over her shoulder, she lay down with her back to the others.

Phoenix watched her for a few moments, annoyed by her petty arguing. Why was she so hung up on being a smartass know-it all? What did it matter who knew the name of a stupid sea? When he looked up, he found Marcus returning his gaze gravely.

"She's frightened," the Roman commented, putting his sword aside and stoking the fire.

Phoenix shrugged. "We all are. Does she have to take it out on me?"

"You're the only connection she has to your world," his reply was cryptic.

"So?" He blinked at Marcus, confused.

"You died. She was stranded here when she thought she'd be home. She was angry, scared and alone." Marcus leaned back on his furs and crossed his legs at the ankles, staring into the fire with an oddly wistful expression on his face.

"Oh." Phoenix paused, suddenly understanding. It was exactly how he'd felt when his father had died: angry and scared. He rotated his shoulders, still feeling a faint ache between the shoulder blades. "I'll try not to let it happen again. It wasn't much fun, anyway." He grinned at Marcus, who smiled a little in return.

"I think we'd all appreciate that."

*****

Many thousands of miles away, Long Baiyu smiled. Staring into the cold blackness of his cell, he let his mind drift. Zhudai's shields around his cell were strong but flawed - as was much of his work. It cost Baiyu dearly to keep a light link with his rescuers over such a distance - enough to know they were safe but not enough to communicate. Now he knew they were truly on the path to complete their second quest, he could afford to rest a little.

They had yet to realise their true goal, of course but that would come in time. With each new experience, they grew and learned – and their chances of surviving to find and free him increased. Many of the obstacles they faced were in their minds, anyway. Only when these were overcome would they truly be able to release him and themselves from bondage.

As he let his thoughts float, Baiyu became aware of

something else: the gossamer touch of another mind seeking his.   Before he could withdraw, it seized him, striking and tearing at his mental shields with fearful force.

Zhudai!

Baiyu wrenched his mind free and withdrew into the weak shelter of his exhausted body.   Shivering, he strengthened his inner defences.   How could he make such a stupid mistake?   Zhudai's shields were not weak. The flaws were simply a temptation.   How could he let himself be lulled by the belief that his rescuers were safe away from Zhudai's influence in Britain?

Now Zhudai knew through which land the four travelled.   He had plucked that much at least from Baiyu's incautious thoughts.   He wouldn't know exactly where but it would not take him long to find out.

Unable to restrain himself, Baiyu released a howl of anguish that echoed off the uncaring stone walls.

CHAPTER FOUR

A soft, sighing sound from one of the others roused Jade from a semi-doze. She had woken when the fire died down in the wee hours. It was the first night they hadn't set watches and she'd been too uneasy to go back to sleep after stoking the flames. The storm gentled sometime after midnight but cold seeped through the walls of their shelter. It was now hours later and dawn eased grey light beneath the door.

She glanced at her companions then down at the pile of fur on her lap. She was almost finished making warm clothes for their little group. When she couldn't sleep, she'd started turning the remaining pile of furs and skins into cold-weather gear. In all the fantasy books she'd read, no-one ever had to make their own clothes. It was either not mentioned, or some kindly villager just turned up and handed the hero what he needed. Here, there was no-one. Luckily, she seemed to know how to sew in this world and she'd found a small sewing kit tucked into a chest of furs in the corner.

The bone needle slipped through her cold fingers as she cast a troubled look at Phoenix's sleeping form. Guilt twisted her stomach into knots. She'd heard Marcus' comments last night and, unhappily, faced her own childish reactions toward Phoenix. She was finding this all much, much harder than she'd thought it would be. He seemed to see the whole thing as some big, exciting lark of an adventure. He enjoyed bouncing from one fight to the next; one perilous situation to another. He treated it like it really was just a computer game they would inevitably win.

For Jade it seemed much more real – too real. She was scared almost all the time and far less certain of victory. Phoenix clearly didn't see the infinite number of things that could go hideously wrong here. His unwavering nonchalance was annoying – and reassuring, too. As long as he thought they could win, she carried a faint hope he was right.

When he died, it had terrified her. For the first time her life, she was completely alone. Marcus and Brynn didn't really count – they were part of this world. With Phoenix gone, there was no-one to rely on; to believe in. Only herself and that wasn't enough; she wasn't enough.

Sniffing, Jade blinked away stinging tears and refocused on her work. She misjudged the next stitch and caught a breath as the needle stuck into her finger. Blood welled and she put it into her mouth, trying not to cry again.

She was good enough. She had to be.

The others slept on.

*****

Sometime later, as sunlight brightened the room, Brynn sat up and shoved his bedding aside with a yawn. Phoenix sat up too and nodded at the boy, noticing the tracks of tears on his grubby face. He recalled that Brynn had lost his last brother in the battle at Stonehenge. There wasn't much he could really say, though, so he didn't mention it. The kid was strong and he had them as a family now.

"What's for breakfast?" The boy stretched, yawning again.

"Errr." Phoenix glanced around the small timber hut but there were no convenient refrigerators or vending machines to be seen. He sighed. Time to hunt – one of the major drawbacks to living two thousand years in the past. That and a complete lack of flush toilets – speaking of which...

"C'mon," he jerked his head toward the door, "let's go find a...ahh....tree.." Brynn flashed him a knowing grin and nodded.   Phoenix squared his shoulders. "Then I guess we'll have to rustle up something to eat and see where we are, too."

"We're going out to hunt up breakfast," he calmly informed Jade as they headed for the door.

She opened her mouth, signs of worry clouding her green eyes.   Phoenix just looked at her and raised an eyebrow. Something in his face must have told her that he wasn't in the mood for discussion, so she shut her jaw with a snap and nodded.   As they eased open the door she touched him on the leg. He glanced down.

"Phoenix..." She seemed hesitant and he guessed she was feeling bad for sniping at him last night. Strangely though, he didn't need her apology. He just smiled at her and gave her the thumbs up before slipping out the door.

When they returned and thrust open the door Phoenix stepped out of the crisp, cold air and into the warm room with some relief.

"Hey!" Jade exclaimed, shivering as she sat hunched over her stitching. "Born in a barn?"

"Sorry," he apologised cheerfully, shutting the door again.

He swung a large bird off his shoulder, onto the dirt floor near the fire. She stared at it, openly astonished. Phoenix hoped it was edible. There wasn't much other game around and they'd seen signs of the wolves so they didn't want to stay out long. The bird looked like some sort of turkey – grey with a black head and bright red bits above its glazed eyes. It had a long tail that looked like it would fan out.

"Oh!"   Truda's sleepy voice called out.   "An auerhuhn...umm...a wood-grouse you call it. Yummy. My Ma roasts them with lots of tubers and wild onions." Her stomach rumbled loudly and she looked surprised. "I'm so hungry!" She scratched her head. Her thick braids were in disarray, creating a fuzzy halo of red hair about her face.

Phoenix grinned at the girl. He was hungry too, although a bowl of Corn Flakes would be better. He could almost taste orange juice, cereal, toast and milk; and sighed in regret. Not today. Heck, electric toasters wouldn't even be invented for at least eighteen hundred years.

In a short space of time, the fire was refuelled and the game cleaned and baked in the hot coals. After the bones were picked clean, they dressed in the new fur clothing and packed their gear. As a group, they sat in a small circle to discuss what to do next.

"When we went hunting, Brynn and I climbed the tallest tree we could find on a hill." Phoenix looked around at the others. They waited expectantly. "We're in the middle of a huge forest. Really huge, I mean," he warned. "It looks like there's a big lake off to the east and another off to the west. Lots of hills and valleys in between. Rough walking no matter what direction we take."

"So did you see any towns?" Jade said.

Phoenix exchanged glances with Brynn. "We think we saw a faint smoke trail off to the northeast, near the lake but it's so glary today with the new snow that we can't be sure."

"So that sounds like our only option." Jade's tone suggested she wasn't very happy with the lack of choices.

"Well, I sure can't guide you anywhere else." Brynn sounded disgruntled.

Phoenix cast him a narrow look, making a mental note to keep an eye on the boy. He needed to be useful or he might be tempted into mischief.

Truda jumped up and brushed off her new fur pants, clearly excited to be moving closer to home. "Lets go then!"

The others gathered their gear and filed out of the hut and squinted around at the tall white-dusted trees.

"I just wish we knew where we are now," Jade sighed.

Truda tucked a cold hand into hers and smiled trustingly up at her and then at Phoenix. "As long as we're not anywhere near Trolltiven or Thursvidur I don't mind."

Everyone looked at her in silence.

"Do we want to know why?" Brynn finally asked.

Truda shook her head, making her braids bounce. "Trolls and ogres live there," she said darkly, her blue eyes wide. "Big trolls and really nasty ogres."

"Are we there now? Would you recognise those places if you saw them?" Phoenix asked, not expecting much joy from her answer.

Truda looked around and shrugged. "I don't think so. I've been to Trolltiven once – or near it, anyway – but it was ages ago, so I don't know."

"Oh good," Jade groaned. "Trolls. Ogres. Wonderful."

Phoenix caught Marcus' eye and grinned, laying a hand on his sword. Marcus inclined his head, his lips twitching into a small smile.

"We'll keep an eye out for them then. Think you can keep us going northeast, Brynn?" Phoenix clapped a hand on the boy's shoulder.

He straightened with a nod. There was a brighter, more determined look on his thin face as he led them away from shelter and into the unknown.

Once away from the clearing around the hut, the vast forest swallowed the little band of travellers. Enormous pine trees towered overhead, their evergreen needles filtering weak sunlight into a thin, greenish gloom. Footfalls were muffled by snow and a thick bed of brown needles. In the cold, muted stillness, each breath rasped harsh and loud. The only other noise was the constant trickling and dripping of water – and once, in the distance, the desolate howl of a solitary wolf.

Brynn led, followed by Marcus, Jade, Truda and

finally Phoenix. It was hard going. The route could have possibly been a deer path, or perhaps a track beaten to the hut by a fur trapper. Faint and torturous, it twisted around giant tree trunks and huge, grey boulders. It took all of Phoenix's concentration just to keep his footing. The ground lay ankle-deep in snow that quickly turned slushy as the sun rose higher. Hidden beneath, moss-covered rocks and patches of ice made the path treacherous to the unwary. Truda stumbled and almost fell a dozen of times. Each time he caught her up, straining to keep her from landing face first in mud and ice.

The track led them down a narrow streambed that sliced between two high ridges. Darker and colder, the forest grew wild and ominous; full of creaking tree branches and strange shadows. A light wind sprang up high in the treetops, sounding like a thousand people whispering in the sky.

As they followed the little stream downhill, the air grew moist and very slightly warmer. At the base of a particularly steep stretch of ravine, the stream widened and joined another. Now a small river, it turned directly northeast and rushed whitely over large, dark grey boulders. Every so often, Phoenix thought he smelled the faintest hint of woodsmoke but it was never strong enough to be sure.

He watched in amusement the puffs of white breath erupt from everyone's mouths. Their heads steamed in the cold air. Inside the fur clothing he stifled, hot from the exercise of walking, but it was too chilly to take them off. His fingers and nose were cold. He sniffed, wishing for tissues as his nose began to dribble. Irritably, he wiped it on the back of his leather sleeve and smiled. His mother would have a fit.

Phoenix looked up, intending to tell Brynn to call a rest halt, and caught sight of Jade's expression. She sent harried looks back over her shoulder in the direction from which they'd come. Her green eyes were intense with an anxious effort to pierce the half-light of the forest floor.

"What is it?" He tensed, hand automatically settling on his sword hilt.

She bit on her lip, hesitated then shrugged. "Not sure. I…I just feel like we're being followed."

He sucked in a slow breath and deliberately released the tension in his chest. He looked about, seeking the source of her disquiet. The area appeared no different to any other section of the woods they'd passed through. The ground levelled off a little, improving visibility. There was practically no undergrowth between the massive tree trunks. It would be almost impossible for anything or anyone to sneak up on them. Nothing that his warrior mind could see as a potential threat or ambush site presented itself; but Jade's Elven intuition had served them well before. He'd be stupid to ignore it.

"I can't see anything. You're sure?"

She shook her head. "No. I just feel…edgy. I'm not even sure if it's something behind us or in front."

"We'd best keep moving then," he said firmly. "Keep a sharp lookout, guys," he addressed Marcus and Brynn in a low tone, "Jade thinks we're being watched."

Jade tilted her head to one side and pressed her mouth into a line. "I don't think it's anything right here. It's something about..." she waved a hand about, indicating their surroundings, "everything. I don't know," frustration was clear in her tone, "there's just something not right." She grimaced. "Sorry."

Phoenix laid a reassuring hand on her shoulder. "Hey, don't beat yourself up. You've warned us, now it's up to us to be alert. Let's get a move on." He glanced up at the thin blue sky far above. "I'm guessing the days will be a bit shorter if we're further north. If you're right, we don't really want to be caught out in the forest at night."

She opened her mouth as though she were going to

argue with him just for the sake of it but apparently changed her mind. She shut her mouth sharply and nodded.

Phoenix felt oddly elated by that short interchange. He was getting the hang of it this leadership thing now. He just had to be firm and decisive, rather than bossy. Of course, it probably helped that he'd listened to her fears and taken them seriously. Smiling to himself, Phoenix took up his position in line. Maybe there was hope after all.

A wolf howled. It sounded close.

Moments later, another answered. Definitely closer.

"The wolves from last night?" Phoenix asked sharply. "Is that what you're sensing?"

Jade's knuckles were white on her staff. "Maybe? Part of it, at least. Yes, I can feel them now. There are more than twenty, this time. They're coming at us fast. I just don't know if that's the only thing..." She shook her head helplessly.

"One thing at a time." He gripped his sword hilt. "Let's move a little faster people. Keep an eye out for shelter or, at a pinch, a big rock we can climb onto."

They picked up the pace, stumbling over the uneven, slippery ground, watching for shadowy forms in the trees as well as where their feet were going. More howls followed them then soft, sharp barks and curious whines that carried clearly in the crisp air. It sounded like the pack was communicating. Still the wolves were hidden from sight, even though their noises came from everywhere.

"There!" Jade panted, pointing off to the right.

The others caught the merest flicker of movement; and another. The pack closed in.

Truda sucked in great, sobbing breaths as she struggled to keep up the gruelling pace. Time after time she slipped, held up only by Phoenix's hand under her arm.

Lean, grey wolf bodies finally showed themselves. They slid in and out of faint patches of sunlight; sometimes nearer, sometimes further away - as though taunting their prey. All around, the barks, whines and growls continued.

Three animals on the right surged closer, almost within weapons reach. They snarled and growled, dashing forward then scurrying back with flattened ears and tucked in tails as sword or staff struck at them.

Brynn veered to the left, away from the sharp, white teeth snapping at his arm.

Phoenix pounded grimly on behind Truda and the others. What the hell were the wolves waiting for? Why didn't they just attack? It was almost…as if they were just herding the humans - but that made no sense at all. Wolves didn't behave like that, did they?

Beneath their feet, the ground levelled. Ahead, the woods opened to reveal a small lake, glassily reflecting the pale blue sky. Brynn skidded to a halt at the waters' edge, turning to cast a desperate look first at Phoenix then left and right along the gently-sloping shore. There was no sign of shelter: no rocks, no caves and no huts this time.

Twenty four wolves eased out of the shadows, sliding into a perfect half-circle around the travellers. Pink tongues dangled over wicked, pointed teeth. Lean grey legs bunched, ready to spring.

There was nowhere left to run.

CHAPTER FIVE

One more wolf padded out of the gloom to sit directly before the children. Jade drew a quick breath. It was the same grey-eyed, black wolf from last night. His ears twitched toward her and, for a second, those grey eyes stared right into hers. He sat before them with regal poise and, somehow, amusement on his long face; radiating power and alpha-control. It was clear the pack awaited only his command before attacking.

Phoenix slid out his sword, its metal-on-metal slither bizarrely out of place in this isolated forest. Marcus unslung his bow and drew an arrow forth from its quiver. The black wolf began a low, almost subsonic growl. The rest of the pack took it up until it thrummed through Jade's body. She clapped her hands over her ears, trying to shut out the sound; the sense of strangeness; the unnerving weirdness of the whole situation. It didn't work. There was something very wrong.

"Why haven't they attacked?" Phoenix whispered.

Jade shook her head. "I don't know. I….I can't think clearly. I don't know what's wrong with me." She clung to her staff, using it to hold herself up. Her head spun with the weight of foreboding and fear.

"Can't you put them all to sleep or something?" Phoenix urged.

Jade shook herself, trying to focus. "I'll try." She half-closed her eyes, attempting to keep her skittish mind on the task at hand.

"Sleep," she Commanded, pointing at the alpha wolf.

The black wolf blinked at her, opened his mouth wide

in a toothy yawn and shook his head but stayed disappointingly upright.

She gasped. The others cast her puzzled looks. She shook her head.

"It didn't work. There's something blocking me. I...I don't think any of my spells will work!"

Phoenix looked quickly about, pointing to where the sun hung, ominously low, behind the trees to the southwest.

"We'll just have to think of something else, fast. It'll be dark soon and we can't stay here all night watching wolves. Suggestions?"

"We could head north along the lake edge," Marcus offered. "That way we can keep watching them and they can't outflank us."

"Sounds good," Phoenix agreed. He hadn't to taken his eyes off the wolves.

Jade couldn't think of an alternative, so she went along with the others as they began to move slowly north. The loss of magic shook her to the core. She tried several spells, muttering them under her breath at the oblivious wolves. Nothing worked. Deeply frightened, she trailed behind Phoenix and Brynn, bereft and lost.

As they approached the closest wolf, it eyed Phoenix, before glancing at the black wolf. The alpha jerked his chin up and gave a sharp yip. The wolf backed up, opening a gap along the lakeshore.

They let their prey go.

Or did they?

Just as Jade began to hope they would all back off, the pack formed into a line and began to pace alongside, picking up speed, pushing the humans to run faster but always keeping a cautious distance, just beyond swordpoint.

"They're herding us." Jade caught up to Phoenix, unable to keep fear out of her voice.

He nodded in reply. "I just wish we knew where.

Can't you do anything?"

"I've been trying but it seems like the further we head this direction, the worse my control over magic gets. I can barely think coherently, let alone formulate a spell correctly." She leaned on her staff as she ran, drawing deep, shuddering breaths, glancing forward. "It's as though whatever it is we're going towards has some way of scrambling my brain and my magic. I'm scared, Phoenix."

"Tell me about it," he muttered, frowning. "This is turning out to be one of the less enjoyable adventures we've had so far in this world."

"How can you make jokes at a time like this?" Jade demanded, angry that he just didn't seem to understand how dire the situation was. She had no magic!

Phoenix cast a quick, quizzical look at her as they ran. "It helps me cope. Does worrying actually fix anything?"

Unable to think of an answer, Jade dropped behind, glaring at his back.

The group ran north, always with half an eye on the silent wolf pack padding alongside like ghostly bodyguards. As long as they ran in the right direction, the animals kept their distance but as soon as they made any attempt to deviate, a flurry of snarling and growling resulted.

The banks of the lake steepened, becoming a rocky cliff with crumbling edges. Still the wolves pushed them on, hounding them right to the edge of a deep gorge. Skidding to a halt, the five weary travellers peered into its freezing depths without enthusiasm. Rocks, loosened by their weight, tumbled down into a stream that fed the lake. The sides were sheer and slippery, the water a jumble of black pools, swift white water and shadowed grey rocks still topped with snow and ice.

"It's too deep and fast," Jade yelled above the noise of rushing water. "We can't cross here. Truda and Brynn will get swept away and we'll all freeze in seconds. There has to be-"

"There."   Brynn clutched at her arm, pointing upstream.   Sure enough, his sharp eyes had spotted a possible crossing: a thick log. Fallen in some past storm, it lay askew from bank to bank.   The closest end was anchored precariously in place by a tangle of roots still clinging to the eroded bank. Dead branches protruded from the trunk in awkward directions. Moss, lichen, snow and ice covered every inch of bark. Hardly a three lane bridge, it would be a dangerous and difficult crossing.

Jade saw Phoenix glance at the tree, down into the stream-bed and over his shoulder at the wolves behind. He swallowed hard.

"Oh man," he murmured. "I hate heights."

She laughed nervously, perversely glad that he showed some anxiety.   Served him right for being so superior before.

"You can always stay here and play with the nice doggies," Brynn said.

Phoenix sent him a sour look. "Just for that, you can go first."

The boy shrugged. "Suits me. I'd rather be on that side anyway." Eyeing the waiting wolves warily, he edged toward the dirt-clogged rootball. The wolves backed away, giving ground.   The black wolf sat on his haunches, watching them all in a disdainful manner; as though he had better things to do and just wished they'd get out of his territory.

Marcus kept an eye on the wolves as the others watched Brynn. The boy picked his way, clambering over exposed roots, onto the thickest part of the fallen trunk. There were no branches there, so he moved slowly, arms outstretched like a tightrope walker, feet shuffling inch by inch along the slippery bark.

Shadows lengthened. Jade held her breath.

Reaching the halfway point, Brynn wrapped his arms

the first branch. He jumped a little, making the entire tree flex and creak. Jade couldn't help the little sound of fear that escaped her throat. Phoenix groaned. Truda clutched at Jade's arm, hiding her face. Brynn jumped again, grinning at them.

"It'll be-"

His foot slipped and he lost his balance, yelling as he slid half-off the rotting wood. He held on, fingers barely clinging to end of the thin branch. It bent under his weight. Phoenix took off, outdistancing the others as they hurried to help.

Wolves forgotten, Jade and Truda watched helplessly as Phoenix scrambled onto the log. Brynn slid further, both feet now dangling high above the whitewater below. His cry for help vanished in the roar. A mist of droplets clung to his hair and fur clothing, giving him a strangely ghostly appearance.

Jade wracked her brain for a spell – anything that might help. Her mind was blank. She had nothing. It seemed that every spell she knew had been wiped. She was just an ordinary person again. Her body shook with fear and the effort to remember. Nothing. Despair gripped her.

Phoenix, visibly pale and sweating, wobbled his way along the fallen log, arms extended, eyes firmly fixed ahead. He reached down to grab Brynn's arm. Hauling the boy up, Phoenix waited until he'd steadied himself then the pair continued to the other side, both breathing hard. Even from a distance, Jade could see Phoenix's hands shaking. At least he had done something, though. If it had been left to her, Brynn would have fallen.

Numb, Jade barely heard Marcus' low-voiced urging, barely remembered the perilous, slippery walk across the log-bridge. She had failed. When her friends needed her most, she hadn't been able to do anything. She really was useless, just as her mother had always said.

The minute Jade set foot on the opposite side of the

river, the feeling of helplessness doubled until she felt physically ill. She saw Phoenix and the others eyeing her with concern but couldn't make herself voice words of reassurance.

Behind her, the others talked about the departure of the wolf-pack. She ignored them, watching the forest, instead. Truda yelled something in her own language at the black wolf, stamping her little foot in anger as it bared yellow teeth at her. Phoenix made some sort of comment about the pack's odd behaviour but Jade ignored that, too.

Something was wrong. Something worse than wolves. She just didn't know what.

She trailed along as the others turned away from the ravine to continue the hunt for a settlement or shelter before darkness fell. What else could she do? There was nothing definitive she could go on to warn them. An all-pervading fear of the unknown was hardly a threat they could stick their swords into.

"We'd better find a safe campsite soon," Marcus called out over his shoulder to Phoenix.

Phoenix nodded and pointed at a fallen log near the lake edge. "We need a few minutes to rest, though. Those wolves pushed us hard."

The two youngest companions, rednosed and exhausted, lurched a few more metres to sit on a rotting log. Jade however, filled with nervous energy, strode back and forth before them, casting anxious glances in all directions. Her breath clouded the air in great, white huffs.

She eyed the sun. It sank lower. Unless the village was within a few hundred metres, there was no way they were going to reach it tonight – if it even existed. Marcus was right: they needed shelter. For some reason, the thought of being out at night sent a paralysing wave of fear through her, making her stomach lurch.

Desperate, she hauled Phoenix & Marcus to one side, digging her fingers into their arms like clamps.

"It's getting worse – that feeling, I mean," she said urgently. Letting go she wrung her hands around the smooth wood of her staff. "I can't think. I...it's like...like when you're about to walk into an exam you haven't studied enough for and your stomach is all churned up and sick – but much, much worse." She looked away from their blank, puzzled expressions, searching for something in the woods. Something she couldn't see but knew was there.

Phoenix and Marcus followed her glance.

"I can't see anything, Jade." Phoenix laid a soothing hand on her arm.

She shook it off impatiently. He was right. There was nothing to see – maybe that was the problem. She narrowed her eyes in suspicion. The woods seemed very bare in this part of the world. There was no undergrowth and not even any reeds around the edge of the lake – just bare earth, patches of slushy snow and brown pine needles. That could be because they had arrived before the true beginning of spring and the vegetation simply hadn't sprouted yet. Otherwise, nothing seemed amiss.

"We got away from the wolves." Marcus spread out his hands to indicate a total absence of danger. "What else is there?"

Jade sucked in a shaky sob and turned a wild look on Phoenix. Her hands trembled uncontrollably now, fingertips white. She ran a hand through her hair.

"I...I don't know...I..." She darted a look around again, half-expecting an attack any second. "I can't concentrate. There's something...here...somewhere. It's...blocking my magic. It's horrible; destructive. I can't stand it much longer!" She wrapped her arms around her body and shivered.

Phoenix frowned, hesitated then shrugged. "Alright. You sit down a moment. I'll keep watch." He turned to peer into the empty forest as the others rested.

Jade sank onto the log next to Truda. The girl leaned her head on Jade's shoulder and patted her leg with gentle concern.

"It's ok," Truda's childish voice interrupted Jade's fearful thoughts. "You just need to eat. Here," she pushed something into Jade's fingers, "try this."

Distracted, Jade ate automatically, watching the surrounding forest for signs or enemies. There had to be some reason she was feeling so jittery.

It was several seconds before her brain registered that what she was chewing wasn't dried or smoked meat. It tasted like bitter lettuce. Confused, Jade glanced down at the food Truda had given her. It was a flower; its many pink petals dewed with sparkling drops of water. Large and cup-shaped, its heart darkened to the deepest scarlet, dusted gold with pollen. A vivid splash of exotic colour in this otherwise grey-green place, it rested like blood in her cold, white hand. A red water lily.

With growing horror and bewilderment, she stared first at it then at Truda's innocent, smiling young face. Did Truda know what the chemicals in this flower did? Was she deliberately trying to sabotage Jade's ability to function? Jade shook her head, trying to think straight. She blinked. The world began to blur. Slowly, a strange feeling of peace settled over her turbulent thoughts; muffling her fears until she couldn't remember why she'd been so worried in the first place. Everything seemed distant and unimportant. What a relief.

What had she been doing?

Oh yes, eating something. That's right. She was very hungry. Vaguely, she lifted another petal to her lips.

*****

Phoenix turned to glance over his shoulder at Jade. She seemed a little calmer, at least. As he watched, she placed something pink into her mouth and chewed slowly. Truda sat beside her, patting her hand and nodding like a wise old lady. Jade blinked, the frown clearing from her smooth brow, her expression turning blank and serene. He looked more closely. What on earth was she eating?

Two long strides brought him to her side. With an angry exclamation, Phoenix snatched the flower from her hand and tossed it to the ground. It lay there, a broken, bleeding heart on a patch of dirty white snow.

"What is that?" he demanded angrily of Truda.

The child shrank from him, her big blue eyes wide.

"Just a waterlily," she said. "They just make you happy when you chew them. Everyone knows that. Jade was all worried and look," she pointed at Jade's beautiful, now-calm face, "see, she's fine."

Catching Jade's face in his hands Phoenix slapped her cheek gently. She turned glassy green eyes on him.

"Oh!" She smiled with childlike delight, her words slurring almost unrecognisably. "Red water lily! Of course. Now I know where we are..." She giggled and her eyes drifted closed.

"Jade!" Phoenix shook her slim shoulders. Her head rocked a little but her blissful expression remained unaltered. When he let her go, she simply sat there, smiling. He rounded on Truda, fear lending sharpness to his voice. "You drugged her! She said she knows where we are!"

Truda ducked behind Brynn, who half-turned as though not sure if he should protect her.

"But Uncle Loki gives it to my brothers, Magni and Modi, all the time," the god-child wailed. "He says it settles them down. Jade was getting so upset..." she bit her lip, burst into tears and hid her face in her hands. "I'm s.sorry. I didn't know it was bad. It usually takes heaps to make Modi go quiet."

Phoenix stepped forward, reaching out a hand to throttle her. He checked himself, threw up both hands and made a noise of sheer exasperation. Girls! Why did they have to cry at you?! How did he explain to a six year old that a worried, anxious, alert Jade was better than a peaceful, stupefied one who couldn't do anything now to save herself – or them.

Aaarrrgh!

Taking several long, slow breaths, he tried to calm himself. OK. Truda was just a kid. She didn't know any better. So, with Jade in la-la land, they would have to be extra cautious and really watch out for whatever she had been scared of. Knowing exactly where they were would have to wait until Jade was back to normal.

"Is there an antidote? How long will the effect last?" he demanded, trying to speak calmly when he wanted to shout at Truda.

The girl shrugged. "I dunno but it won't hurt her." When Phoenix scowled at her, she hastened to add more. "Unca Loki gives Mag and Modi two or three flowers each and it just makes them kinda dopey for a little while." She gave a sheepish little smile. "He hates it when they make a racket and tease him. He says he just wants them to stop being pests."

"I know how he feels," he muttered, glaring at her. "But," he frowned at Jade's blank stare, "she only had a small part of one, so why should she be so out of it?"

"Perhaps," Marcus' deep, thoughtful voice intruded, "she's more affected because she's a half-elf?"

"You could be right," Phoenix agreed.

Elves were closely bound and connected to all things natural. It made sense that Jade would be more affected by a natural sedative than the children of a god.

"Dammit!" He slapped his hand on a tree trunk. "Talk about bad timing! OK," he drew a long breath and tried to think logically. "Brynn," he laid a hand on the youngster's thin shoulder, "you'll have to keep us heading northeast as planned. Think you can? Keep an eye out for any kind of shelter, though."

In a flash, the young boy's troubled expression cleared. Giving Phoenix a mock-salute, he skipped a few steps in the right direction. "Course. Follow me."

Phoenix grinned at the youngster's infectious enthusiasm. "Marcus, you go next with Jade." The Roman nodded and took Jade by the hand. She moved without resisting, like a sleepwalker.

"You, young lady," Phoenix shook his finger at Truda, "will stay with me where I can keep an eye on you. No more surprises like that, understand?"

She bit her lip and nodded, falling into step with him.

"By the way," he asked after a few moments, "where did you get that lily?"

"Oh, they grow in the lake." She waved a hand in that direction.

He glanced out across the water. The lake was just as empty as before. There were no scarlet flowers anywhere. No plants of any sort; not even any birds.

He eyed the girl suspiciously. "There's nothing there. Where did you find it?"

She blinked up at him and shook her head. "I didn't find it," she said, "I growed it, silly."

CHAPTER SIX

Phoenix stopped short, grabbing Truda by the shoulder and spinning her to face him. "You grew that lily flower? When? How?"

Ahead, Marcus and Brynn halted and turned back, pulling Jade docilely along with them.

Truda scuffed a toe in the damp earth. "Just now. S'what I do." She shrugged a shoulder. "Y'know?"

Phoenix crouched in front of her and gripped her arms. She looked back at him, her eyes huge.

"No, Truda," he replied with barely curbed impatience, "I don't know. You'll have to explain it to us. How did you grow that flower?"

Brynn gasped. "The Power! Remember? The druids said something about us wanting the Jewel of Asgard for its power. The druids draw their magic from nature and they said they had used the Jewel's power to fight the Romans. This must be what they meant. I mean," he stared at the girl in thoughtful fascination, "she is the daughter of a god, after all. She must have some sort of abilities."

"Is Brynn right?" Phoenix straightened up. "Are you some sort of deity?"

Truda blinked in confusion. "Deity? Oh, you mean a god." She tilted hr head to one side. "I guess, but I don't have any like...y'know...worshippers or anything."

"What can you do?" He tried to keep eagerness out of his voice. Perhaps he'd just found a weapon of mass destruction; or a way to instantly transport them all vast distances in some magic chariot of the gods.

There was a long pause as they all stared at the girl in

hope.

"I can make plants grow," she finally replied in a small voice.

Phoenix's rising hopes fell with a resounding thud. He sighed and dropped his hands from her arms. "That's it? You're some sort of minor goddess of plant growth?"

"Hey!" Truda was indignant, "I help Gefjun to make Hodr go away and then I help the plants grow again." She put her hands on her hips, "This year Gefjun said I was going to be helping the farmers' crops grow – all on my own! And if I don't get back to do it in time, Hodr will stay and Ragnarok will come!" She nodded sharply and raised her button nose in the air.

Phoenix sighed again, wishing Jade were alert enough to tell him who was who in Norse mythology. She was the reader. He had no idea. Thor, he'd heard of but the other two...

"And Gefjun and Hodr are...?" he prompted.

"Gefjun is goddess of fertility and farming." Truda rolled her eyes like he was stupid for not knowing. "Hodr is the god of winter, a course. Without me, Hodr keeps the snows too long and the farmers can't plant their crops." She looked critically at the frost-hardened, bare ground. "If I don't get back by my birthday, the seasons will be all unbalanced. Hodr will stay and there'll be Winter then Fire then Ragnarok will come and the gods'll-"

"Yes, yes" Phoenix interrupted, "we know the drill. Four more days or Gods and giants will fight; mankind and the world will be destroyed; ra-de-ra-de-ra." He bowed. "Well, after you my lady. Must get you home so you can send Hodr packing and get those plants sprouting. Can't have Ragnarok happening on our account, can we?"

Brynn tugged on his arm, frowning. "Truda just said something about things being unbalanced. 'Member when the druids talked about having to send Truda away to keep the 'balance'? What do you think it means?"

Phoenix shrugged, too irritated to worry about philosophical ideas at that point. "I haven't got a clue. Personally, I think the druids were just sick of her and wanted to get her out of their hair as fast as possible – and I have to agree with them. C'mon. We need to get moving if we're going to get her home before the whole damned world explodes."

Far from getting Truda home, they managed only a few more kilometres before the short northern day dwindled into grey evening. The village they'd hoped to reach was nowhere in sight and the forest bore no indications of human use – no wood-chopping, no clear paths, not even much animal life.

Phoenix peered through the darkening dusk and swore. He'd come to rely on Jade's superior, half-elven vision at these times. The moon was rising, and they couldn't travel much further without food, anyway. They had to find shelter before nightfall but darkness crept in mighty fast.

"There!" Brynn called. "Up ahead there's a cave, I think."

"Great!" Phoenix was relieved but as Brynn dashed off, a sobering thought occurred to him and he yelled out, "Be careful! Watch for..um..bears and stuff!"

The youngster waved an acknowledgement over his shoulder and approached the cave mouth from the side, rather than front on. Marcus and Phoenix drew out their swords. Truda huddled against Jade, holding one lax hand. Jade swayed gently, still not alert enough even to run if there was trouble.

Brynn struck a spark with his flint and coaxed a small amount of brushwood alight. He then lit some sort of rag and wrapped it around a thick branch. The boy peered cautiously around a protruding rock and flicked the branch deep into the cave.

After a few tense moments, Brynn glanced back over his shoulder and gave a thumbs-up sign. Phoenix nodded and they all advanced. Inside the cave, the torch was still alight, its flickering golden flames sending shadows dancing across sloping stone walls. A small chamber off to one side of the larger front cave was safe and big enough to shelter them all easily. Best of all, it was dry and empty.

Brynn inspected the floor and sniffed the air. He frowned and shook his head.

"I don't think anything lives here." Hesitating, he looked around again. "It doesn't smell like an animal den, anyway. But..." He sent a worried glance around.

"I know what you mean." Phoenix eyed the rear of the cave where a large opening showed only vast darkness. "The ground is packed down here like something often walks through but it doesn't smell like an animal den. People?" He raised an eyebrow at Marcus.

Surprisingly, it was Truda who answered.

"Oh no," she assured them, "all the people live in houses, not in caves. The only time they use caves is for sacrifices to the Æsir but there's no bones or anything, so it can't be that."

"Æsir?" "Bones!" Marcus and Brynn spoke at once, asking exactly the questions Phoenix wanted to. He was kind of sick of Truda's little surprises.

"Oh," she giggled, "I keep forgetting you're from Albion, not here. The Bretons have different gods. The Æsir are the gods, like me," she pointed a finger at her chest, "but the people who live in Midgard," rolling her eyes, she stopped Brynn's question before it started, "Midgard is this world, Asgard is where the Æsir live – where I live. Anyway – the people who live in Midgard sometimes make sacrifices to Grandpa Odinn."

"Sacrifices!" Brynn squeaked.

Truda grinned at his fear. "Silly, they don't sacrifice people – at least, not much any more - just goats and stuff. It's a bit gross, really." She made a face. "It doesn't look like they do it here, anyway."

"That'll do," Phoenix interrupted, hoping to turn the discussion away from bloody animal sacrifices to pagan gods.

It was almost full night and they had yet to find food. This was no time to stand around discussing religious practices. Ushering his little band into the cave, he made another of Brynn's torches then set him and Truda to gathering firewood. Marcus settled Jade on a stone ledge off to one side, well-wrapped in her furs and cloak. Much to Phoenix's disgust, she promptly fell into a deep sleep from which no-one could wake her.

"I guess she'll just have to sleep it off," he grumbled, standing over her inert form.

Marcus cast her an anxious look. "I'll try and find some game." He glanced out the cave entrance. "I don't like my chances at this time of night, though. Strange," he frowned, "I haven't seen many traces of small animals – or even big ones – since we crossed that river."

Phoenix exchanged worried looks with him and, together, they both gazed back at Jade.

"Do you think it has anything to do with whatever she was afraid of?" Phoenix gave voice to the question they were both considering.

"Possibly," Marcus said, "but if something's taken all the local game, we're going to go hungry tonight."

"Well," Phoenix sighed, "go hunt. But if you're not back in an hour I'm coming after you."

The Roman gave a half-smile and gripped Phoenix's forearm in a gesture of friendship and equality. Unslinging his bow, he turned and ran lightly out the entrance to be swallowed by the thin, cold darkness.

Truda and Brynn returned with great armfuls of brushwood and branches. Most of it was damp, so the result was a smoky, smouldering fire that did little to heat the cave. Without complaint, Brynn bullied Truda into coming closer to dry her soaked boots and thaw her chilled hands. She pouted, coughed and complained about being hungry. The grumbling of their stomachs was audible across the room.

Phoenix pulled out the Hyllion Bagia, thrust his hand in and hopefully requested food. Nothing slapped into his hand so he tucked the bag back into Jade's pack. The endless bag had Roman javelins, money and who knew what else in it but obviously they'd eaten all the food. Oh well, it had been worth a shot.

There were a few meagre strips of baked bird-meat left in his pack. He handed them around with the advice to chew slowly as it might be all they got. Again, Brynn simply nodded while Truda groused. Brynn pushed his own share into Truda's hand but Phoenix said nothing to him. The boy had proven himself tough enough for this journey over and over again. He wasn't going to humiliate him by acting all fatherly and making him eat his food.

When the hour was almost up, Phoenix moved to the entrance and stared out into the silent blackness. The first silvery rays of moonlight filtered through the canopy but shadows still outnumbered any faint patches of light.

Something wasn't right. The feeling had crept irresistibly over him ever since they'd entered the cave. Something was very wrong and it had nothing to do with the gnawing hunger in his gut.

Brynn appeared at his side, looking outside. Truda pattered up to huddle behind both of them, her face peeking out over Brynn's shoulder.

"I don't like this. Marcus is taking too long, but if I go you two will be unprotected with Jade still comatose." Phoenix growled. "I wish we'd reached that village. At least we'd know where we are. Then, maybe, we could work out where to go next."

"Oh dear," Truda hispered, "I hope he hasn't run into a Troll."

Phoenix forced a laugh. "Don't be silly. Of course he

hasn't run into a Troll." Truda's big eyes blinked solemnly up at him. "There're no trolls around here!" he said sharply, hoping she would agree. "We don't even know where we are. How could you know if there are trolls here?" Despair sank into the pit of his stomach as she continued to stare at him. "Please tell me there are no trolls here?"

"But we're in Trolltiven," she said simply. "Of course there are trolls."

"Of course there are trolls," he repeated, slapping his own forehead. "Oh man!" He paused, eyeing Truda. "Hang on a sec. You said you didn't know if you'd recognise Trolltiven. How can you be so sure now?"

She widened her eyes. "Jade told me just before she fell asleep that we're in Svealand, so then I rec'nised it from when Pa took me hunting two summers ago. We're in the great Tiveden forest. Trolltiven's the bit in between Geatsland and Svealand. Nobody comes here – 'cause of the trolls."

Phoenix growled and she ducked behind Brynn.

Phoenix clenched his fists together and shook them silently at the stone ceiling. *Preserve me from all irritating, know-it-all, superior and yet amazingly stupid females,* he yelled inside his head. It wasn't safe to make that sort of request out loud in a world where gods really did exist and might just grant it. Right at this very moment, though, he would be very, very tempted to say 'yes, please' if some handy god offered to take both Jade and Truda away.

Jade was an over-anxious brainiac sometimes but Truda was worse. She seemed to know instinctively exactly when to reveal bits of information so they would cause the most chaos. Telling them about Trolltiven *before* they'd let the wolves herd them headlong into it would have been a whole lot more useful!

He should have paid more attention to Jade's fears.

Trying to get a grip on his frustration, Phoenix paced

the short length of the cave a couple of times while Brynn and Truda watched him in wide-eyed silence. Sucking in five long, slow breaths, he finally put a lid on his emotions and faced the pair calmly.

"OK, Truda." He stood before her, arms folded. "Talk to me. Tell me where we are and where we need to go to get you home. No!" He put out a hand to cover her mouth as she opened it. "Belay that. I have to get my priorities straight. Tell me about trolls. If Marcus is in trouble, I need to know how to defeat them."

She shook her head. "The only way I know of is daylight. They can't be killed by anything else." Her voice was muffled by his hand. Phoenix took it away and wiped it absently on his shirt.

"Nothing?" He glared at her.

She shook her head again.

"What about iron weapons?" He drew his sword. "If they're magical creatures then they should be susceptible to iron like Jade is."

He half-turned to look at Jade's peaceful features and remembered how Agricola's iron blade had scalded her cheek in Britain. The druid's Spring Rite had smoothed the mark away. Damn, if only she were awake, she could fight the troll with magic – or maybe not. Maybe this troll was what had been blocking her before.

"Oh, no." Truda said with horrible cheerfulness. "Trolls aren't like Elves. They aren't affected by iron or magic. In fact, Trolls have such thick skin that weapons just bounce off and magic just doesn't even work around them. Nope," she shook her head blithely, "only sunlight kills them. Turns them to statues straight away."

"Fabulous. It's only…oh…ten hours or so until morning." He scrubbed both hands through his hair, trying to physically pull an idea out of his head.

Jade. He needed Jade awake. She always seemed to come up with the brilliant schemes at the last minute. All he knew how to do was fight and apparently that wasn't an option this time.

Striding to Jade's side, he shouted at her to wake up then reached out and shook her roughly. Her whole body flopped and her head, too. Brynn rushed over to push him aside.

"You'll break her neck," the boy yelled. "Stop it!"

Phoenix turned away and snatched up a waterskin. He poured liquid over her face. Surely that would work. Freezing water dribbled down her white cheeks and made little puddles in her ears and at the base of her throat. She slept on.

"Dammit, Jade," he whispered. "What do I do?"

Outside, a hoarse, masculine scream sounded in the distance. It was followed by a sound like large rocks being forcibly ground against each other; and then another yell tinged with despair and fear. With one last, hopeless glance at Jade, Phoenix gripped his sword and strode toward the cave entrance.

"What are you going to do?" Brynn peered up at him, his own little knife held tightly in one hand.

Phoenix stared out into the darkness. "I have no idea but I have to help Marcus." He laid a hand on the boy's shoulder. "Whatever it is, we'll try and kill it or lead it away. Hole up in the small cave and if we're not back by morning, take Jade to find that village and…I don't know," his mind was numb, "do whatever she says."

"But weapons won't work if it's really a troll," Brynn reminded him.

"I know that but Marcus doesn't. I have to help him. Look after the girls. I'm counting on you."

The boy swallowed and nodded. Swiftly, he made another torch from a rag and a thick branch. Handing it over he whispered, "Good luck."

Phoenix grinned through gritted teeth. "I think I'll need it. You too."

Brandishing the torch before him, he stepped out into the inky night.

CHAPTER SEVEN

Phoenix walked into the crisp, cold darkness and shivered. The torch in his hand cast an uncertain orange light on the ground. Overhead, just visible through the sighing treetops, the waning moon shone in a star-dusted sky. Its pale light served only to make the shadows blacker and the trees bigger.

Again the ominous sound of huge rocks grinding together echoed through the silent forest; and again Marcus yelled his defiance. Phoenix turned toward the noise and ran - carefully. The torch sputtered and sizzled as he peered ahead, trying to pick the safest path. Once he stumbled and almost dropped the torch into a shadowy snowbank. Soon his breath came in sharp spurts as he pushed himself harder and took more chances. He had to get to Marcus before he was slaughtered.

The grinding noise grew louder and Phoenix skidded to a halt as he came up to a large boulder. Holding his torch behind him, he edged forward and peeked around the corner. There, just visible in the centre of a large clearing, stood Marcus. His sword drawn, three dead hares at his feet, the Roman stared upward with a mixture of fear, defiance and resignation on his face. Phoenix followed his gaze and almost dropped his sword in shock.

Towering over his friend was what appeared to be an enormous stack of grey, lichenous rocks, teetering in a strange, gravity-defying formation. The grinding sound he'd heard came from the very top. The piles moved. Phoenix swallowed a gasp of terror. With movement, the heap of rocks resolved into a horrendously huge, living thing. It was over twenty feet tall, with a body that appeared to be made of granite and limbs that were more of the same: lumpy, chunky, hard, stone. He supposed the misshapen pile of boulders on top could only be its head. It had to be a troll.

From high above a long arm descended, thick fingers bunched into a fist. Marcus skipped aside and the fist smashed into the ground with the sound of a small earthquake, splattering the hares. As he turned Phoenix saw Marcus clutched only the hilt of his now-shattered blade. His bow was slung over his shoulder; the quiver empty of arrows. Again the arm smashed down; again Marcus danced away; again that crunching, grinding noise sounded – this time almost rhythmically. With a start, Phoenix realised it was the troll: laughing. The beast wasn't trying to kill Marcus – it was playing with him!

Marcus had to be tired. He had had little sleep after fighting the Romans in Stonehenge and the wolves had pushed them hard through the forest today. Phoenix heard his breath coming in ragged gasps as he spun away once more. It was only a matter of time before Marcus lost his footing on the wet earth and was crushed to death beneath that juggernaut fist.

Desperately, Phoenix looked around for inspiration. Where was Jade with her ideas when he needed her? Nothing leapt to mind. There were no convenient solutions lying around. His heart raced and his brain seemed to swim in stupidity. Thumping the heel of his hand against his own forehead, Phoenix cursed himself. Think, think!

If he were sitting safely in his chair at home and this were on the computer screen, how would he handle it? Impossible leaps and ninja karate kicks wouldn't help against a giant made of rock. What would? Not weapons or magic. What was left? Daylight. Phoenix glanced up the silvery moon. Hours away. What was a substitute for daylight then?

A fragment of smouldering cloth fell from his torch, biting into the back of his hand. He absently pressed the small burn to his cold cheek then pulled it away to stare at the scorch mark. He looked at the burning torch.

Well, it wasn't daylight but, if the trolls were truly creatures of the night, perhaps they hated flame almost as much. It was worth a try. He glanced around. What could he burn, though? Everything was soggy with the recent snow. Everything except... Phoenix looked up at the nearest pine tree and grinned wickedly. Pine forests. Lots of flammable oils in pine needles. His mother was forever telling him, at Christmas time, to be careful in case their tree went up in flames from a carelessly held candle. So, now it was time to see if her worry was justified.

Reaching up Phoenix touched the torch to the lowest branch of a tree and held his breath. The needles sputtered and sparked, flared and went out. Thin grey spirals of scented smoke soared into the air. No! It had to work. Resolutely, he pushed aside the horrible thought that their Christmas tree might actually have been plastic. Everyone knew that pine trees burned easily. He risked a quick look at Marcus. The boy half-knelt on the wet ground, shoulders heaving. He staggered back to his feet just in time to dodge another thunderous blow from the chortling troll.

Phoenix thrust the torch right into the midst of a dense patch of needles. This time they caught, flickered, dimmed and then burst into bright little flames that ate their way quickly up to the base of each needle. He held his breath, watching, hoping. Just as he thought the fires would stutter and die, a gust of wind fanned the little flickers into bigger ones that jumped up to the next branch and the next. With a massive whoomph that seemed to suck the oxygen from his lungs, the whole tree overhead blazed and came alive with dancing golden light and heat. Startled, Phoenix shielded his face and backed away, afraid the whole thing might start dropping fire on him.

There was a horrific, deafening avalanche of sound. He spun. He'd backed into the clearing. Marcus ran full tilt toward him. The troll roared again and took two large steps toward them but the burning tree was right behind, warming their backs. The troll put his hands up to protect his craggy face and stayed where he was. He turned his ponderous head to and fro in an effort to see past the glare and find his quarry.

Panting, Marcus grabbed Phoenix's arm. "Thanks," he gasped.

"It's not over yet," Phoenix warned. "The only thing that kills them is sunlight and there's still quite a few hours of night left, I'm afraid."

"What..." Marcus puffed, frowning. "are we supposed to do then?"

"I think...," Phoenix turned to look up at the tree. Its burn-time had been short. Even now the last of the oil-rich needles were sizzling into extinction. There wasn't enough wind to make the fire jump to the next tree. "I think," he repeated, "we're going to have to run for it."

Can't you just," Marcus waved an arm at the tree, "set a few more alight and drive it away?"

"Sure," he replied, "but that might set the whole forest on fire or even send it straight back toward Jade and the others."

"Can't Jade do anything?"

"She's still asleep. We couldn't wake her up – believe me, I tried. Besides, Truda tells me magic doesn't work on trolls either. Must've been what was causing her so much trouble before."

"Is that what that thing is?"

Phoenix nodded. "Evidently we're right in the middle of troll-country."

"Oh, this keeps getting better and better," Marcus muttered.

Phoenix quirked a quick grin. "Ain't it great? Can't

have things getting too dull."

Marcus sent him a sardonic look. "Dull would be a nice change. I'd even opt for boring."

The troll chose that moment to roar at them in its unintelligible, gravelly voice.

Phoenix gripped the torch tighter and pointed with it in a direction away from the cave.

"I don't like your chances of dull or boring happening any time soon," he said. "Let's take turns distracting it and hope it's too stupid to realise what we're doing. We've got to keep it away from the others until morning."

So began the longest night in Phoenix's life – either of his lives, in fact. For hours the two ran, staggered and fell through the cold forest. They took turns hiding and resting while the other carried a torch and ran in a different direction, making enough noise to attract the troll's short attention. Whenever it looked like losing interest, they would yell or light another tree to get it stirred up again – always careful now to choose isolated trees. It had occurred to Phoenix only after setting the first one alight, that a full-scale forest fire might not be such a great idea.

Always the troll thumped after them remorselessly, untiringly; sometimes roaring, sometimes laughing as though this were a hilarious game these puny humans had invented just for its enjoyment.

Late in the night, the moon set and the boys could no longer tell what direction to run. They were exhausted, cold and soaked from the knees down. Phoenix couldn't feel his feet or fingers any longer. He wondered if they were frostbitten. The ground was treacherously slippery underfoot. They stumbled and fell more and more often. At last, even their torch sputtered and gave up, leaving them in utter darkness. Starlight gleamed off to their right. Water. A lake. Considering how many lakes and streams they had seen, it was a miracle they hadn't fallen into one.

"I can't keep going," Marcus whispered. He rested in

the deep shadow of a tree just to Phoenix's left. Phoenix stood with his back pressed to another tree, head down, hands on bent knees taking weight off his legs, breathing hard.

"Me neither," he admitted.

Not far away, a loud crunching, crashing sound told them the troll was close on their trail. Although made of rock, the beast seemed to have the nose of a bloodhound and the night vision of an elf. It delighted in sniffing out their hiding places.

"We could try the lake," Marcus suggested.

"I don't think you can drown a rock," Phoenix said. "Besides, we'd freeze to death in that water."

"Got a better idea?" The Roman sounded aggravated.

"Actually," he tried to sound confident; hoping he was right, "I do. We need to make for high ground. Dawn's not far away now."

That, at least, was true. In the last few minutes, black shadows had lightened to dark grey. A hint of pale sunrise colours showed in the east. If they were really lucky, they might be able to keep the troll occupied for another half an hour. Then, if they were really, really lucky, it would be too far from its home to run back when the sun rose.

Unfortunately, Phoenix had become so turned around during the night that he had no idea in which direction his friends were. He did, however, have a very bad feeling that the cave that currently housed an unconscious Jade and two children was the home of their friendly little troll.

The tree holding Phoenix up shook violently. With another grinding chuckle, the troll grabbed and pulled it back like a giant slingshot. Fear gave both boys a spurt of adrenalin and they sprinted away just as the rock-hands released the trunk. It twanged and creaked in an arc toward them, the tip of the pine dipping low before snapping upright again and swaying to and fro, showering them with ice and snow.

Phoenix scrambled uphill as best he could, picking his way between huge boulders. Hopefully none of them would turn out to be trolls as well. Marcus' uneven breathing rasped close behind. Too close for comfort, came the sound of enormous rocky feet stomping on the slope below.

"Have you..." Phoenix panted, "got your...flint and...tinder?"

"Yes!"

Phoenix paused to glance up and then back over his shoulder. The beast gained on them but so did the light from the eastern sky. It would be close. Resolutely, he gritted his teeth and pushed on his aching thighs to force himself up the slope.

"When we get to the top," he called breathlessly, "I'll distract it while you find something to set fire to. I don't care if it's your own clothes. I want it trapped in a circle of fire when dawn comes, got it?"

"Right." Marcus wasted little breath on the acknowledgment.

Abruptly, the slope levelled out and they emerged from beneath the canopy onto a strangely level hilltop. It looked like a small mountain had been sheered off cleanly by an enormous sword. Phoenix searched rapidly for a hiding place. Unfortunately, the area was not only perfectly flat but also perfectly clean. Not a tree, rock or even a bush broke the unforgiving openness of the space before them. Not even a convenient patch of long grass or ferns.

There was nowhere to hide.

Phoenix had no breath to spare on swearing. He staggered to the very centre of the clearing and cast a desperate glance over his shoulder at the eastern horizon. It glowed beautifully pink and grey in a way that early-rising joggers would have admired. For Phoenix and Marcus, however, it had a worrying lack of bright, shimmering sunshine. Sunrise was at least twenty minutes away and there remained absolutely nowhere they could hide from the troll for that long.

Phoenix stood a few moments longer in the middle of the space and exchanged despairing glances with Marcus. His legs were jelly and each breath stabbed at his lungs. Sometime during the night he'd fallen badly on his side. He suspected one of his ribs was fractured and was sure his right ankle was seriously twisted. As long as he didn't actually look at the bruising, he could convince himself the pain was irrelevant.

"Go," he managed to gasp at Marcus. "I'll try and keep it busy."

The Roman nodded and stumbled off to the other side of the clearing. Phoenix prayed he would find enough dry tinder and willing trees in time. The top of this hill was bigger than he'd hoped. Marcus would have a difficult job to get the entire thing encircled by flame in time for sunrise. If he didn't, this could be the first and last sunrise that Phoenix would ever almost see.

Even as the morbid thought of his own death by flattening occurred, relief spurted through the exhaustion and fear blanketing his mind. He had already died once. His knife still had six jewels on it. Hypothetically, he could die five more times and still come back to life. But one death had been more than enough and he wasn't even slightly keen to test this hypothesis. Besides, there was always the chance that the troll would simply squash him repeatedly with that enormous fist until all of his remaining lives were gone.

What would happen then? Would he be truly dead, or would he find himself back in the real world? Was that an option? Could they just die enough times to get free of this game? No, they had a task to complete as well. Stopping Feng Zhudai was more than just winning this game – it would save both worlds from a horrible future.

From just beyond the edge of the plateau, thunderous

footsteps and that crunching laugh sounded, ominously close. Phoenix saw the troll's ugly head and massive fingers appear as the beast idly brushed aside a fifty foot tree like it was made of spider web.

Phoenix sighed and squared his shoulders as the troll spotted him and chortled roughly. OK. There could be a chance that dying six more times might launch him back into his real life; but there was an even bigger chance it would just make his world and this one a hell-pit of death and disaster. He couldn't take the easy way out by dying. Easy! Hah!

It was time to duel with Death in a world where Death was programmed to win.

CHAPTER EIGHT

As far as he could tell, Phoenix had three advantages: he was smarter and faster than the troll; and there was nothing on this scoured-flat plateau he could trip on. As long as he stayed on his feet and didn't succumb to exhaustion, he should be able to keep the troll occupied long enough for Marcus to complete his task.

Of course, the troll had at least two big advantages of its own: it was indefatigable and indestructible. Did his three outweighed the trolls' two?

The creature trundled closer, looming over him like a mobile cliff-face. Phoenix looked up and swallowed heavily. From this angle, it was hard to believe he had any chance at all. His legs shook.

With one more fleeting glance at the brightening eastern horizon, Phoenix uttered the most childish war-cry in history. He stuck his thumbs in his ears, poked out his tongue and yelled:

"Nyah nyah nyah-nyah nyah – you can't catch me!"

He dove and rolled clumsily to the left. Tiredness and pain made his aikido roll awkward and jarring but it served the purpose. A huge cloud of dust roiled up as the troll's granite fist smacked into the ground where he'd stood.

Clambering to his feet, Phoenix clutched at his ribs with one hand and his sword scabbard with the other. He should have taken it off. It threatened to tangle his legs as he skipped aside again and ducked beneath a swinging, stony arm. The hand passed so close to his head that the wind tossed hair into his eyes. Impatiently, he brushed it aside and stumbled back just as an enormous, craggy foot stomped where he had been. This was never going to work. The troll was simply too big and too strong for him to keep being that lucky. He had to change; had to do the unexpected.

Something his aikido sensei often said came to mind: "Avoid the falling rock".

If he hadn't been so exhausted, Phoenix would have laughed at the irony of it. It was a central idea of Aikido: don't be there; don't go places where you were likely to get in trouble; if you did get into trouble then running away was a great option. His sensei probably never expected the philosophy would be taken quite so literally.

Aikido! That was it!

OK, he couldn't actually throw the troll or put it in a wrist lock but there had to be some way he could use its own strength and movement against it. That was the very basis of how Aikido worked.

An idea glimmered.

Dragging long, painful gasps of breath, Phoenix turned and ran twenty long paces away then doubled back towards the troll at full tilt. The beast stopped short, appearing confused by this sudden change of tactics. It stood uncertainly for a moment. Then it raised a thick arm and swung down at Phoenix's darting form. He dived directly between its legs at the last second. The momentum of its own arm carried the troll further forward than it probably intended. It tried to twist its heavy body to follow Phoenix's path, the beast leaned just a fraction too far and overbalanced. It fell to earth with a resounding thump and a roar that shook the entire mountaintop.

Phoenix didn't stop to watch. He only had a brief respite before the beast would be up again – and probably very angry this time. He spotted Marcus working frantically with a smoky branch. Several trees around the clearing were smouldering nicely. The Roman had chosen trees evenly spaced around the mountaintop. But there weren't enough alight and dawn was still at least ten minutes away. There were big gaps. The creature could still escape if it wanted to.

Time for Plan B.

If only he had a Plan B.

"I need a rope!" he yelled.

Marcus nodded and reached beneath his fur coat. Rapidly, he unwound a long, thin rope from his waist. Phoenix decided now was not the time to ask why it was there in the first place. He was just grateful his companion was so well prepared. Snatching it with a brief nod, Phoenix staggered back into the clearing as the troll unfolded itself and pushed to its feet.

Star Wars time, he thought grimly – just like Luke taking out the Empire's Walker on the snow world of Hoth. With hasty, trembling fingers, he knotted the rope into a huge lasso and laid it out on the ground like a giant snare. Next he laid the free end in a long straight line and backed away a few steps.

The troll paused and watched Phoenix with an air of confused stupidity. It clearly couldn't work out why this puny human was laying such an obvious and ineffective trap. There was no way a troll could be snared by the strength of one man. It peered uncertainly at the loop and at the loose, untethered rope. Then, with a rough laugh, it placed one foot unconcernedly smack into the middle of the lasso.

Phoenix darted forward and snatched up the free end and ran backward, pulling the loop taut around the stony leg. The troll laughed again and stepped back, jerking the rope tighter and pulling Phoenix off his feet. He managed a scrappy breakfall that protected his ribs but winded him. Holding onto the rope, he scrambled upright as the troll trod heavily toward him.

Again Phoenix rushed suicidally toward the monster; again he launched himself between its open legs. This time the troll was a shade quicker and he barely escaped being hit like a croquet ball by the swinging fist. This time it did not overbalance. Instead, it turned around to face this annoying gnat of a human.

In doing so, it did exactly what Phoenix hoped – it tangled the rope around its own legs. He ran as fast as his burning thighs would carry him around the thing. He stayed just out of reach of those fists, darting in every direction to confuse and encircle the troll. It twisted and turned to follow him until the rope was thoroughly snarled around its legs.

Finally realising its dilemma, the troll stood still and looked down at itself. Perplexed, it reached down to pluck at the thin cord. With perfect timing, Marcus managed to get a dozen more trees to burst into flame right in front of it at that moment. The troll looked up. Heat and flames leapt. Raising rocky hands to shield its face, the troll tried to back away. Then, as the ropes pulled taut, it toppled slowly to the ground with the booming sound of a mountainside avalanche.

Phoenix jumped aside and punched the air with a whoop of joy. He stumbled to Marcus' side and the pair of them watched the troll thrash and twist on the bare earth. More trees flared into life. The circle of fire was complete – but it wouldn't last long. With a loud twang, the thin rope snapped and the troll managed to bend a knee.

"C'mon, c'mon!" Phoenix breathed, staring at the eastern horizon. A thin, shivering slip of sun appeared.

The troll roared. Phoenix imagined he heard a touch of fear in that gravelly sound. Its struggles increased. Rope plunked, broke and fell away in loose segments. The troll heaved itself to its feet and lumbered toward the nearest trees. The fires there were reaching peak intensity. It backed away with a roar of pain and confusion.

Turning, it ran directly toward where Phoenix and Marcus hid behind an unburned sapling. Marcus gasped and backed away. His movement must have caught the troll's eye and it raised a murderous fist right above them.

Phoenix caught Marcus' elbow and dragged him aside. "Run!"

The two bolted. Phoenix's twisted ankle chose that moment to give out completely. He fell to the ground in a heap. Marcus stopped, turning back to help.

"Go!" Phoenix yelled, afraid they would both be killed. "Get out!"

At least with his digital lives he had a chance of surviving. Marcus had only one life in this world. The Roman shook his dark head and bent over to haul Phoenix to his feet.

He was too late. Overhead, branches snapped. Burning pine needles and glowing embers fell around them like fireworks. A fist of unyielding stone descended unstoppably toward their unprotected heads. Phoenix shoved at Marcus, pushing him aside. He stumbled away with a look of horror as he realised what Phoenix had done.

"No!"

There was a flash of brilliant white light, tinged with purple-blues that burnt into the brain and left strange after-images on the inside of Phoenix's eyelids. Marcus' despairing yell was overwhelmed by a horrendous cracking sound. It echoed like the crunching, grinding, snapping cacophony of noise an iceberg makes as it calves into the sea; or the sound of an earthquake destroying whole cities.

Then; silence. Profound, utter silence except for the crackle and sizzle of pine trees fizzling into bare trunks around them. Reddish sunlight poured through the smoky haze. Phoenix slowly turned his head and looked up. Two feet above him, the troll's grey fist hung, frozen in midair. With a gasp of shocked relief, Phoenix dragged himself out from beneath the looming pile of stone. Marcus hurried to help him up and together they hobbled back uphill to get a better view.

Teetering on the edge of the hilltop clearing was an enormous, solid, statue of a troll. Spring sunlight had done its job. The troll had petrified, just as Truda predicted. As the two warriors watched, gravity took charge and the stones disintegrated. An arm shattered and smashed to earth just where Phoenix had lain. Then the other arm; the head; a knee snapped. Suddenly the whole lot imploded into a large, shapeless pile of grey rocks tumbling down slope.

Phoenix coughed as dust rose and added to the smoke already drifting around.

He exchanged looks with Marcus. "It worked."

"Seems that way," the Roman said, but there was a look his dark eyes that hinted he would remember this night forever. "I owe you my life."

Phoenix shrugged, grimacing as the motion sent stabbing pains into his chest. "I think we're pretty even."

There was a pause at the two silently surveyed the scene.

"Sorry about your rope," Phoenix said.

Marcus shrugged, still watching rocks roll away. "Easily replaced."

"And your sword."

"Now that is going to be more difficult."

There wasn't much else they could really say. Now was the time for some witty quip like, 'well, he took the rocky road to enlightenment' but Phoenix was too tired to summon up the energy to utter it. Come to think of it, the idea of enlightenment was probably not a Roman one, anyway. Marcus would just give him a blank look and a perfectly good pun would go to waste.

Where was Jade when he needed her?

Speaking of which...

Phoenix turned a slow circle. The sun had cleared the horizon and the last of the burning trees was dwindling into smouldering sticks. The hilltop looked like it had been hit by a bomb.

Squinting through the smoke and sunlight, he tried to work out where they were. He'd become so turned around there was no way of telling. He thought about following the path of destruction left by the troll, but they had lead the creature in circles last night and it would take hours to get back to the cave. By then the others would have left for the village.

Water glinted off to the east, through the glare: probably the same large lake they had been aiming for yesterday. Their best bet was to head in that direction with the hope of finding Jade and the others along the shoreline. It was a long shot but he couldn't think of anything else.

Belatedly, Phoenix remembered his own resolution to be a better leader. He swung about to find Marcus gazing at him gravely.

"Any idea which way to go to find the others?"

Marcus gave him a rare, small smile. "I'm sure you'll think of something."

Phoenix laughed, feeling a twinge in his abused ribs. "East then? Toward the lake."

Marcus nodded agreeably. He slung Phoenix's arm over his shoulder and together they staggered toward the distant lake.

The pair made their way down the steep, rocky slope they had climbed so recklessly an hour before. Neither of them commented. Already the hazards of the night faded into a dream. The fact they had survived was so outrageous that Phoenix began to wonder if, perhaps, one of Truda's godly relatives watched out for them. Weirder things had happened here - and would probably keep doing so.

It took two solid hours of walking and hobbling before they again saw a hint of water through the trees. They were utterly exhausted and it was only the fear of what might have happened to the others that kept them going. Phoenix had no memory of most of the walk. He relied on Marcus to keep them going as he concentrated on putting one foot in front of the other. Pain shot though his ankle and chest with every step. The world beyond his feet blurred. It took all his willpower just to stay upright. If something attacked them now, they were dead.

Hearing Marcus' sharp intake of breath, Phoenix raised his head. Tall and barbarically-dressed, a dozen heavily armed men stepped out from behind the trees and encircled them. Their long, blond hair lay loose over thick fur cloaks, which were flung back to reveal rough cloth shirts, sturdy leather pants and heavy boots. There was nothing barbaric or rough about the sharpness of their swords, however. One of them stepped forward and growled what might have been a challenge or perhaps a question, but it sounded like gibberish. Phoenix blinked vaguely and looked at Marcus. The Roman shook his head to show he couldn't understand either.

The circle of long, unpleasantly pointy broadswords closed in. The leader repeated his words in a singsong voice that sounded almost familiar. Phoenix smiled dreamily. Truda had said they were in Svealand. Marcus had named the Suebian Sea. Which meant they must be in...Sweden. Knowing where they were didn't give him the power to speak ancient Swedish, unfortunately. A sword jabbed at his chest. He raised his hands above his head, trying to ignore the sharp pain in his ribs. Marcus did the same.

A second man came forward. He was smaller and darker than the others. He spoke to them in broken Latin.

"You will come with us."

Phoenix blinked as the world spun in front of his eyes.

"Are we your prisoners?" he managed to ask, also in Latin. The man nodded curtly, gesturing with his sword. Phoenix swayed. "Are we being taken to your village?" He wasn't sure if the words came out clearly but the man nodded again. Marcus cast his companion a perplexed look.

"Oh good," Phoenix murmured, "but I think you'll have to carry me."

He slid to the ground, welcoming the darkness that enveloped his exhausted body and mind.

CHAPTER NINE

At the sound of male voices outside their prison, Jade drew Brynn and Truda close. She pushed them behind her and faced the door boldly, trying to hide a shiver of fear. The rough timber door flew open and a tall warrior stepped through, sword drawn. He glanced at Jade then nodded to someone and moved aside. Jade shoved her charges back against the timber wall and glared at him but the warrior ignored her.

A man stumbled through the door and sprawled on the dirt floor. Jade squinted against the light, trying to see. Two more warriors strode in, bearing a limp body between them. They dumped it unceremoniously on the floor and left, closing the door. Outside, there was a short conversation, laughter then silence.

Inside the hut the gloom was broken only by thin streams of dusty sunlight sneaking through cracks in the door and thatched roof. A sunbeam fell onto the face of one of the young men lying prone on the floor.

"Phoenix!" Jade dashed across the room and almost fell onto her unconscious companion's chest. Tears of relief started in her eyes as she felt his heart beating strongly beneath her hands. He was alive! She turned to the other prisoner. "Marcus? Is that you too?"

"Yes." The Roman replied, clambering to his feet to move stiffly to her side.

Jade threw her arms about his strong shoulders and hugged him ruthlessly. He stayed still for a second then returned the embrace briefly before letting her go.

"I can't believe you're here!" She sniffed, wiping her

wet cheeks.

Brynn and Truda ran up, delighted smiles on their faces. Brynn clouted Marcus on the arm with rough affection before crouching beside Phoenix. Truda smiled happily on all of them as though she had somehow arranged their reunion.

"What's wrong with him?" Brynn asked Marcus.

"We spent all night leading the troll away from you," the Roman boy replied. "He's exhausted." Fatigue roughened his voice.

"Any injuries?" Jade asked professionally. There was undoubtedly more to the tale but Marcus wasn't one to brag and she wasn't going to push him. Phoenix would tell them all the details when he awoke.

Marcus shook his head. "A few cuts and bruises on me. Phoenix did most of the work and took the worst hits. He was limping and I think he's hurt his ribs."

"Well, I'd better check while he's unconscious then." Jade nodded at an earthenware jug in the corner of the room. "Brynn, bring Marcus some of that water and food the villagers gave us. Truda, get some blankets for Phoenix."

Jade worked on Phoenix's injuries, trying to clear her mind but it was difficult. Phoenix was injured and exhausted because she had been reckless and scared and had done something truly stupid. If she hadn't been so jittery and brainless, she would have at least looked before eating those lily petals. She knew exactly what they did. If she'd just glanced at the flower before stuffing it in her mouth she wouldn't have eaten it at all.

Was that true, though? After all, she did know that waterlilies contained a sedative and she had been overwhelmingly frightened. Would she really have refused if she'd seen what Truda offered? Would she have had the strength to say 'no' when she was desperate to dull the crushing fear? It was awful to admit but she may not have:

she might have let fear overcome her judgment. She might have eaten them anyway.

Shivering with self-loathing, Jade wrapped her arms around herself and stared at her tired companions.

Now they were prisoners because of her, too. This morning she'd awoken with a sick headache and guilt weighing heavily on her conscience. She'd allowed Brynn to talk her into following Phoenix's last instructions to find the village - and regretted it as soon as they'd walked into the hamlet of scattered thatched huts. A dozen warriors had captured them, taken away all their gear and put them in this hut.

They hadn't even had a chance to explain anything. Truda had tried to speak to them but the burly men had just laughed at the young girl's efforts. When Truda had stomped her little feet and imperiously told them she was Thor's daughter, they'd just laughed harder than ever.

It had taken Jade ten full minutes to calm Truda down after that.

She shook herself, focussing on using her powers to heal the worst of Phoenix's hurts. Without her herb bag she couldn't cure him totally, but he would mend with a little time. Two fractured ribs; one badly sprained ankle and a broken little finger. It could have been worse but she still felt awful. When it was done, she sat back, drained.

Marcus lay beside Phoenix, soundly asleep on a thin blanket. His eyes were ringed with purple-black circles, his face and hands filthy with soot. He hadn't even bothered to remove his smoke-scented, grubby furs.

Jade stared at the two for a long moment then sighed. She turned to the youngsters and gestured them closer.

"You two didn't sleep much either, I know." She smiled as Truda tried to cover a yawn. "Why don't you get some rest now? I've slept enough. I'll keep watch."

Truda nodded amicably and curled up with her back against Phoenix. Her eyes drifted closed and she was asleep in seconds. Brynn reached out and squeezed Jade's fingers.

"It's not your fault," he whispered.

Jade pressed his thin hand gratefully. She didn't trust herself to say anything. It was and she knew it. It had been pure luck that nothing awful had happened to anyone while she was under the influence of the lily; luck and Phoenix and Marcus' skills. Next time, she mightn't be so fortunate. Well, there wouldn't be a next time. She would never, ever do anything as dumb as that again.

*****

A voice penetrated layers of sleep and drew Phoenix slowly back from a warm, comfortable place. He groaned in protest and tried to push away a hand that stroked his forehead.

"Go 'way, mum," he muttered irritably. "I don't wanna get up yet. School's not for ages."

There was a girlish giggle from somewhere nearby. What was a girl doing in his bedroom? Memories of the last week came flooding back: amulets; Romans; druids; Stonehenge; death; snow; wolves; giant killer troll; barbarians. Phoenix sat straight up in shock, eyes wide.

Sure enough, Jade, Truda, Brynn and Marcus were all gathered close, peering at him with varying degrees of anxiety. Well, Truda giggled, the rest peered. He put a hand to his head as it began thudding. It seemed like every muscle in his legs ached and his ribs felt bruised. He prodded them and wriggled his sprained ankle at the same time. Surprisingly, there were only slight twinges of pain. He felt amazingly healthy, apart from a headache and sore muscles.

"How're you feeling?" Jade's worried voice intruded.

He stared up at her then around at the room. They were in some sort of small, windowless hut with a high, thatched roof.

"Fine. Mostly," he replied absently. "Where are we?"

"We're in a Svear village called Olshamarr on the edge of Lake Vatn in Sweden. They call it Svealand," Jade replied.

Truda giggled again, covering her mouth with her hand.

Jade sighed. "What?"

"You just said Lake Lake," Truda said.

"But that's what you said it was called, 'Vatn'." Jade rolled her eyes.

"That's because the word for 'lake' is 'vatn'."

"Oh, good grief," Jade moaned, dropping her head into her hands. She looked over at Truda with an expression of resigned irritation that reminded Phoenix strongly of how his mother looked at him sometimes.

"I never realised what a pain it is not to be able to speak the language," Jade complained to him. "Truda's the only one who can understand what the men outside are saying but she doesn't know the Latin or Breton words for half of it, so she can't translate correctly. Although," she grinned and sat down on the dirt floor, forearms resting on her knees, "by the tone of their voices, they are probably not saying anything fit for small ears anyway."

Brynn sniggered. Truda looked confused then giggled.

Jade sighed again, a frown pulling her slanted brows together over her nose. "The problem is, if we ever get out to see anyone, we don't stand a chance of getting help or pleading our case to be let free. What are we going to do?"

It took Phoenix a full thirty seconds to reply as he tried to clear the last of the sleep-fog from his aching head. He was thirsty, tired, starving and bursting to go to the toilet. Now he was awake, he remembered to he was also seriously annoyed with her for going zombie on them with the lotus flower. How the heck was he supposed to know what to do about translating an obscure ancient dialect?

"Ummmm," he stalled, rubbing his hand over his wild, smoke-smelling hair. "Couldn't you just..." he made a gesture in the air like a magician waving a wand, "y'know, magic us some translation ability?"

Jade shook her head. "I've tried everything I know but I just don't have any spells that apply to the situation. The closest I could come was to give us all my ability to understand what trees are thinking and somehow," she grimaced, "I don't think that will help much."

"No," he snorted a laugh, "I see your point. Hang on," he frowned, trying to remember the moments leading up to his capture, "wasn't there a guy who spoke Latin?"

Marcus nodded. "There was but he's a trader to the lands south across the Suebian Sea. He was only here until yesterday. He left as we entered the village."

"Helpful," Phoenix muttered. "Look, I can't think properly. I'm half-asleep, starving, thirsty and desperate for the loo."

Jade apologised. She pointed out the primitive leather slop bucket in one corner and, when he'd used it, handed him some water and the stale remains of some bread and smoked meat. The others went to sit by the door, listening to their guard's conversations in hope of gaining something useful.

After he'd assuaged the worst of his needs, Phoenix sighed and prodded his injuries again. He cocked his head at Jade, pointing to his ribs.

"Your handiwork?"

She flushed vividly red and looked away, nodding.

"Thanks." He was extremely grateful for the healing.

"If it hadn't been for my stupidity," she groaned, "you wouldn't have been injured at all! I should have been awake to help you, not lying in a drugged out coma because I was too cowardly to face my fears!"

"Errr…" He patted her awkwardly on the shoulder, not quite knowing how to deal with her in this mood. His lingering annoyance with her bad judgement faded. "You're not a coward, Jade and it wasn't your fault.

Besides," he added as she glared at him, "you couldn't have helped anyway. Didn't Brynn tell you?"

Jade sniffed, shook her head and wiped her nose on her sleeve.

"Your magic wouldn't have worked on a Troll. They're immune." He smiled as her mouth dropped open. "I'm guessing being in the troll territory was what caused you so much grief with your magic. And that's another thing: those wolves obviously knew where they were pushing us." He frowned at the memory. "If we ever see them again…"

"You mean the wolves herded us into the troll's territory deliberately?" Jade blinked at him. "But wolves aren't that smart. I mean, I knew they were driving us somewhere but I thought they were just…I don't know…I mean, why didn't they just kill us and eat us? Why go to so much trouble?"

"Don't ask me." Phoenix shrugged. "There was something weird about that big black one. It seemed to me like he wanted us dead but didn't want to do the deed himself. Maybe they were spies for Feng Zhudai? Who knows?"

Jade bit her lip then replied but with a note of uncertainty in her voice. "No. My spell - he can't find us here, remember? Anyway, forget the wolves. The point is: I still shouldn't have been stupid enough to eat that lily. I let you down. I'd never forgive myself if something happened to you both."

Phoenix grimaced and held up his hands. "OK, OK. You shouldn't have eaten the flower. You made a mistake. Welcome to the real world – sort of. Build a bridge and get over it, Jade. We don't have time for wallowing in self-pity." He knew he was being harsh but there really wasn't any room here for this sort of silliness. They needed Jade to be her usual capable self if they were going to survive.

For a moment he thought she was going to lash out at

him in anger. Her fists clenched at her sides and her jaw clamped shut. Her brilliant green eyes flashed fire and he wondered if she would do magic on him without thinking.

"Hey," he warned, "don't get angry at me for telling you a truth you already knew. Remember the amulets? We have to finish this level and three more if you want to get home. Learn from it and move on, that's my motto." Some of the fire went out of her face, so he continued more quietly, "Let's concentrate on getting out of this village and on our way."

She swallowed hard a couple of times then let her hands relax. She nodded.

"But where do we go from here?" she asked hopelessly. "We don't even know how to get to Asgard or Bilskirnir."

"Well, let's work on getting out of here first," Phoenix shrugged, "then we can worry about Asgard. Besides," he twisted his lips into knowing smile, "I'll bet Truda can tell us how to get there."

"Why should she know?" Jade sounded defensive.

"Well, to start with, it's her home," he pointed out mildly. She was being very touchy. "Plus, I've noticed she's pretty darned good at springing little surprises on us at the most inconvenient times. Watch." He caught Marcus' eye and waved the others over.

The group sat in a tight circle on the packed earth floor, huddling around a small, central hearth fire that provided meagre warmth. Phoenix looked around.

"So, any ideas on how we can get out of here?"

Truda shook her head solemnly, as did Marcus.

Brynn shrugged and, with a wicked gleam in his eye, picked up a stick from the fire. "We could set the place alight and escape in the confusion."

Phoenix tried to think of a tactful way of telling him what a bad idea that was. "It could be tricky to avoid being burned ourselves," he pointed out. "Besides, I think

Marcus and I have had enough fire for awhile - and they still have all our gear and weapons."

Brynn threw the stick back into the fire and slumped with a defeated sigh. "No idea then."

Phoenix raised an eyebrow at Jade, flicking her a knowing look.

"Anyway," he asked in a deliberate, disappointed tone, "even if we could get out, how on Earth are we supposed to get to Asgard to return Truda to Thor? I mean yes, we know we're in Svealand but we don't know which way to go from here."

Marcus cast him a puzzled look. Brynn blinked in confusion but Truda's blue eyes lit up and she gave them all a blinding smile.

"Oh, don't be silly. Everyone knows that all we have to do is get to Uppsala, find the Yggdrasil and go down the Urdarbrunnr into Asgard. Of course," she added blithely, "we'd have to be careful to stay away from the guardians: Nidhogg, Graback, Grafvolluth, Goin and Moin."

"Ha!" Phoenix grinned triumphantly at Jade. "See, I told you she'd spring the answer on us." Then he frowned at Truda's bright, dirt-smudged face. "Of course, it would help if anything you just said made any sense at all. I understood about the first ten words, after that it was utter gibberish."

Jade chuckled. Brynn clutched at his stomach and howled with laughter.

Truda pouted and opened her mouth to speak but she never got the chance. The door to the hut flew open, crashing back against the wall. All five companions jumped, hands automatically reaching for absent weapons. Little bits of disturbed thatch fell on their heads as they sprang to their feet.

Silhouetted in the afternoon light, a strange, hideously-deformed man-thing stepped toward them. They couldn't see its face clearly but it seemed to have a long snout and pointed ears on top of a furry, vaguely man-shaped body. It growled something in a low, harsh voice and began limping forward, leaning heavily on a thick ash staff.

Truda gasped. "It's the Lífbjóðr!"

CHAPTER TEN

"Oh, man," Phoenix muttered, "stop it with the gibberish, already."

Truda gurgled a laugh. "No, silly, he's the village lífbjóðr: the lifebringer." She didn't seem the slightest bit afraid of the thing walking stiffly toward them but then, she was a goddess.

The shape moved into the gentle orange glow cast by their fire and its frightening features resolved into something much less scary: an older man, wearing loose furs and carrying a staff. Draped over his head and back was a wolfskin. Complete with head, fangs and sunken, empty eyes, it created the illusion of monstrosity that had startled them. Beneath that gruesome relic, was the much more normal face of the Lifebringer. He raised thick, white eyebrows and said something incomprehensible.

Truda translated. "He asked if he can sit down."

Marcus and Brynn moved aside to make room around the fire. Their unexpected guest eased himself creakily down to join them. He laid his staff on the ground and held out his hands in a gesture of peace. Cautiously, the companions sat as well.

The Lifebringer spoke again, his mouth almost hidden by a coarse, white beard and moustache. Above, his pale blue eyes sparkled with intelligence. He pushed back the wolfskin hood to reveal a mane of grizzled grey hair.

Truda struggled to translate. "Ummm," she squinted in thought, "he's asking something about the Troll but I don't know the words for it in your language. I think he wants to know where it is and what happened to it." She spoke something rapidly to the old man, her high, clear voice a contrast to his gruff, deep one. The Lifebringer nodded, frowning at her. Truda smiled.

"Yes, that's it. He wants to know what happened to the mountain Troll." She looked expectantly at Phoenix and Marcus.

The two young men exchanged glances. Jade thought quickly. She was fairly sure this society was patriarchal. The old man obviously resented having to talk through a girl-child and he probably wouldn't appreciate it if Jade answered instead of Phoenix or Marcus. She leaned over and whispered a warning in Phoenix's ear. His answer had to be the right one or they could be in serious trouble. He nodded his understanding but gave her a look that clearly said he thought she was nuts.

"Err," he began, "it depends. Is having the troll around a good thing or a bad thing?"

Truda raised her eyebrows at him but asked the Lifebringer the question anyway. The old man blinked at her in astonishment then, to Jade's amazement, burst out laughing. He had a nice laugh and his face creased into a thousand wrinkles, making him much less intimidating. He looked like a slightly grubby Santa Claus.

Truda giggled, too. "I'm pretty sure it's a bad thing to have a troll around."

Phoenix cast Jade an irritated, 'I-told-you-so' look. She ignored it. You never knew. It was stupid to own up to something until you knew if the person asking was happy about it or not. You learned that fast growing up in a family of seven kids.

"Well then," Phoenix waggled a finger at himself and Marcus, "he'll be glad to know it's gone. We killed it."

Once Truda translated, the old man laughed again, this time with joy. He bent his wiry body in a bow toward both warriors and rattled off a series of sentences. Everyone looked at Truda.

"Ummm," she frowned, "he says the village is grateful and he's sorry we've been put in here. He's going to speak to the yfirmaðr....um...the chieftain... about getting us out." Turning back to the older man, she asked him a question.

"It's about time," Phoenix murmured. Jade nodded.

Truda spoke over the top of their soft exchange. "He says his name is Ásúlfr."

Jade leaned over and whispered to Phoenix, "We'd better introduce ourselves. You do it."

Phoenix shrugged again. He introduced them by the simple means of pointing to each person and naming them. Marcus bowed his head; Brynn gave a small wave; Truda smiled chirpily. He introduced Jade last. She pushed back her fur hood and nodded.

Ásúlfr stopped in mid-greeting, staring at her, apparently hypnotised. "Ljósálfar!" He breathed the word reverently, as though Jade were something he had never seen and never expected to see.

Jade looked at Truda for a translation. The girl was also staring at her strangely, as though she'd suddenly understood something important and wasn't quite sure she liked it.

"It means 'light-elf'," she said in a wondering tone. "You are, aren't you? I hadn't really thought about it, but that's what you are: one of the light-elves."

"What's a light-elf?" Jade asked sharply, once again not sure if it was a good or bad thing.

"They live in Álfheim near Asgard, under the roots of Yggdrasil – the World-tree I was telling you about," Truda explained. She frowned up at the old Svear man. He kept staring at Jade with awed admiration. "The Light elves don't come to Midgard very much, so I think he's a little surprised. Even I've only seen them a few times, when they take Pa along on the Wild Hunt."

Jade laughed uneasily. "What would he say if he knew who you are?"

Truda shrugged. "Not much. My pa and the other gods are always turning up in Midgard, so the people are used to us. They never see the Ljósálfar." There was a hint of resentment in her voice and Jade wondered if the god-child were jealous. She was probably used to being the centre of attention with the Druids.

Just then, Ásúlfr made a sound of extreme frustration. He peered at their faces, obviously trying to follow their conversation. Now, he climbed stiffly to his feet. The companions did the same, not sure what to expect.

He raised gnarled hands, fingers flat and splayed. In a low, gentle voice, he began to chant. The hairs on the back of Jade's neck rose. Flickers of purple-blue danced around the old man, gathering in strength as his voice grew louder. His body shook. The long ash staff jumped from the floor to his hand of its own accord.

Brynn yelped. Marcus stepped in front of Jade, pushing her and Brynn back toward the wall. Phoenix did the same for Truda. There was nowhere to go. No place to avoid the buildup of magic in the tiny hut. Desperately, Jade tried to create a shield strong enough to deflect the old man's magic but the after-effects of the lily weakened her powers. When he finally released the spell, her thin safeguard shattered into a thousand invisible, purple-blue shards. She flinched, feeling its destruction a fraction before the enchantment struck.

When it hit, Jade felt almost nothing. She expected pain or death. Judging by the wary, incredulous looks on her friends' faces, they did too. Instead, something twisted inside her head. It fiddled around in her brain, tweaking it and altering it somehow. Then the sensation disappeared but she felt no different.

Pushing past Marcus, she marched up to the old man. This was no time to worry about social protocols. She had to know what he had done to her mind.

"What did you do to us?" she demanded.

Ásúlfr raised one bushy brow, his blue eyes twinkling down at her. "I simply made it possible for us to understand one another."

Jade blinked at him; and blinked again as she realised she'd understood every word.

"But how…?"

The others looked equally dumbfounded – except Truda, who sulked.

The old man bowed. "I placed the ability to understand all languages into your minds. You will never again have this problem."

"But why…?" She stared at him. "Why didn't you just do it to yourself, instead? Why give us this gift?"

"Alas," he spread his hands regretfully, "I cannot perform even the simplest magic on myself, only on others. It is the limitation of my form of power."

Feeling a little shell-shocked, she hastened to thank him. "Th..thank you. It will help us immensely in the future."

"You are most welcome, my lady. It is a small repayment for the service you have done our humble village." He inclined his grey head.

Jade smiled and blushed. "I don't think I rate being called 'my lady', Master Lifebringer. Please just call me Jade."

"You may call me Ásúlfr." The old man bowed.

As he straightened, he grimaced and placed a hand in the small of his back. Jade moved to help him but he waved her away.

"Bone-pain is one of the many joys of old age, I'm afraid. There is nothing that can be done. Now," he pulled the ugly wolf-head up again, "we must talk to the chieftain about getting you out. This is not the place to house Troll-slayers and a lady of the Light-elves." He glanced distastefully around the tiny, dirty hut.

Twenty minutes later, the group had moved into a

guesting house of positively luxurious standard compared to their last accommodation. Their spare clothing already awaited them, laid out on the low beds. Jade was overjoyed to find there was even a sauna and standing bath-room. She instantly dragged Truda into the little rooms and proceeded to sweat, steam and slosh the dirt and filth of the last week off. It felt so good to be clean.

Afterward, she changed into her spare set of clothes and made Truda put on her druid robe again. Then she attacked their clothes and scrubbed them clean as best she could in the standing tub. Finally, she hung them out to dry on a line obviously placed in the room for that purpose.

Emerging from the bath-rooms over an hour after they'd entered; Jade sighed and fluffed out her long, clean hair. Now she felt like a person again. Marcus and Phoenix dragged Brynn, protesting and yelling, into the facilities.

When the boys were gone, a soft knock fell on the door. It opened and a young girl about Truda's age came in carrying a tray of food. Behind her came several larger boys and girls, all carrying foods, drinks, new clothing and, best of all, their confiscated weapons and the rest of their bags. They stared openly at her, whispering and nudging each other.

Jade thanked them, desperate for them to leave. She needed to check on their gear. Was the Hyllion bagia still there? Her herbs; her knife? As soon as the door closed, Jade snatched up her pack and searched it. Sighing deeply, she drew out the ruby-hilted knife and the slippery black bag and hugged them to her chest.

Inside the bag rested the magic horn Aurfanon had given her. She really needed to keep it closer to hand. Twice now she could have used it to summon help. If she'd had her wits about her last night, she could have simply blown it to combat the Troll. Obviously Phoenix hadn't remembered it either; or he wouldn't have had to dash off and rescue Marcus.

Everything else seemed to be there, too. Relieved, she and Truda inspected the new clothes. Two long skirts she put aside as being too impractical for travel. Luckily, there were enough trousers and sturdy shirts for all five companions to have at least two changes of clothes from now on. How wonderful. Jade had never really appreciated the delights of clean clothes and clean skin until now. She must remember to thank her mother for doing so much laundry when she got home. If she got home.

Not long after, all three boys emerged, Brynn still grumbling over his enforced cleanliness. His dark hair stuck out at odd angles, reminding Jade of a wet, very irritated kitten.

Ásúlfr knocked on the door, interrupting Brynn's complaints. Behind him was a small boy carrying another bundle. Ásúlfr bowed and smiled.

"There is to be a feast in your honour. You are to meet our lord, Hrothgar."

Jade glanced at Phoenix, who frowned a little. He and Marcus still looked like death warmed up. A feast was probably not what they really needed.

"That's very kind," she smiled at the old man, "but we are very tired. Please don't go to any trouble for us."

Ásúlfr shook his white head. "There has been little enough to celebrate this winter. It has been long and hard. Even now, Spring hides her head from us and refuses to melt the snows. If it lasts much longer, we will not be able to plant crops."

"All the more reason to husband your remaining food wisely," Marcus said.

The old man sighed. "Indeed but Hrothgar will not be swayed. He feels the news of the troll's death must be an omen and should be celebrated. The gods must be thanked for sending you to us. Come," he nodded toward Jade, "I am afraid that your attire is not appropriate, my lady. You must meet the Chieftain. He will not appreciate your manly garb. Please put this on." He handed the cloth the boy carried to Jade. "It is a gift from the Queen and is far more fitting for a lady of the Light-elves." Bowing slightly, he turned to go. "I will return to escort you to the Virki – the Chieftain's stronghold."

After he left, the five companions looked at each other. Jade frowned thoughtfully at Truda. "So if we don't get you back to Asgard quickly, these people will starve?"

Truda nodded solemnly. "These people and all the others caught in the snows of winter. I must get back to make Spring come - and soon," she said twisting her hands together.

Jade sighed. "Well, I guess we'd better go to this feast and thank the Gods or whatever. Maybe they'll even hear us and take us straight to your parents. That would save a lot of mucking about."

Phoenix grinned at her. "I like the sound of a feast but I don't like your chances of getting any shortcuts to the end of the quest. Skipping the fun bits is not how it works here."

Jade snorted. "Fun bits! You're a nut, you are. That last 'fun bit' almost got you killed again."

She turned away, shook out the gown and gasped in delight. Far from the coarse woven cloths of the peasants, this was of the softest, finest wool. Coloured a deep, forest green and embroidered across the breast, hem and long sleeves with silver thread, it was a dress fit for a Queen, indeed. Jade held it up admiringly. She couldn't hide a small smile at the thought of wearing something so beautiful. In her real-world family, all her clothes were three-times hand-me-downs; worn and tired. Even as a tomboy child, she'd longed for something better. She turned around to show Truda, only to find the others all staring at her. Their expressions ranged from Marcus' mild frown to Truda's outright sulk.

"What?"

Phoenix raised an eyebrow. "Getting the special treatment, are you?" He gave her a mocking bow. "My Lady of the Light-elves."

Jade felt a flash of hurt and pressed her lips together to hide it. She gave an irritated, one-shouldered shrug. "I don't care about it, if that's what you mean. If I play along, we'll probably get better help. Besides, I am an elf – and that's obviously something special to these people."

Truda gasped, her blue eyes widened then narrowed. She huffed at Jade, folded her arms and stomped away. Jade sighed at the young girl's temper.

Phoenix gazed after Truda then turned a cynical expression on Jade. "That was uncalled for. She's a kid. You don't have to make her feel bad just to make yourself feel better. She's important, too."

Hurt and guilty, Jade turned away to hide the quick rush of tears that stung her eyes.

CHAPTER ELEVEN

It was a silent, tense group that followed Ásúlfr from the guest lodge, with Jade clearly still smarting at Phoenix's comment, Truda sulking over Jade's special treatment, and Phoenix annoyed at both of them. Marcus looked grimmer than usual and Brynn stayed uncharacteristically silent, his dark eyes darting between Phoenix and Jade.

They walked for almost ten minutes, up a steep incline behind the village. Darkness slipped in to replace dusk, so it was only when they had almost reached the top that Phoenix realised what they were climbing: an enormous, man-made, fortified hilltop. At the end of the path, a great ditch encircled the top of the hill. Behind it was an earth embankment topped by a tall palisade – a massive, wooden wall made of sharpened logs. A stone causeway led to a timber gate, guarded by two large, blond warriors. They nodded to Ásúlfr and the gate swung outward to admit the party.

Inside, flaming torches lit their path, marching straight toward a huge timber hall that had to be the Chieftain's place. From within came the sound of male voices talking and laughing, dogs growling and the faint, regular thump of a drum.

When the door opened, Phoenix blinked in surprise. The great hall was massive and full of people. Down either side of the rectangular room ran rough wooden tables and benches lined with dozens of hulking warriors. Little bowls filled with burning, oil-soaked reeds - rushlights - cast a mellow, flickering light on the faces of everyone present. A large fire crackled in a central hearth, the smoke rising up to seep out through the thatched roof. Huge, round wood-and-iron shields hung along the walls. At the far end was a head table, slightly raised on a dais. Seated there were three men and one woman.

Ásúlfr thumped the end of his staff on the packed-earth floor three times.

"My lord Hrothgar, builder of the great hall of Heorot, ruler over Svealand," he bowed deeply to the silver-haired giant of a man at the head table. "I bring the strangers before you." Waving them forward, he introduced them one at a time.

"Brynn, Alun's son, of the Bretons."

Brynn stepped to the front, bowed jerkily then retreated behind the others.

"Marcus Gnaeus Agricola, Trollslayer and son of Gnaeus Julius Agricola, Governor of Britain for the mighty Roman Empire."

Marcus bowed. His face was blank but Phoenix saw his jaw working as he heard his father's name linked with his own. Phoenix took a moment to wonder how the old magician knew so much about them - and whether such knowledge was a potential threat.

"Thrudr, Thor's daughter, Goddess of Spring."

Truda curtseyed regally as the buzz of talk amongst the assembled warriors increased. The child looked extremely pleased at the excitement her name generated.

"Phoenix Drake Carter, Trollslayer!" The old man's voice was exultant as he gave the title.

Phoenix felt himself flushing as spontaneous applause broke out amongst the men. He bowed awkwardly and stepped back. It was ridiculous to feel so thrilled by impressing a bunch of barbarians he didn't even know, but he couldn't help a surge of pride as they all gazed at him in admiration. No one, except his mother, had ever been impressed by him before - and hey, that was her job.

"And," Ásúlfr waved Jade forward, "Jade, daughter of Eleri, Lady of the Light-elves."

She stepped up and removed the long, fur coat she'd worn over her dress. There was a collective gasp from the audience. Phoenix looked at her critically but had to admit she was worth gasping over. Her pale skin was clean now and the green dress matched her eyes perfectly. Long, silver-blonde hair rippled down her back. She was beautiful; haughty; queenly.

Phoenix gritted his teeth and glanced at Truda. Sure enough, the young girl's mouth was set in a mulish expression of anger and hurt. If Jade weren't careful, she would alienate the young goddess and make their journey much, much harder.

The old man led them around one side of the hall. Heads turned as they passed; whispered comments were made; laughs followed. Phoenix chose to ignore them. He laid a hand on Brynn's shoulder when the boy opened his mouth to reply hotly to a less-than-polite comment. Leaning down, he murmured,

"We're outnumbered ten-to-one, Brynn. Don't start anything."

Startled, the boy looked around. He had to be noticing what Phoenix spotted the moment they walked in the room. Every man in the place was armed with a dagger and built like an Olympic weightlifter. Between the five of them, they had a bow with no arrows, a quarterstaff, one sword, a sling and four daggers. Unfortunately, they'd been forced to leave all but the daggers outside the hall. Weapons were not allowed on the King's presence.

Out of the corner of his eye, Phoenix saw Marcus lean forward and mutter something into Jade's ear. She looked briefly startled, glanced around the room then nodded. Her eyes narrowed and mouth firmed. Good. At least Marcus had jolted her out of dreamy princess-land. He'd been worried that she was going to drop her guard, just because they'd given her a pretty dress and a flowery introduction.

So far, these people of Olshamarr had not yet shown any overwhelming reasons to trust them.

Dinner passed jovially enough. They were seated at the high table: Phoenix, Marcus and Brynn sat on King Hrothgar's right; Jade and Truda on his left, beside his Queen, Wealktheow. Food arrived and the companions ate the best meal they'd had for days. Roast auerhuhn, roast boar and salted fish were the main ingredients, but there were all sorts of root vegetables and breads as well as a few dried fruits – the last winter stocks of summer gathering. It was worrying to think that this might be the last of their stores, though. Truda had to get to Asgard.

While the meal progressed, there was little talk between the king and his guests. Everyone seemed more interested in eating, much to Phoenix's relief. He had no idea what to say to a king.

Jade didn't seem to have the same problem. She and the Queen chatted away like old friends. Thankfully, they included Truda in their conversation. The girl looked happier, anyway.

All too soon, the food scraps were cleared – either tossed to dogs scavenging around the floor or taken back to the kitchens by serving women. King Hrothgar leaned back in his high wooden chair and slewed around to stare, with piercing blue eyes, at Phoenix. He stroked his beard, eyeing the young man shrewdly.

"So, my young hero, you are the Trollslayer? Tell us the story then," he demanded.

Other warriors nearby took up the request, yelling "Story! Story!" until the whole lot chanted it and the rafters shook with the sound.

Phoenix gulped. He hated public speaking. In fact, hated was an understatement. He'd been known to skip school just to avoid having to speak in front of the class. He looked toward Marcus. The Roman's eyes widened and he shook his head with a half-smile, clearly refusing to do the job. Phoenix understood. If he were bad with words, Marcus was surely worse. He seemed to have a fifty-word per day limit. Glancing to his left, Phoenix saw Jade scowling at him. Go on! she mouthed, jerking her head at the impatient mob before them.

There didn't seem to be any option. He could hardly refuse. The palms of his hands began to sweat as he shoved his chair back. His heart pounded in his ears and his stomach felt like it was about to violently eject his dinner. Dozens of expectant faces turned toward him. He swallowed hard, his mind a complete blank.

"My lords, ladies and good thanes!" Brynn's voice cut through the babble, rescuing Phoenix from one of his worst nightmares.

Brynn sent him a cheeky wink before jumping onto the high table in one lithe bound. The boy put his wooden, recorder-like pipe to his lips with a flourish and blew an intricate run of pure notes. Silenced, the audience turned their attention to him.

"By my lord's and Phoenix's leave," Brynn bowed to Phoenix and then to the king, "I shall tell the tale of high adventure that occurred just one day ago." He blew another quick tune, this one seeming somehow haunting rather than joyful.

Astonished, Phoenix stared at him. With a relieved sigh, he nodded to the Breton boy and relaxed. Whew. He was off the hook.

For twenty minutes, Brynn held the Svealanders enthralled: alternating between music, cavorting re-enactments with the pipe substituting for a sword or torch, and thrilling, hypnotic words. He kept fairly close to the real story but there were a few embellishments here and there. It all sounded a lot more gripping than terrifying. There also seemed to be quite a few more cliff-hanger moments than Phoenix remembered. The audience loved it.   They cheered the "successes" and gasped at "near escapes". He just hoped nobody asked him for his version. It was much less exciting than Brynn's. The boy was a born story-teller. Embarrassed, Phoenix exchanged rueful glances with Marcus as the hall erupted into thunderous applause.

Hrothgar pounded the wooden table with a stein, calling for silence. "Truly you have done us a great honour this day, boy." Hrothgar flicked Brynn something and the boy caught it deftly, bowing his gratitude. "You are a princely sagatala, lad. Any time you wish to cease your journeying and join my court, you will be welcome."

Brynn bowed again. "I thank you my lord but the true heroes of this day are my lords: Trollslayers!" He gave one last, triumphantly joyous run of notes on his whistle then scooted back to his seat, flushed and starry-eyed.

Phoenix leaned past Marcus and gripped the boy's shoulder. "Totally amazing, Brynn. I had no idea you could do that."

"Me neither," he grinned, "but you should have seen the look of terror on your face when he asked you. I figure if you can kill Trolls, this is the least I can do to contribute."

Phoenix laughed. "Thanks. I know which one I'd rather do!"

The king spoke again, addressing the whole room in his deep, rich voice.

"These strangers have done our village a great service. We must reward them suitably for they have destroyed the troll, Grendel, which has plagued our people for two long years. Surely it is an omen that Spring will come and our land will once again be rich, fertile and free from fear." He had to wait a few moments for a fresh wave of cheers to die down.

Phoenix snuck a look at Jade, wondering what she thought of all this, whether she resented being left out of the recognition. He saw an expression of astonished horror on her face that sent a chill down his back. He looked around, expecting to see invaders, minions of Zhudai, Roman soldiers – something to justify that face.

The room seemed normal – well, normal for a hall full of half-drunk, mead-quaffing, sword-waving barbarian warriors. Hrothgar continued and Phoenix had to quit trying to catch Jade's eye. Whatever bothered her would have to wait until they were back in the guesthouse.

"Phoenix Carter and Marcus Agricola, approach," Hrothgar summoned them. Hesitantly, they moved to stand before the imposing figure. Hrothgar stood and placed a hand on a shoulder of each. "It is difficult to know what reward to give you, for there is little that can compare to the freedom you have bestowed upon my people. Ask what you will and, if it can be done, I will give it to you. What would you?" The king frowned, "My daughter's hand?" There was a faint, startled protest from his Queen. "No, 'tis true, she is already pledged. A place at my side then, as sons and heirs to my kingdom?" This time, there was a low muttering from several warriors at the top of one of the long tables. The Queen gasped.

Phoenix guessed that neither of these choices would be popular, so it was a good thing he wasn't interested in either marrying or becoming a Svear prince. He thought for a moment.

"My lord," he bowed, trying to find the right words, "we are on a great journey so, alas, we cannot stay in your fair land." A relieved sigh came from several nearby people. Phoenix suppressed a smile. "However, if you would be kind enough to give us fresh supplies, perhaps horses, a sword for Marcus and directions to Uppsala, we would consider ourselves amply repaid."

All up, he was quite pleased with that speech. It sounded humbly regretful and grateful while at the same time getting them what they needed to continue their trip.

This time, when he looked up, Jade smiled at him. She nodded a little and gave him a tiny thumbs-up signal. There was still a faint, worried look around her eyes that said she knew something she wasn't happy about, though.

Hrothgar hesitated then inclined his head in agreement. "You shall have that and more, my young friend. Gifts will be prepared and delivered to your quarters in the morning but surely you will stay in Heorot a few more days and enjoy our hospitality?"

There was nothing Phoenix would have liked better than to stay and be pampered and fed for a few more days. Well, almost nothing. He didn't need Jade's quick frown or Truda's scowling, pouty look to remind him of the tight schedule they were on to get Truda home. Ragnarok had to be prevented and it seemed they were the only ones who could do it. So he expressed suitable apologies to the king and tried to pretend he was pleased to be going off into the unknown to die a few more times. Well, at least he still had five more times he could die. He'd managed to avoid being "killed" by the troll, and was perfectly happy to avoid being killed by anything for as long as possible.

The celebration finally dribbled to a halt at around midnight when the last of the king's thanes and warriors drank themselves into oblivion under the tables. The worst part was how truly awful their singing became as the evening progressed. There seemed to be a direct connection with their inability to stay in tune and the amount of mead consumed. The poor court musician's ears must have been bleeding.

Jade had long since taken Truda and Brynn off to bed. Marcus and Phoenix only stayed because Hrothgar insisted. Somehow, they managed to stay fairly sober by tipping more mead and ale onto the floor than into their mouths. The dogs were now staggering about, howling drunk but at least Marcus and Phoenix weren't.

By the time they picked their way through the

sprawled, snoring bodies and down the hill to the guest hall, they were completely exhausted. Phoenix was looking forward to a decent sleep – in a bed for once.

His luck was out. The minute they pushed the door open, Jade pounced on them. She had changed back into travelling gear. Her expression said she'd been pacing the room anxiously and had something important to say.

Phoenix groaned. "Not now, Jade. I'm totally wrecked. Can't this wait until morning?"

"Shhhh!" Jade hissed. "Don't wake the others." She glanced over her shoulder at Brynn & Truda's blanketed forms. Clutching at Phoenix & Marcus' arms, she dragged them into a corner. "No, it can't wait until morning."

"Why not?" Phoenix yawned. She was being very dramatic. "What can possibly happen between midnight and morning?"

"You don't understand," she said fiercely. "You are Beowulf!"

He stared at her blearily, having no clue at all what she was talking about. Tired of the drama, he said so. "I have no idea what you're talking about, Jade. I'm Phoenix, remember? P.H.O.E.N.I.X." He patted her arm. "It's been a long day. You're tired. Get some sleep and you'll be fine in the morning."

"Aaaargh! You moron!" Jade thumped his chest. "Don't patronise me, just because you don't read books. Beowulf is the hero in a story."

"So?" Phoenix yawned again. Marcus began removing his outer furs and boots, having wisely decided to stay out of it.

"So!" She took a deep breath, visibly trying to calm herself. "Beowulf killed Grendel the Troll in the old Norse story of 'Beowulf'. Grendel had been terrorizing king Hrothgar, his wife Wealktheow, his hall Heorot and his people. See, everything fits."

He raised his eyebrows in an effort to seem amazed.

"Huh, well what do you know? So the programmers wrote an old story into this world. Cool. So what? We did kill Grendel. Story over."

She threw up her hands in frustration, somehow managing to yell in a whisper, "Grendel had a mother! A big, fat, angry mother troll who came to take revenge on Beowulf for her son's death!"

CHAPTER TWELVE

Marcus dropped a boot onto the floor with a thud that seemed loud in the silence following Jade's words. She glared at Phoenix. Surely he understood the danger they were in, now?

"Ah," he expelled the word on a sigh, "so you're saying there's another one of those walking mountains out there?"

Jade nodded. It was hard to stay calm when he was being so stupidly relaxed about it. She wanted to thump him on the head to try and get the idea into his skull. Honestly!

Phoenix ran a hand through his long, dark hair and scratched his scalp.

"So will it come after us like, right now?" He cast a longing glance at an empty bed.

She bit her lip. She'd never read the original Norse poem, only a Rosemary Sutcliff book based on the fifteen-hundred year old saga. So she couldn't say exactly when Grendel's mother was supposed to attack Hrothgar's hall.

"I'm not sure," she admitted.

"Excellent." Phoenix arched in a bone-cracking stretch. "How about you stay up for this first watch, just in case? Marcus and I will get some more sleep. That way," he waved a hand, "we'll be ready to give mother troll the run-around as well."

"Well," she hesitated. Glancing at Marcus' face, she saw he and Phoenix both had heavy, dark circles beneath their eyes. They needed sleep. She felt another twinge of guilt for letting them bear the burden of defeating Grendel.

She owed them. "OK," she sighed. "You sleep, I'll keep watch but…"

Phoenix slapped her on the back, making her cough. "Don't stress. I'm sure we'll have at least one night's grace."

"Famous last words," Jade muttered. She moved to station herself beside the front door, opening it a fraction so she could see the moonlit village outside.

In the long hours that followed, she wondered how much more she could take. The strain of actually living this adventure was wearing her down. She really needed to get a grip. This game was challenging everything she once thought she actually might be good at. She'd always daydreamed about how perfect she'd be if she were thrown into this sort of fantasy land; always imagined being a brave warrior princess. Now, her deeper fears about not being able to cope in this game were being played out. She was making mistakes – lots of them. It was terrifying.

Not surprisingly, this thought did nothing to improve her confidence.

Jade spent the night with her hands clenched on her quarterstaff, eyes on the door; head awhirl with confused, worried thoughts and doubts.

In spite of her fear, the night passed peacefully. Everyone, except her, slept soundly until sunrise. Jade let them all rest the night through. As a half-elf, she could go longer without sleep than humans. She was a little tired but she knew she could cope until the next night.

At dawn, she roused them all and started the packing. The morning had brought a little composure to her thinking. At least she was able to plan for their next trip. That was something, anyway. The other doubts she pushed aside, not yet ready to deal with them. She had to focus on getting Truda home in time to stop Ragnarok. That was the most important thing now.

Carefully, she stowed a small amount of gear into each

backpack then shoved the bulk of their new clothes into the Hyllion bagia. For extra security, she asked Brynn to also remember the name of each item she stuffed into the magic bag. To get things back out of the bag, you had to give it the correct name: like "bear fur coat" or "leather pants". There was no point in having a bag full of things nobody could get out.

Who knew what was already in there. In his more treasure-hungry moments, Brynn tried random words. Generalities like 'gold' or 'silver' didn't seem to work. His more specific, frustrated attempts had so far produced only a chair, a bolt of coarse cloth and five pairs of baby shoes. He often repeated his suggestion that they cut it open and see what came out.

A servant brought breakfast of thick porridge laced with honey, which they ate quickly. A polite knock fell on the door. Ásúlfr's aged voice called to them.

"My friends, King Hrothgar and his lady await you without. They bring gifts and wish to give you a good fare well."

The five companions stepped out into brilliant spring sunshine, blinking. Arrayed before them were five sturdy horses: three for riding and two loaded with stuffed provisions bags. King Hrothgar himself came forward carrying two swords. The first, a long sword, he handed to Marcus with a warning to use it well. Marcus murmured his thanks and swung it, frowning at the difference between it and the shorter gladius he was used to.

"It is made of the best steel by the best craftsmen in the world. You will not find a better sword, except perhaps this one." Hrothgar handed the second over to Phoenix with a look of pride and regret. "It was given to me by Thor himself. I don't really want to part with it but I am getting too old to do it justice. Now I have found a hero worthy of it." The older man pushed the sword away as Phoenix automatically tried to return it. "No. You keep it but use it wisely. Its name is Blódbál. It means, 'blood-fire'."

Hrothgar drew a breath and released it on a sigh. "There is power in this weapon for one who can use it with a clear head. However, if you use it in blind hatred or anger, that power will consume you and you will become a berserker." The old king raised a warning finger. "You will not know friend from foe and you will not stop until all are dead around you. So be careful, my young hero. Of course, it doesn't work on trolls or I would have used it years ago."

Phoenix stared at the weapon, clearly more than a little excited by the idea of wielding a magic sword. He drew it from its worn, leather scabbard. It was exquisite. There was nothing flashy or fancy: no jewels or goldwork in the hilt, just a plain, leather-wrapped grip and metal crosspiece below a long, broad blade. The blade did not have the high polish that Marcus' new one did but it looked sharp and well-kept. He swung it experimentally.

"Wow," he murmured, catching Jade's sceptical look. "It's like I don't even have to think; it just knows what I want to do next." Bemusement flickered over his face and he looked away into the distance, as though he heard something no-one else could. Then his eyes refocused and he blinked at Hrothgar. "It's singing to me. Is it supposed to do that?"

Hrothgar roared a laugh and slapped Phoenix on the shoulder, making him stagger. "That means it likes you, boy. It's getting the damned thing to stop singing that's the challenge."

Phoenix turned to show the others. Brynn touched the flat of the blade hesitantly, as though expecting it to shock him. Jade inspected it in a different way, looking for any signs of magic. There it was. When she looked at it right, the whole sword positively glowed and pulsed with the telltale purple-blue aura that indicated a powerful magical tool.

"Magic?" Phoenix said.

She nodded, a little worried. "Quite strong, too. Be careful with that thing."

Phoenix resheathed Blódbál and strapped it onto his left hip. After a moment's hesitation, he presented his own, shorter, sword to Brynn. The boy took it reverently and tied it to his hip. He walked with a definite swagger. Jade made a mental note to ask Phoenix to teach him how to use it before he accidentally cut his own leg off.

Hrothgar presented still more gifts. Jade watched, feeling guilty and worried. She hoped he wouldn't give her anything - she hadn't done anything to earn gifts. Besides, if Grendel's mother came, they would have accepted them under false pretences. To Marcus, he gave a quiver full of new, iron-tipped arrows. Phoenix received a small, round shield to replace his own, lost in Stonehenge. To Brynn, the king gave a whistle made of bronze. It's pure, clear notes sounded out across the village as the boy piped his joy. Truda received a gown of blue to match Jade's green one, a bracelet of bronze and a small, iron dagger. The girl was delighted and hugged the old king. His lined face softened into a smile and he patted the child's head.

When it came to Jade, he beckoned Ásúlfr forward. The old magician came stiffly up, holding a slender, leather-bound book in his hands. He stroked the cover reverently once then handed it to Jade. She accepted but protested that she didn't need anything but the gift of languages he had already given them.

"Lady," Ásúlfr said with a smile, "you have made my long life complete just by your arrival in our village. You and your companions will be remembered in saga-songs for generations to come. This," he tapped the book with his finger, "is a copy of my research: spells and enchantments that might help you in your travels."

Jade gasped, awed. "This is too much. I can't take

this."

He laughed softly. "It's only a copy. I still have the original. Besides," he patted her hand, "everyone's magic is personal. My spells may not even work for you."

She gazed at the old man and suddenly missed her father terribly. He was the only other person who ever treated her as special and important. Ásúlfr had given her an incredibly valuable gift – trust. Trust that she would not misuse his spells for dark purposes; trust that she would keep his knowledge to herself; trust that she was a good person.

In the depths of her heart, Jade vowed not to let him down.

Following Truda's example, she hugged the old magician. As she did so, her healer self sensed the aches and pains of arthritis in his joints. He was not really so old after all but the pain of the disease had aged him. Well, she could do something about that.

Rummaging about in her backpack, Jade brought out her herb bag and extracted a couple of dried juniper leaves from it. She poured a few drops of water from her waterskin into the palm of her hand and crushed the leaves into a paste. Next, she drew Ásúlfr aside from the throng of people seeing the companions off.

"Will you let me help you once more?"

The old man frowned at her. "How?"

"You said you couldn't do magic on yourself?"

He shook his head.

"Let me ease your pain." Jade smiled at the flicker of hope in his eyes.

He nodded hesitantly. She dabbed a little of the herb paste onto his forehead and hands then took his twisted fingers in her own and closed her eyes. A few, soft, Elven words spoken under her breath; a surge of power that tasted like copper and juniper in her mouth; the flicker of purple-blue energy behind her eyelids - and it was done. Smiling in satisfaction, Jade let go of the Lifebringer's hands and stepped back.

Ásúlfr stared at her. He straightened up slowly. A look of pure joy and amazement flowered on his wrinkled face. With an exultant laugh, he executed a funny little dance step on the spot. He gazed at her wonderingly then bowed.

"I have no way to thank you. You have changed my life."

Jade blushed and shook her head. "I'm glad I could help but..." She drew him further aside. Glancing around to make sure nobody overheard, she decided to warn the old magician. "Please be careful."

"What of?" Ásúlfr flexed his fingers, admiring the way they moved.

"I'm sure Grendel wasnt alone." she whispered.

The old man's eyes jumped to hers, his white brows snapping together in a frown. "What makes you say that? In all the years Grendel terrorised our people, he did so alone."

Jade bit her lip. How could she say she'd read it in a story? It would sound ridiculous. Finally, she decided she'd have to tell a small lie and hope he couldn't read her very well. She'd always been able to fool her family.

She reached up and tapped her temple with one finger. "My Elven senses warned me about Grendel and now I feel the presence of another. It is angry. I'm worried it may take revenge on Olshamarr for Grendel's death. Please," she laid a hand on Ásúlfr's sleeve, "warn Hrothgar to be wary."

Ásúlfr stared at her in horror for a moment then shook himself and nodded.

"Thank you for your warning. I shall pass it on to the king." He opened his mouth then shut it with a regretful look. "I cannot ask you and your friends to stay when you have already done so much. You have your own quest to pursue. Now that we know a troll can be killed, we will be able to do it ourselves, if we must. Go with our thanks, Jade. Be safe." He held her shoulders and placed a light, whiskery kiss on her cheek. Jade hugged him again and moved back to the others with a heavier burden of guilt.

It was her fault Phoenix and Marcus had taken on the troll alone; her fault that Grendel's death now put Ásúlfr and his people in danger. She just couldn't afford to make any more mistakes.

CHAPTER THIRTEEN

Jade's strangled gasp of fear made Phoenix look sharply around. They were only a few minutes outside the village and he already wondered where and when the next attack would come. Blodbal leapt to his hand before he thought about it. He twisted about, trying to find the source of her sudden exclamation of shock. There was nothing.

As he looked a question at her, she leaned forward, clinging to the mane of her horse. The mare, startled by her rider's fear, tossed her head nervously and trotted for a few jarring steps. Jade buried her face in the horse's neck and held on.

Phoenix reined his own mount in and leaned over to grab the back of her coat. Truda, sitting behind him with her arms wrapped around his waist, squeaked and grabbed tighter.

"What on earth are you doing?" he demanded, hauling Jade upright. "Two minutes ago Marcus and I were just talking about what a good rider you are. What's the deal?"

Her knuckles were white on the reins. She stared around at him. "I...I...can ride?"

"Duh," he said sarcastically. "It's what you've been doing perfectly well for the last fifteen minutes. Why did you suddenly decide you couldn't...oh." He realised, a little, late that Jade from the real world must not be able to ride but Jade gan Eleri obviously could. As long as thirteen year old Jade had let her avatar have control, she'd been fine. Once she'd actually thought about what was going on, she'd freaked.

Phoenix sighed. When this whole weird adventure

began, Jade had been a very reluctant heroine but heroine she undoubtedly was. After her initial doubts, she'd coped beautifully with magic, Romans, dryads and druids. Now she was falling apart and Phoenix had no idea why. It might have something to do with how badly she'd been overwhelmed by the presence of the troll – and how stupid she'd been to eat the lily leaves. It had shaken her confidence and now she was second-guessing herself.

He did know that if she didn't get herself together pretty fast, they were stuffed. In this land of magic and gods, they needed someone like her – someone who understood the supernatural and who'd read a lot of stupid fantasy adventure novels. He knew computer games and fighting; she knew the books they were based on.

"Jade," he tried for patience but managed slight sarcasm, "get a grip would you? You might not think you can ride but *you* can." He frowned at her, trying to get the message across without prompting awkward questions from Truda. "Relax. You'll be fine." He kneed his horse and hers followed his.

She sent him a quick, worried look before closing her eyes. Phoenix watched as she took a long, deep breath and released it. Her whole body relaxed and she sat back in the saddle like a seasoned rider. He nodded in satisfaction.

"Didn't you tell me your uncle owned a farm," he said, finally assured she wasn't going to fall off.

"A dairy farm," she replied tartly. "I can ride a motor bike without a problem, thanks."

Phoenix grinned. "Well, just think of the horse as an old-fashioned kind of motor bike – a bit bumpier and more temperamental, that's all."

"Helpful," she shot back, but she smiled a little.

The three were silent awhile, watching Marcus who rode ahead with Brynn clinging on for dear life behind. Marcus rode as if born in the saddle – which was not surprising, considering how many years he had followed his father around the Roman Empire. Brynn, however, rode badly. The boy's thin legs stuck out stiffly over the stallion's round belly and he winced at every bump and jolt. The pockets of his new clothing bulged and Phoenix briefly wondered how he could diplomatically ask the boy what he'd stolen from the village. After a moment's thought, he decided not to ask at all. He was better off not knowing.

From the corner of his eye, Phoenix watched as Jade slipped back into deep thought and chewed her lower lip. Something was really bugging her. Eventually, she sent him a troubled look.

"Do you think we did the right thing, leaving them like that?"

Mindful of Truda's curious ears right behind, he shrugged. "Who knows. From a..er…Player's point of view, yes. We did what we were obviously supposed to do there and we have to keep moving. Anything more would have been just bonus points. Remember where we are?"

She sighed. "I just don't feel good about it. I know it wouldn't have got us any closer to Asgard but it seems wrong to leave them and not know if they'll be ok. It doesn't feel like the right thing to do."

Phoenix frowned, hearing an echo of his father's words. He shifted uneasily in the saddle. If he'd just been playing this game on the outside, he definitely would have stayed. On the outside, these decisions were easy: you fought the badguys, collected points, treasure and weapons along the way and eventually either got killed or you killed the big badguy to win the game. In fact, he probably would have gone looking for Grendel's mother, just for the bonus points and possible treasure.

Being in the game added an extra layer to every decision. It wasn't just his life on the line and, as much fun as all these adventures were, it was always in the back of his mind that Jade didn't really want to be here. Marcus and Brynn were part of the team, too and he couldn't justify putting them in danger just to chase some extra Experience Points or treasure they didn't need. No, they were better off on the move than waiting to get tromped by another troll for absolutely no gain. His job was to get Truda back home and prevent Ragnarok.

"I know what you mean," he finally said, "but we don't even know for sure if this matches up with Beowulf. Keep in mind the…quest we're on. We can't get sidetracked. Who knows, maybe it's just a co-incidence. Maybe the…" he hesitated, glancing at Truda's wide blue eyes over his shoulder, "powers that control this world just like the same sort of stories you do. Maybe it's no big deal to them," he said. "You know how easily amused those geeks are." That was a word that shouldn't translate.

Jade stared at him for a second then nodded with obvious reluctance. "I suppose."

After a few minutes, she shook herself and made an effort to be her old self again. Phoenix breathed a soft sigh of relief. She wasn't quite back to normal but at least she wasn't sunk in depression. He just hoped nothing bad happened to Olshamarr. If it did, she'd be sure to blame herself and he'd never hear the end of it.

They didn't discuss it any further and the day passed without incident. Hrothgar's directions had them travelling northeast. They aimed to be at Orebro a large town about fifty kilometres away, on the shore of a lake called Hjalmaren. However, because of their late start, the shortness of the northern spring days and the slow pace of the pack horses, they had not yet reached their goal when night swept in.

As dusk turned everything softly grey, the companions slipped stiffly down from their mounts and lead them off the narrow road. To the east was yet another of the many small lakes and ponds that dotted this area. Nearby, they found a small thicket of saplings growing in a rough circle.

It seemed like a good place to set up camp.

Phoenix was surprised and a little guilty when one of the packs opened to reveal two tents made of thin, waterproofed leather. It was certainly a change from sleeping in makeshift lean-to's or caves and a very welcome relief from the chilly spring night air.

Marcus and Brynn took charge of cooking, bantering light-heartedly over who would clean up afterward. Jade, still subdued, didn't protest. Phoenix eyed her uncertainly. He definitely wasn't going to ask why she wasn't cooking as she usually preferred to. He might not read books but he wasn't stupid enough to ask a modern girl why she wasn't doing domestic chores. She'd probably whack him over the head with her quarterstaff and call him a pig – or worse, turn him into one. That didn't change the fact that he was worried about her.

The night was perfectly clear and calm. Stars glittered brightly until a gibbous moon rose to dim them. The companions set watches, as usual. Truda was the only one exempt. When told, she complained so much that Jade eventually sighed and agreed to let her stay up with Brynn for first watch. Then she slipped quietly away into one of the tents.

Marcus, Phoenix and Brynn exchanged concerned looks. Phoenix raked a hand through his hair and decided there wasn't much they could do. He went to the other tent. It was still early but there wasn't a whole lot to do other than sit around watching the campfire and stress about stuff over which he had no control. Anyway, he was tired enough to welcome the extra sleep.

The night passed and they were disturbed only by the distant sound of a single, lonely wolf-howl. Phoenix took last watch, shivering in the early morning chill, poking at the fire and watching yet another spectacular sunrise. At least this time there were no rocks falling on his head.

They had breakfasted and were striking camp when

Jade held up a hand for silence. Obediently, the others stopped. She listened for a moment, an intent look on her face that made her sharp, Elven features seem strangely pronounced. Then her eyes widened and she stared across at Phoenix.

"There's a horse coming fast," she glanced over her shoulder, "from the direction of Olshamarr."

Phoenix grimaced. "Marcus, would you please go out to the road and wait for it while we finish packing? It's probably nothing but if it is a messenger for us then he'll go right past."

The Roman nodded and disappeared into the pine forest. Jade sent Phoenix a stricken look that showed just how bad she felt about leaving the villagers. He gestured for Brynn to keep packing the gear and sent her a reassuring smile.

"It's probably nothing. Could be someone sending for a midwife; a bandit attack; just a message for the next village – the Queen suddenly craving blueberries," he said, trying to sound positive. Inside, he couldn't ignore a sinking feeling that it was something quite different.

"Yes," Jade said quietly, "it could."

For the next several moments, no one spoke. They all went about their duties silently, listening for the sound of hoofbeats. Sure enough, within seconds they all heard what Jade had picked up: the sounds of a horse galloping full pace down the road, heading north. Abruptly, they thudded to a stop and Jade lifted worried eyes toward the road.

Marcus appeared again, followed by a breathless messenger boy leading a sweating horse. The Roman shook his head gravely as he entered the clearing.

"We must return. The village has been attacked. Hrothgar is slain. Grendel's mother has taken her revenge."

"Ásúlfr? The Queen?" Jade's hushed question fell in

the silence that followed.

The messenger held up a reassuring hand and nodded. "By virtue of his new health, he was able to escape, my lady. He lives, as do the Queen, the princess and the young princes. But twenty thanes and warriors were slain as they slept in the great hall, Heorot, last night. Hrothgar took a party and followed the beast back to its lair but he was killed when they attacked it." The boy swallowed and scrubbed tears from his red face. "My brother was the only survivor. He sent me to fetch you and beg you to help us once more, Trollslayers." His blue eyes beseeched them as he glanced back and forth between Marcus and Phoenix.

Phoenix sighed, glanced at Marcus, then drew Jade and Brynn nearer for a whispered conference. Truda sat on a stump looking mulishly annoyed.

"I hate to go backwards. We ought to be getting on with finding Asgard. We've only got two days left, remember," Phoenix murmured.

Marcus frowned and Brynn scowled.

Jade looked outraged. "You can't mean it, Phoenix. It's our fault those people are dead. We have to help them."

He grimaced. "I know how you feel, Jade, but remember where we are and who they are." He tapped the amulet lying beneath his shirt and rolled his eyes significantly, trying to remind her that they were just part of a digital world, not a real one. She had to be objective about this. If she kept getting emotionally involved with the characters in this game, they'd end up taking forever to get to Level Five, if it were even possible. "We have to get Truda home before her birthday, remember?"

"No, Jade is right," Marcus stated. "It's our duty to help these people. I could not be easy if we left without trying. I don't believe you could, either." The Roman gazed straitly at Phoenix, his dark eyes solemn.

Brynn hesitated, one hand covering a pocket

possessively. Jade glared at him. Finally he sighed and shrugged. "I guess we could go back if we have to."

Phoenix echoed his sigh. This 'do the right thing' stuff was going to get them all killed one of these days. Having a conscience was a pain in the butt. Logically, he knew their best option was to go ahead to Uppsala without wasting time but that was just too cold-blooded for any of them.

"Alright, we go back but," he raised a warning finger, "if we try and it looks like we have no hope of killing this thing, we evacuate the village and get the heck out of there. Agreed? We don't want to lose anyone on this little side trip."

The other three exchanged glances and nodded.

So they turned deaf ears to Truda's complaints, packed and rode as fast as they could south, toward Olshamarr.

After a while, they decided to put Brynn and Truda on the packhorses and ride on ahead. Brynn protested until Phoenix laid a heavy hand on his thin shoulder.

"I'm asking you to take care of Truda, Brynn. You know she's the most valuable thing we have. She's the whole purpose of this quest. We have to take care of her, first." He tightened his grip until the boy winced. "We need to help these people, too. You ride with Truda and the messenger. He'll find you somewhere safe to stay outside the village until we come back. Guard her with your life, Brynn. We're counting on you. Plus," he grinned, "I'm not sure you really want to go back to the village anyway, do you?"

After a brief attempt to look innocent, Brynn had the grace to give an ashamed shrug and a half-grin. Turning serious, he glanced at Truda, nodded curtly and gripped Phoenix's forearm. He set his jaw and turned away to clamber onto the pony without another word. His dark eyes were fierce with awareness of his new duty, one hand clamped onto his new sword.

Marcus lifted Truda up on the packhorse, tucking her in amongst their baggage. She grumbled bitterly the whole time until Marcus gave her a stern look and a short, sharp lecture on how a goddess should behave toward her people. After that, she subsided, bottom lip quivering. The messenger led her horse and Brynn's as neither knew how to ride well enough to control their mounts. After giving the village boy final instructions, Jade, Marcus and Phoenix put heels to their horses' flanks and galloped toward Olshamarr.

Rank upon rank of huge, sombre pines zipped past, even as time seemed to drag. To Phoenix, it seemed to take forever to cover the distance back to Olshamarr. Shoulder to shoulder with Jade's fleet roan mare, his grey stallion flew over the rutted dirt track. Close behind, Marcus' bay pushed to keep up.

Finally, they slowed to a trot as the village came in sight. Even from a distance they could see the destruction wrought by the troll. Houses lay flattened as though the beast had simply kicked down the thick walls. Workshops and stables were just piles of matchstick tinder. High on the hill a column of black smoke rose above Heorot. In the village, people either wandered about as though they had no idea where to start, or worked tirelessly, with blank expressions, to restore their property.

As the three companions approached, Ásúlfr came striding toward them, his face alight with relief. Beneath that, Phoenix could see pain and remembrance of fear and suffering that would last for years. A baby wailed somewhere nearby.

Jade clutched at his arm, her expression distraught. "If we hadn't rushed off yesterday we'd have been here to help them last night, Phoenix. We have to make things right."

He nodded, knowing there was no argument this time. They shouldn't have left.

"Well, we've done it once, we can do it again." He

swung down off his horse and squared his shoulders, clenching his teeth against bile that rose at the sight of the devastation in the village. "And this time we'll have your help, too, so it should be easier."

Jade's fingers tightened. He looked down to see her guilt had turned to fear.

"But you said my magic won't work against a troll, Phoenix." Her nails dug into his arm. "I can't help you. Grendel's mother is supposed to be even worse than Grendel…and I can't do anything!"

CHAPTER FOURTEEN

Much later that day, led by the sole survivor of Hrothgar's doomed group, the three companions, Ásúlfr and a party of ten warriors rode the last few metres toward the enormous lake east of Olshamarr. They dismounted at the top of a rocky cliff overlooking the water.

Jade followed Phoenix and Marcus toward the edge, away from the war party. Silently, the three stared down. Below was a small, stony cove. A tiny stream trickled down a deep gorge to spill sparkling droplets into the lake's dark waters. It was late afternoon now, and the surface of the lake rippled under light, cold winds. A million wavelets glittered red in the sunset. The water looked deep and unforgiving; the grey rocks sharp and slippery. It was an ominous place.

Phoenix stepped back, staring out across the vast expanse of water.

"OK, Jade." He turned to face her, glancing over as though to make sure the Svear warriors were well out of earshot. "You said you know this story. How does it go from here?"

Jade swallowed and glanced down over the edge. She could once more sense the presence of a troll and it played havoc with her thinking. Fear swelled up from her belly, trying to take control of her brain. A sense of impending doom pushed into her mind like a dark fog. Her legs began to shake.

Desperately, she took a deep breath, closed her eyes and tried a small spell on herself. Relax, she willed the Command spell on herself. Amazingly, it seemed to work.

A gentle reassurance spread from a warm spot on her chest. It seeped into her limbs and brought clarity back to her mind. The amulet. Touching a fingertip to the gleaming metal, Jade felt a sudden surge of strength and power. She was ok. The fear was still there but she could think through it now.

Delighted, she opened her eyes to find Phoenix and Marcus staring at her in bewilderment.

"What…?" Phoenix began.

Jade waved the question aside. There was no time. The sun sent golden fingers of fire across the lake as it set in spectacular fashion behind them. Grendel's mother would emerge soon. They had yet to come up with a plan.

"In Beowulf's story, he's given a sword, Hrunting, and he dives into the lake. Under a headland," she indicated one of the rocky points jutting out into the water, "he finds the cave where the troll lives."

He fingered his new sword. "But this isn't Hrunting, it's Blódbál – which is a way cooler name, by the way - and Hrothgar said it didn't work against trolls."

"Exactly," Jade said, ignoring his comment about the name. "Hrunting doesn't either but Beowulf doesn't find that out until he actually tries to kill her. Then he has a huge battle of strength that he knows he's losing. Luckily, he finds another magic sword lying about in the cave and this one can and does kill her. Unfortunately, her blood dissolves the blade and Beowulf comes out with only the hilt."

"So he does survive then?" Phoenix asked. "You're sure?"

"As much as I can be." She bit her lip and laid a hand on his arm. "I'm guessing here, Phoenix. I mean," she shook her head, irritated, "the programmers have mixed up their dates. I'm pretty annoyed with them, if you must know. The story of Beowulf isn't supposed to happen for another five hundred years or so – and it's set in Denmark, not Sweden."

"Remind me to speak quite firmly to them about historical accuracy when we get home," he said, raising an ironic brow.

Jade sighed and chose to ignore the sarcasm. "The point is: how can I be sure they've stuck to the plot? I mean, Hrothgar gave you the wrong sword, he wasn't supposed to die, and the way you killed Grendel isn't part of the original story, either. You were meant to rip off an arm so that he bled to death."

Phoenix made a face. "Gross - and," he added, as an afterthought, "impossible, I'd say." Marcus nodded in wholehearted agreement.

She gave them a worried half-smile. "Beowulf was amazingly strong."

"I rolled a twenty for strength, if that helps." Phoenix shrugged.

"Really?" Jade blinked at him.

He nodded and she could see he was pleased he'd surprised her.

"Well," she said firmly, "I still don't think you should rush into the cave and just hope there's a convenient, magical sword lying about – even one with a cool name. We need a plan."

Phoenix looked at the dark, rippled water below and shuddered. "Sounds good to me. I'm not a very good swimmer anyway. Got one?"

"Ah," Jade grimaced, "that's where we have a problem. I was hoping you might."

"Me? You're the one with the big ideas all the time."

"But you're the one who defeated Grendel, remember?"

"Don't remind me." Phoenix rubbed his ribs. "It was sheer luck. I don't think we could do it again if you paid us."

Jade gave an exasperated huff, losing patience with his

ill-timed humour. "Well you're the only ones with experience at this. Think of something! The sun's going down and that troll is going to come out and flatten us as soon as it's dark."

He growled. "I do know that. Geez, Jade. You're not the only one with a brain, you know."

"Well, sometimes it seems like it," she snapped. "Think of something."

"You think of something!" Phoenix shot back at her. "You're the one who so keen to be important. Come up with another smartass plan to save the day."

"I am not a smartass." Her voice broke and she turned her head away, fighting tears.

"Well stop acting like it then." Phoenix crossed his arms over his chest. "You keep trying to rub our noses in how smart and how special you are. Now's your chance. Save us all with your brilliance."

They glared at each other. Jade felt her throat clamp shut as she struggled not to cry. Why was he being so horrible? It was just like being back at home with her sisters and mother. No matter what she did, it wasn't good enough. Would she ever be able to make everyone happy?

There was a long, uncomfortable silence until Marcus stepped between his friends. He laid a hand on each and pushed them apart.

"Stop behaving like children," he ordered. "You are adults, both."

Jade flushed and exchanged a guilty look with Phoenix. They still hadn't told Marcus that, although their avatar bodies were in their late teens, their real bodies were just barely into double-digits. Sometimes she just couldn't help acting like the kid she still was – at least partly.

"Jade," Marcus turned his dark, solemn gaze on her and she squirmed inside, "you know he deserves better. Phoenix," he addressed the warrior sternly, "you know Jade has saved us several times already. She does not need to prove anything."

Annoyance then reluctant agreement flickered across Phoenix's face. He opened his mouth, probably about to apologise. He never got a chance. Inspiration hit her.

"Oh!" Jade clutched at Marcus' arm. "That's it!"

Both boys turned puzzled gazes on her. "What?" they asked in unison.

"The dryads. The magic horn Aurfanon gave me! I keep forgetting we have it." Jade dropped her pack on the ground and yanked the Hyllion Bagia out of it. Reaching in, she named the item and felt its cool, smooth curves slap into her hand. She pulled it out, balancing it across her palms.

In the rapidly-fading sunlight, the three examined their prize, differences forgotten. It appeared to be some sort of curled sheep or goat horn. Both ends were edged with thin layers of beaten gold, the small one in the shape of a mouthpiece. The cream-coloured horn between was carved with a thousand, intricate drawings that seemed to twist and shift in the greying light.

"How does it work?" Phoenix poked it with a grubby finger.

"I think you just blow into the pointy end and sound comes out the fat end," Jade said with a touch of scorn, still a little hurt by the things he'd said.

"Thank you for that helpful hint."

She stuck out her tongue at him then felt like an idiot when Marcus sent her a mildly astonished look.

"I meant," Phoenix continued, "didn't you say something about being in danger?"

"Oh, yes." Jade thought back. "We have to be in dire peril, we can only use it three times, and the help that comes might not be what we expected."

"Fabulously vague." He still sounded like he was mocking her.

"Got any better ideas?"

He sighed and glanced at the sun, slipping rapidly behind hazy, purple mountains. Around them, crickets began to chirrup. The horses whuffled and stamped as the temperature dropped. Nearby, the Svear warriors stared uneasily into the gathering darkness.

"No, but we're not exactly in dire peril," he admitted.

Behind them, echoing out across the dark lake, came splashing followed by an awful grinding, crunching sound. It bounced off the cove's rocky walls, sounding like it came from a dozen directions. Everyone jumped.

Jade whispered a light-making spell from her new spellbook. A feeble, greenish ball of light appeared in the palm of her hand, casting weird shadows on the anxious faces around her.

"Somehow, I don't think it will be long before we are," she said shakily.

"You can do magic?" Phoenix stared at the green light in surprise. "Even with a troll this close? Can you do any spells to help the situation?"

Jade shook her head. "It's taking all my concentration just to keep this going. I can't help, I'm sorry." It grated to have to make that confession. She ought to be able to do something.

Phoenix and Marcus exchanged weary, wary glances.

"Here we go again," Phoenix murmured. "Let's get some torches happening. At least we can buy some time."

Marcus nodded. Turning away, the Roman began to instruct the Svear warriors in the 'light-torches-and-trees' method of Troll distraction. The groundshaking grinding grew louder and several battle-hardened warriors paled and backed away. Ásúlfr spoke sharply to them, moving forward with a lit torch in his hand. At the sight of the old man stepping up, the younger warriors took heart and followed his lead.

Phoenix peered over the cliff-edge then withdrew quickly, his eyes wide.

"Man, she's huge!"

Jade peeked over. She could just make out the silhouette of a massive, jagged creature clambering from the water far below. It headed for the gorge, apparently its path to the top.

"You guys outran and outwitted one of those?" Her respect for Phoenix jumped a few notches.

He shrugged. "Ours was a fair bit smaller, though."

"Still…"

Together, they watched the enormous rock-creature as it moved toward the gorge with surprising speed and agility.

"Can we do anything before she gets up here?" Jade asked hopefully.

"Like what?"

"Maybe roll big rocks down on her?" It was a long shot, she knew but the thought of being chased down by that thing sent shivers up her spine.

Phoenix frowned. "Aren't we just going to use the horn to blow for help when we get into trouble?"

"So?"

He raised an eyebrow. "What's the point in delaying it?"

She shivered. "I guess I just want to stay as far away from that thing as I can."

"Good instincts," he said, slapping her on the back, "but we can hardly be in dire peril if we're a dozen miles away. Nope, we may as well get it over with. I'll just go put myself in danger, shall I?" he finished, annoyingly blasé. With a wave, he jogged over toward the narrow gorge that led to the bay.

Jade stared after him for a moment, worried. She tightened her grip on the horn, ready to blow the minute Phoenix yelled for help.

*****

Phoenix felt a whole lot less confident than he tried to

sound. He regretted snapping at Jade but he'd felt under pressure to come up with an answer. Thank goodness she had once again pulled a viable plan out of her hat - or Bag, in this case. Unfortunately, he had a really bad feeling that, for the magic horn to work, he would have to put one of his lives on the line. All too clearly, he remembered the fearsome size of Grendel. Vivid images of that wild night reeled through his head until he had to grit his teeth and force his feet to move forward. Even worse, twinges of pain shot through his ankle, ribs and the healed arrow-wounds on his back. Dying again was the last thing he wanted to do. The very last.

His legs felt leaden as he reached the lip of the gorge. Blood thundered in his ears and his breath grew shallow and quick at the thought of what was coming. Below, the grinding and crushing of great rocks told him the troll was climbing steadily upward, growling as she came.

Instinctively, Phoenix reached for his sword. Its song burst into his mind, urging him to rush into battle, to die in glorious, bloody defeat. Shaken, he slowly re-sheathed it. He knew it wouldn't work but its insidious song was hard to resist. There was no point in breaking a perfectly good magic sword. Still, he felt naked without something in his hand.

On cue, a burning torch was thrust into his palm. He gripped it gratefully.

"You're using yourself as bait?" Marcus sounded almost angry.

Phoenix gave a half-shrug.

"I'll join you."

Alarm shot through Phoenix. "No way! I'm not really in any danger but you are! Get away from here, Marcus. I mean it." He glared at his friend.

Marcus shook his head. "I can't, in good conscience, leave a sword-brother to face such danger alone. You would do the same for me."

Phoenix wasn't so sure of that. He had the security of knowing he had more lives. If he didn't he wasn't certain he'd be brave enough to offer what Marcus did. He pulled out his dagger and brandished the ruby-studded hilt at his companion.

"I'll be ok. Remember?"

Marcus stared at him then down at the dagger, obviously unwilling to believe in his ability overcome death. "Are you certain?"

Phoenix swallowed hard and nodded, trying to ignore a flicker of doubt in his guts. "Go keep the villagers from panicking and getting killed."

The Roman stood still for a moment, staring at him, clearly undecided.

Phoenix felt a surge of gratitude for his loyalty. No-one in his world had ever shown him such unswerving support. The Roman had been brought up in a world where such unshakable loyalty was expected. Phoenix found it uncomfortable and hard to accept. He reached out and gave him a shove.

"Go, Marcus. Be safe."

Marcus gripped his arm. "And you, my friend."

Phoenix turned his back on his friend and stared into the darkness, afraid his face might give away how alone he felt.

Would dying hurt this time? There was no doubt he was destined to die at least once tonight. How could being squashed by a ten-tonne foot not be painful? The question was: how long would he have to stand it before he "died"? How would he come back if he were squashed flat? For a brief, silly moment, he felt an insane urge to giggle. A cartoon-style vision came into his head: himself squished perfectly flat then blowing on his own thumb to pop himself back to full size.

Unsure, he checked his dagger again. Yes, there were still six glowing rubies in the hilt. Surely that had to mean he had six lives left. Doubt flared again. What if, somehow, the Druid's spring rites had actually cured him last time? What if it was just a coincidence that one ruby in his dagger was broken? What if the seven-lives rule didn't apply to him and Jade because they were actually in the computer game, not just playing it?

An inborn fear for his own life gripped him. It was just stupid to deliberately let himself be killed again. Totally nuts! Slowly, he retreated from the edge of the gorge. There had to be another way.

Then he took a deep, slow breath and a tightened grip on his torch. There was no other way. Someone had to be in danger for the Horn to work. He could do this. He could. He'd outrun and outsmarted one troll already with just Marcus to help. This time he had a whole backup team. He was not alone. Hard as it was, he just had to have faith in them and in himself. Phoenix stepped back toward the gorge, listening and watching. Sweat trickled down his forehead as he strained to see the troll in the darkness.

Something was wrong. It took a second for the change to register. While he'd been thinking about dying, the troll had taken a different path. The sounds of her climbing no longer echoed up the rocky gorge. She had moved around to the cliff face.

As he turned, a shrill scream pierced the darkness. Peering past the light of his own torch, Phoenix saw Jade stumbling away from the precipice. The greenish witch-light she had cast bobbed at her shoulder, illuminating her terrified face. She wasn't looking in his direction. She was looking at the sheer drop before her.

There, hauling itself awkwardly over the edge, was the troll. It was now less than twenty metres away from where Jade stood.

"Jade!" "Run!" Phoenix heard Marcus' yell echo his own as they both started toward her. She half-turned but glanced back over her shoulder at the beast. It loomed closer. There was no way they could reach her in time to distract it.

"Phoenix!" Jade's despairing, urgent cry tore at him.

He ran faster, legs pumping, Marcus thudding beside him.

"The horn!" Marcus shouted.

Phoenix looked up hopefully. Jade put the golden mouthpiece to her lips as she ran. A wobbly, faint note sounded – like the muffled tone of a distant trumpet. It sent a shiver down his spine and made the hair on the back of his neck stand up.

Phoenix glanced around, expecting instant results. Nothing happened. It was too late, anyway. Phoenix and Marcus could do nothing as a great, rocky arm swung in an unstoppable arc toward Jade's sprinting form. They could do nothing as it connected sickeningly and carried on swinging. Nothing, as Jade's limp body flew through the air toward them and landed, broken and twisted, at their feet.

CHAPTER FIFTEEN

"Jade!" Marcus' hoarse cry echoed across the dark lake.

He and Phoenix reached her motionless form at the same time. Phoenix risked a quick look up at the troll, relieved to see it turn away from them. Several Svear warriors taunted it; waving their torches about; yelling abuse and curses at it; trying to lead it away.

Marcus crouched beside her, his fingers on her throat. The Roman looked up at Phoenix and shook his head. His jaw was clenched, dark eyes stricken.

"She's dead."

Phoenix crouched too, elbows resting on his knees. Jade looked as if she were sleeping – except that her neck was twisted in a way that would not be possible if she were alive. Her right leg and arm both lay at awkward angles. A thin line of blood trickled from her mouth.

He swallowed hard, trying to stay calm. She wasn't really dead. She had just lost one of her seven lives. He struggled to reassure himself but worry welled up in him. Maybe he'd been right before. Maybe the seven-lives thing wasn't part of the game; maybe she was, truly, dead and he was alone; maybe he would have to fight with this weird world on his own. Dammit, he'd gotten used to having Jade around. How was he supposed to win the game without her? How could she do something so stupid?

Phoenix shook all over. He fought the urge to hit something; to run somewhere – anywhere but here. Trying to think logically, he drew a deep breath. A quick look at the handle of her dagger showed that one of the seven rubies had, indeed, cracked and dulled. His shoulders slumped in relief. Maybe there was still hope. If she was going to recover, they would have to at least give her body a chance to heal itself. It had to be impossible to come back to life all twisted up like that.

Resolutely, he reached out and turned her onto her back. Her limbs flopped unpleasantly. Marcus uttered a wordless protest then reached out to help as he realized what Phoenix did. Together, the boys laid their friend out straight on the rocky ground, hands crossed on her chest, eyes peacefully closed.

"Will she…?" Marcus asked in a choked voice. He laid calloused fingers gently against her cheek, staring at her serene countenance.

"I think so." Phoenix's voice shook. "I hope so." She had to. Had to. He couldn't bear to think of the consequences if she didn't.

From somewhere behind them came a frustrated, gravelly roar from the troll-mother; followed by the crackling sound of a burning tree and the strong scent of pine-smoke. Then the ruckus of shouting warriors and thunderous troll-feet was coming closer again.

"We have to get her somewhere safer, though."

Stooping, he picked up the horn of Aurfanon and jammed it into Jade's pack. Fat lot of good blowing that stupid thing had done. Where was the help it promised? How were they supposed to kill the troll now? Damn Jade for coming up with such a brainless idea anyway!

With teeth gritted against the anxiety that thudded in his chest, he handed the pack to Marcus and scooped Jade up in his arms. Her head lolled back, pale hair almost touching the ground. She was lighter than he thought; her skin still warm. He almost expected to feel a heartbeat beneath his fingers. She couldn't be really dead. His thoughts seesawed between helpless denial and unreasonable resentment at her foolhardiness. Please,

please don't let her be dead, the chant ran ceaselessly though his head as he turned away from the cliff.

A cold, swirling wind sprang up around them. With it came the fresh scent of earth, horses, dogs and, oddly, a hint of sweet wine. Eddies caught at their hair and clothes, fluttering Jade's cloak and hair like butterfly wings. It carried the faint, haunting sound of a hunting horn, followed by the baying of hounds and the soft drift of wild laughter and music.

"What is it?" Marcus' hushed voice sounded at his shoulder.

Phoenix stared into the darkness, puzzled. "It sounds like there's a hunt of some sort going on out there."

"A hunt?" Marcus was incredulous. "At night?"

"Strange, alright," he agreed, "especially since it's coming from out over the lake."

He peered into the purple gloom. Again the eerie wail of a hunting horn echoed thinly through the cold air, closer this time. The hounds bayed louder but the thunder of hooves was strangely absent. Distant, greenish lights flickered over the dark water. Laughter and song ebbed and flowed with the wash of lively music but it all had a weird, other-worldly quality that set Phoenix's teeth on edge.

"There!" Marcus pointed out across the lake toward a host of bobbing, pale green lights.

"I see, but what exactly are they?" Phoenix squinted through the darkness.

"I have no idea."

Several tense moments passed. The swaying lights drew nearer as the two boys watched, spellbound. They barely even registered the now-distant noises of Svear warriors leading the troll away through the forest.

Finally, the lights were close enough to illuminate the folk who bore them aloft.

"By Jupiters' beard!" Marcus swore softly.

"What the...?" Phoenix had no idea what to say, so he let his words trail off as they stared in awe.

A multitude of merrymaking hunters galloped majestically toward the cliff. Seated on horses that practically glowed white were twenty or more of the most beautiful, frightening people Phoenix had ever seen. Impossibly tall, severely elegant and unbearably handsome, each rider wore a shimmering, midnight-blue, belted tunic over breeches tucked into high boots. Many of them had grey cloaks, falling gracefully from their shoulders to drape across their horses' withers. All had long, white-blond hair, pale skin and high, sharp cheekbones.

Several carried torches burning with an eerie, greenish light that echoed the magic radiance Jade had cast. Did cast, Phoenix corrected himself. All bore hunting bows and swords or daggers of some silvery metal, glinting purple-blue in the torchlight. Some also held and played a strange assemblage of musical instruments: harps, flutes and drums he'd never seen before. Their eerie music plucked at Phoenix's brain, distracting him and filling him with a deep sense of unease.

Gambolling about the riders were a dozen enormous dogs. Pure white, with red ears and glowing red eyes, they were a frightening sight as they came closer. By far the oddest thing though, was that both their steeds and dogs pranced at least fifty feet above the surface of the lake. As the moon began to rise in the east, they rode on air and moonbeams.

Marcus dropped a hand to his sword. "They are Elvenkind – Jade's folk. They must be."

Phoenix saw the similarities – and the pointed ears. Jade did look like them, but in a more human way. All the exaggerated, almost alien beauty of these riders was, in her face, softened into loveliness more acceptable to humans.

"You're right," he whispered back, "but that doesn't explain who they are or why they're here."

At that moment, the whole cavalcade spilled over the cliff edge and reined to a halt only metres away from the two warriors. On a curt command, the dogs sat obediently beside their masters. The group formed a rough wedge behind one person: a terrifyingly tall, elegant male dressed similarly to the others but with a cloak of silver and a thin, silver coronet around his forehead. His eyes were the blackest pits of boredom, his expression faintly contemptuous.

Phoenix felt distinctly at a disadvantage. He still held Jade's limp form in his arms but he didn't dare drop her to snatch at a weapon. Keeping half an eye on the newcomers, he tried to look casual and non-threatening as he laid her gently on the cold ground at his feet. Resting a hand on his new sword, he stepped over her.

The music stopped. The horses and dogs came to a complete halt. Phoenix felt as if twenty pairs of slanted, Elvish eyes were focussed on him which, unfortunately, they were. He gulped, wishing for Brynn's roguish tongue. Remembering his manners, he bowed jerkily. He had a vague idea that Elves were a lot more powerful than Jade and a lot more arrogant. Probably best to be polite.

"My lords," he began.

The leader held up a slender hand and stared coolly down at him.

"What mortal dares summon the Wild Hunt?" Disdain chilled his voice.

Caught off guard, Phoenix exchanged frantic glances with Marcus. Then the Roman's eyes widened and he glanced at Jade's backpack, dangling from his fingers. The horn, of course! Jade's use of the magic horn had summoned them.

Relieved to have cleared up that mystery, Phoenix bowed again.

"We did, my lord," he managed.

"By what right do you possess the Horn of Aurfanon?"

the Elven leader demanded.

Phoenix thought fast. If he gave the wrong answer, would they leave without helping?

"By right of gift, my lord." He waved a hand at Jade's inert shape. "Our companion met and was befriended by Queen Aurfanon, in Albion. The Queen lent us the horn to help us complete our quests. We used the horn to summon help but we didn't know what form the aid would take."

The Elven king leaned forward in his saddle, staring past Phoenix at Jade. His expression tightened to something close to dismay. Phoenix felt his heartrate jump. What if he thought they'd killed Jade, a half-elf? They stood no chance at all against twenty well-armed Elves.

The Elven king swung down off his mount. His followers exchanged startled, wary glances. Phoenix and Marcus moved to protect their fallen comrade but the king raised one thin eyebrow at them and stared until they edged aside. He knelt gracefully beside Jade, his frown deepening as he brushed hair from her face.

"What colour were her eyes?"

Phoenix stared at him blankly. The question was so unexpected he didn't know what to say. The king stood swiftly, towering over him, his expression bleak.

"Green, sir," Marcus put in quietly, coming to his rescue.

At this, the king's already-pale face turned ashen. He closed his eyes briefly, glanced back down at Jade then drew himself up, his face once more cold and haughty.

"If you have called us to save her from death then we are too late." With a swirl of his cloak, he turned away and placed a foot in the stirrup, preparing to mount.

"No!" Phoenix called. "We called for aid in destroying a troll."

The Elven leader paused for a second, considering. He shook his head. "We are not interested in hunting trolls. Farewell."

"But this troll killed the Svear king and many of his people," Phoenix said urgently, "and it did this to Jade." He couldn't explain why he'd said it; he just hoped the Elves would want to be revenged on whoever killed their kin. He was right.

A frightening sternness came over the king's narrow face. His dark eyes blazed with anger. In one smooth movement, he swung onto his horse and gathered the reins. Rapidly, he spoke over his shoulder in Elvish to quick for Phoenix to catch. Half of his troupe nodded, smiled with devilish delight and spurred their steeds toward the distant sounds of troll-wrought destruction. Their horses' hooves made no sound as they skimmed above the earth. The dogs followed, baying again.

Phoenix, Marcus and the rest of the Elves stood frozen, listening. Moments later came the satisfying sound of trollish frustration and the spine-tingling laughter of Elves on the hunt. The two warriors gaped as ten Elven hunters appeared above the forest. Bound in a dozen slender, silvery ropes, dangling between the horses and dogs, threshed the roaring shape of Grendel's mother. Still laughing, the Elves galloped overhead, out across the lake, heading east. As the grinding sound of the troll's anger faded, Phoenix managed to shut his jaw and turn back to the Elven king. The Elf gazed down at him with faint humour. He inclined his head regally.

"It is done. The troll will be carried into the morning sun then dropped into the sea. Now may we go?" His question was tinged with irony.

Phoenix flushed. Obviously his little ploy to involve the Elves by appealing to their desire for revenge had not gone unnoticed. Plucking up his courage, he managed one more request.

"We need to get to Uppsala, quickly. Can you help us?"

The king frowned again, his slanted brows snapping

together. "What of your fallen companion? Is she worth no more than a cold grave above ground? Will you not bury her with dignity?"

Phoenix took a deep breath. Here was the crucial moment. Would the king be angry when he found out Jade might not be permanently dead?

"I believe she can be returned to us, good sir, if you will give us further aid this night. Will you?"

"Returned to you!" The Elven king's face showed quick series of emotions that baffled Phoenix: anger, disbelief then finally hope. "By what manner of magic can you, a mortal, restore life?" he asked haughtily.

"She and I are...unique... in this world, my lord." He searched for the right words. "I can only say that I believe she will recover if given a chance. It's worth a try."

"A non-answer if ever I heard one, warrior." The king was not deceived. "However, we all have our secrets, do we not?" He glanced one more time at Jade's still face. "Very well. We shall take you to Álfheimr." He paused for a moment, staring over Phoenix's shoulder at the forest behind. A thin smile pulled at his lips. "Shall we also take the little godling who lurks among the trees, watching? She would appear to be far from home."

Phoenix and Marcus sighed in unison and turned around.

"Truda!" Phoenix yelled. "You can come out now!"

There was a moment of silence, and then two small figures stepped out from the shrubbery. In front strode Truda, proud as any princess. Behind her, looking sheepish, came Brynn. He led their pack horses and cast awed glances at the glowing Elven host. When they were close enough, Truda exchanged stately nods with the king, who luckily chose not to take offence. Brynn bowed deeply and received a scornful glance from his young companion.

"How did you get here?" Phoenix demanded. "I

wanted you two safe outside the village."

"That messenger didn't want to miss out on the fight." Brynn was breathless. "He led us here. What were we supposed to do?" He spread his hands, giving his best innocent look.

Phoenix didn't believe him for a moment but whatever he'd intended to say was cut short when the boy caught sight of Jade's body. Brynn gasped in horror, his eyes wide. He dropped the reins and threw himself over her with a wail of despair. He grabbed her slim shoulders and shook her.

"Jade! Jade! Wake up!" When she didn't, he buried his face in her neck and sobbed.

Truda stood by, looking troubled. Marcus hurried over to Brynn, dragging the boy aside, murmuring explanations and reassurance into his ear. Slowly, Brynn's tears dried. He sniffed and wiped his face on his sleeve.

"Do you really think...?" He cast hopeful glances between Phoenix, Marcus and the Elven king.

"I'm hoping we can bring her back," Phoenix said for at least the third time – and hopefully the last, "but I think we need to do it fast, or she may be gone forever." Truthfully, he had no idea if this was right but he was getting pretty tired of explaining and he wanted to get moving. Each time he thought about Jade, he had to suppress the fear that he might be wrong; that she was already gone forever.

Even if she weren't then it was time to move on. The troll was gone. They'd done their duty by the village. Now they needed to get on with their own quest before Zhudai found them or something else nasty decided to get in their way.

Glancing up at the Elven king's cold, aloof eyes, Phoenix wondered briefly if they hadn't jumped into the proverbial fire. The Elves didn't exactly look thrilled to be taking on passengers.

*****

Drifting in and out of sleep, Long Baiyu felt death like a hot needle in his mind. He awoke with a groan, eyes wide in the darkness of his cell. Cautiously, he cast his thoughts out. He needed help again. In her between-life state, she could be reached...taught...helped without Zhudai's knowledge. He couldn't risk reaching that far again himself. Zhudai had sealed the breach in his mental shields. There was one close by, however, who could again be of assistance...

CHAPTER SIXTEEN

Jade swam slowly up from great depths. Shying away from the memory of shattering pain; of utter blackness; of nothingness; she moved into a familiar, grey world of shifting fogs and whispered, half-heard voices. She drifted for what seemed like eternity in limbo, chasing voices, peering into the mists, wondering how to find her way home.

At last, a voice murmured her name clearly. A vaguely familiar voice: kind, tired and patient. She turned toward it eagerly, hoping to see a face but finding only more fog. The voice called again, whispering reassurances at first, then instructions. Information she'd never read about this game-world: what the next three 'quests' entailed; what countries they would encounter; a basic idea of what they needed to do in each.

The voice faded, fainter and more exhausted until it stopped altogether. Jade called out, hoping to find out more but to no avail. She was once again alone, trying desperately to remember everything she'd heard.

Now, a different voice called. One she recognised but couldn't put a name to. Puzzled, she turned toward it. Drawn by a green-gold glow, she floated reluctantly out of suspension and back to life.

With a gasp, Jade sat up, blinking in the light. She felt her body, patting it to make sure she had all her arms and legs, her head, her face. Everything felt ok. Tentatively, she rotated her shoulders, expecting pain. After all, her last memory had been of a massive troll fist crashing into her frail body. Nothing seemed amiss. Everything appeared to be functioning fine. How strange.

"Jade?" Another familiar voice drew her attention. This one she could name. Phoenix knelt beside her bed, looking both anxious and thankful. Behind him stood Marcus, his normally-solemn expression one of glad relief. Next to him, Brynn clutched at Phoenix's shoulder with wide-eyed disbelief. Suddenly, the boy threw himself into Jade's arms.

"I thought you were dead," he howled. "Don't ever do that again! I don't want to lose you, too."

Jade patted his thin back, wondering how to remind him it was probably going to happen at least another five times - if she couldn't avoid it. Finally, his sobs subsided and he moved away, wiping his grubby face with an equally grubby sleeve.

"Where are we?" she asked, bemused.

She was in some sort of bedroom that much was obvious. It was a room unlike any she'd ever seen. The walls were some sort of pale, almost translucent white stone. The blocks fitted so smoothly that she could barely see the joins. The bed on which she lay was an enormous, canopied affair that dripped velvet curtains and gold tassels. All around stood exotically-designed pieces of furniture ornamented with plant designs picked out in gold leaf. Through a huge, arched window, she could only see darkness and faint stars.

"We're in Alfheim," Phoenix replied. "The Elves only just let us in to see you."

"Alfheim..." She frowned, trying to connect the dots. "Oh! 'Elf-home', the home of the elves in Norse mythology. How did we get here?"

Phoenix told of the arrival of the Elven Wild Hunt; the destruction of the troll; his plea to the Elven king. Jade stared at him with amazement. Asking Elves for anything was either impressively brave or astonishingly ignorant. They were known to be tricksy, fickle folk when dealing with mortals. She was pretty sure Phoenix'd been oblivious to the danger, although he had shown a fair amount of bravery in the last couple of weeks.

When he finished, she frowned. "So how did we get to Alfheim then?"

The others exchanged glances, all three looking a little paler.

"The king gave our horses the ability to fly – temporarily, I hope," Phoenix added with a shudder. "We travelled over what he called 'Bifrost, the Rainbow Bridge' – kind of a solid rainbow into the sky then...somewhere else. Here, I guess." He shook himself again as if to be rid of a bad memory. "Honestly, I hope we never have to do it again. It was...a long, long way up and there were no handrails."

"Terrifying," Brynn put in, shivering.

"Most unpleasant, I must admit," Marcus agreed.

"Oh, yes." Jade recalled what she knew of Norse mythology. "Bifrost connects Midgard to Asgard. I didn't know it went to Alfheim, too."

"I thought we had to go down the roots of that tree Truda told us about: Igdrizzle or whatever," Brynn complained.

"Yggdrasil," Jade corrected. "Yeah, that's the other way to get here. I guess this was easier."

"Debatable," Phoenix muttered.

Jade chose not to dignify that with an answer. She had something more important on her mind. "Where's Truda?"

"She's with the king and his court, why?" Phoenix was puzzled.

"Don't you understand?"

The others shook their heads.

"I've just remembered. The world of Alfheim is on the same level as Asgard, under the roots of the Yggdrasil tree. From here, we should be able to get across to Asgard!" Jade fidgeted with excitement as she recalled soft words whispered while she floated in limbo. They were finally nearing the end of Level Two. "Don't you see? All we have to do is get there, return Truda to Thor before her birthday and...steal...his..." Her words ground to a halt as she met Phoenix's sceptical gaze. "Yes, I suppose we're not really that much better off, are we? Stealing the hammer was always going to be the hardest part." Sighing, she slumped back on her pillows as exhaustion swept over her.

Marcus leaned in, concerned. "You probably should rest."

Phoenix nodded and quirked a knowing grin at her. "Being dead sure takes it out of you, doesn't it?"

Jade smiled a little. "Speaking of being dead, where's my knife?"

Marcus handed over her belt knife. She inspected the handle. Sure enough, one of the rubies was blackened and cracked through the middle. Only six left. Scary.

Phoenix grinned again. "An old friend of yours gave us some help. She and her ladies have been looking after you." He glanced at the door. It opened and a familiar figure entered.

She sat up, surprised. "Aurfanon!"

The golden Queen of the dryads glided gracefully toward the bed. Phoenix and the others withdrew a little, leaving her space to sit beside Jade. The queen sank onto the mattress with hardly a sigh of her fine linen dress. She smiled, the corners of her amber eyes crinkling pleasantly. Reaching out, she placed a cool hand on Jade's forehead.

"You are well, child?" Her voice was a whisper of wind through autumn leaves.

Jade nodded. "Thank you. How did you get here? You were in Engl...Albion, in Anoeth – the Timeless Land of the Elven folk there. How can you be here, so far from your oak tree?" As far as she knew, dryads were tied to their trees. Surely Sweden was too far away for Aurfanon to travel.

The Queen smiled again. "Silly child. The Anoeth is not like the mortal world. It is everywhere at once. What is Alfheim to the Svear people, is Anoeth to the Bretons. My tree is here, too. When the king told me of your need, of course I came."

"Th...thankyou, your majesty," Jade stuttered, humbled. "I don't know why you're being so kind to me. I'm nobody to you or the king."

Aurfanon sent her a sidelong glance beneath long lashes. She smiled a secret little smile, shook her head and patted Jade's hand. "When you are better, you must come to the dining hall and meet his majesty." Standing, she swept the others with a cool look. "Your companions will dine here."

"But..." Jade protested.

"I'm sorry but mortals are forbidden to enter Vídbláinn, the king's own hall," Aurfanon said firmly. "Your companions will await your return. That is the king's will." With that, the golden queen swept out of the room, leaving the four companions speechless.

After a few moments, Phoenix turned to Jade with an ironic smile, his arms folded.

"So you get VIP status again, huh. Happy?"

Jade glowered at him. "Don't be mean. I didn't ask her to do that."

"No, but you sure didn't argue much," he pointed out. "Well, I'm sure you'll love getting the royal treatment again. We'll just wait for you here, shall we?"

She felt hot tears of hurt and injustice sting her eyes. She turned her back and closed her eyes. "Just go away, Phoenix. I'm tired." She heard heavy footsteps. A door slammed but not before Phoenix's angry words reached her.

"Man, she can be such a princess sometimes."

For a long time, Jade stayed curled up, shaking and

struggling to hold back tears. She thought she'd found real friends in Phoenix, Marcus and Brynn. Now Phoenix was treating her just like her sisters did – trying to make her feel worthless. First on the cliff, now here. Why? Why did he do it? She didn't deserve it. It wasn't fair.

She sat up, thrusting the heavy covers aside. It didn't matter. At home she might be the least-loved daughter of a huge family but here she was something special. She wasn't going to lie around in bed feeling miserable. It was time to go meet the Elven king. Phoenix could just get stuffed.

She slipped out of bed. The floor was stone but pleasantly warm to her bare feet. Looking down, she realized she wore only a thin woolen shift. Smiling, she reached for her pack and withdrew the beautiful green dress Ásúlfr had given her.

A few moments later, dressed as ready as she'd ever be, Jade swallowed heavily and opened the door to her room. Outside, with her hand poised in mid-knock, stood Truda. She wore the blue dress that matched Jade's. The god-child smiled brightly up at Jade, her head cocked to one side.

"You're all better! Good." She grabbed her hand and tugged on it. "Come on, I'm supposed to take you to the hall. It's really nice. I haven't been here before." On she went, chattering like a magpie about the wonders of Alfheim and her joy at being so close to home again. The child seemed certain she would be back with her family very soon, although she obviously had no idea how to get to Asgard from Alfheim.

With a laugh, Jade followed her down several confusing, white corridors. In the distance, sounds of revelry swelled. Soon, she saw a warm, golden glow streaming through an arched entrance. The sound of gentle laughter and breathy flute music came with it.

Jade stopped at the doorway, allowing her eyes to

adjust a little. Truda dropped her hand and skipped straight in, leaving her alone. She fought the urge to run away. What if the Elves hated her? What if the king himself banished her from his hall in disgust at seeing a mere half-elf. She had no idea what attitude full Elves took toward half-breeds.

She drew a slow lungful of air, raised her chin and stepped into the room. Stretched out before her was a massive hall made of timber. It wasn't cut timber but the close-planted trunks of tall trees. The roof was their arching, thickly leaved branches. In the centre of the floor was a circular, bare patch of earth. Surrounding it was a vast area of soft, green moss, out of which poked smooth, grey boulders like seats around a stage. Several beautiful dryad women sat on those rocks, strumming and playing instruments of strange design. The music was soft but eerie – not quite what her human ear was used to.

Most importantly, there were a fifty or more tall, fair, exquisitely beautiful true elves. They lounged around three long, stone tables in various attitudes of remote disinterest. All wore long robes of shimmering, purple-blue material and matching looks of slight disdain on their elegant faces. It was difficult to tell if they were male or female, since they all wore their white-blonde hair loose past their shoulders. Only one also wore a thin silver circlet on his brow.

This, the tallest of the elves rose from the table and approached her. It had to be the Elven King. Jade dropped instinctively into a deep curtsy, fearful anticipation stirring in her stomach as he came nearer.

"Rise, child," he ordered quietly.

She stood obediently. Her head barely reached his shoulder. She didn't dare look up but stared fixedly at the trees behind him. Long, white fingers reached out and tipped her chin up with a strength that belied their narrow, delicate appearance. Finally, she was forced to look at him.

His eyes were so dark they seemed black, but were actually a bottomless indigo-purple, set beneath pale, flying brows in a smooth, elegantly-boned face. Long, white hair divided around pointed ears so the front lengths, bound by decorative silver rings, fell onto his chest. Everything about him was cool, yet infinitely powerful; raw wildness restrained by vast intelligence. Where Aurfanon was Queen of the golden dawn, the Earth and new life personified; the Elven King was the glittering, star-strewn sky; the full moon; cold darkness with a taste of death in the final hours of night.

Then he smiled gently and the whole aspect of his face changed. He no longer looked cold and frightening but calm and wise. Jade smiled hesitantly back. With a gesture for her to walk with him, he moved toward the table where an extra chair waited.

"Aurfanon mentioned you visited her in her home tree," he said. "She also said your mother is Eleri, Spellweaver of the great Cyfriniol forest. Eleri daughter of Brychan the hunter. Is this true?"

Jade nodded, wondering why he sounded so amused.

The tall Elven prince turned and smiled down at her. "Of course it is. I can see the resemblance.

She stared at him, astonished. How did he know her avatar's mother? Before she could ask, the Elven King was touching two forefingers on each hand to his forehead, lips and heart.

"I have been remiss, Jade gan Eleri," he murmured and bowed slightly in formal greeting.

She returned the gesture awkwardly. She'd never had to make the correct Elvish salutation before.

"I am Arawn, Lord of Anoeth, the Timeless land of the Faery or, as the Svear people call me: Freyr, king of Alfheim – home of the Elves. I am also," he led her gently to a chair between himself and Aurfanon, "your father."

CHAPTER SEVENTEEN

Arawn? Her avatar's father? After the initial shock wore off and Jade was able to close her mouth again, her first impulse was to deny it. Instead, she bit her lip to hold back the words. There was no reason to doubt him. How would a lie benefit him? She slid her eyes sideways to look at him. He gazed regally over the gathered Fair Folk below, apparently oblivious to the fact that he had just turned her life in this realm upside down.

She shook herself, struggling to keep a grasp on who and where she was. Oh! Jade straightened suddenly, gripping the arms of her chair in amazement. Arawn was the King. Did that make her a real Princess and these her subjects? She looked out over the Faery hall, finding it incredibly easy to imagine living here with these extraordinary people. Something in their languid, arrogant joy appealed to her. Their assurance of their own superiority made it easy to believe she would be safe here.

It would be so simple to walk away from all the unhappiness that stalked both her existences; so easy to live a life of luxury and freedom here in Alfheim with her own kind. Surely not even Zhudai could reach her here, in another realm. She could be safe, free, wanted, accepted.

Overwhelming excitement leapt in her heart only to be dashed a second later by the memory of Phoenix's last, impatient words. *She's such a princess!*

Defiance lifted her again. She might not be a real princess in the real world but here, it seemed, she was a princess; or, at least, the daughter of a king. She wasn't sure if being the half-blood daughter of the Elven king made her a princess or not. Her emotions fluctuated as she tried to get her head around all the implications of this new development. How would Phoenix and the others react when they found out? Phoenix and Truda already resented her. What would happen if she were invited to stay here? Could she be happy? Jade looked at the king again, longing to know him better. His pale, alien beauty seemed strange.

A shaft of homesickness shot through her like a dagger. Oh, how she missed her real father; his gentle smile; his reassuring hugs. Then she remembered her mother's constant criticism and her sisters' merciless taunting and wasn't sure what she wanted.

Arawn turned to her and asked a question. She answered hesitantly but was disarmed by his very real interest. Almost against her will, he led her into a conversation. Time flew and she barely remembered eating from a fabulous feast placed on her plate. Before she knew it, Arawn had skilfully drawn most of her digital history from her. She had the uncomfortable feeling he saw far more than she wanted. As she relaxed, Jade found it ever harder to keep her two lives separate. Several times, she almost referred to her real-world father and sisters. Often she had to steer the talk onto safer grounds – such as botany or magic. He knew a great deal about both of these and she found his knowledge as fascinating as he was.

When, as the evening drew to a close, Arawn finally did extend an invitation for her to stay as long as she liked in Alfheim, Jade gazed around at the exotic, brilliant, incredible, above all safe, Faery world and knew a very real, very deep desire to say 'yes'. This was where she belonged.

Then Aurfanon made an amused comment about Truda's childish antics. The girl was dancing with the dryads. Jade's heart dropped. How could she even consider staying here? They had to get Truda home before her birthday. Ragnarok would destroy everything, Alfheim included. It wasn't just her life she had to consider. It was everyone in this world, the other world, plus those of her trusting friends. Brynn, Phoenix and Marcus were still imprisoned in their rooms. They were probably worried and frightened, conscious of running out of time, while she wallowed in royal treatment. She was behaving exactly as Phoenix had complained: like she was better than they were.

Disgusted with herself, Jade pushed the plate away. The rich food now felt like lead in her stomach. Every moment she wasted here, pretending this was a life she could be part of, was a moment she kept Truda away from her duty; put this world in jeopardy and her friends lives in danger. She might be happy here but she had no right to force the others to stay. Even if Phoenix seemed to get a kick out of playing the game now, he'd eventually want to go home.

Reality was: she was responsible for getting her friends safely out of Alfheim and Truda to Asgard to prevent Ragnarok and the end of this world. Then she was responsible for helping Phoenix to progress through all the levels of the game so they could get home. This was not her real life at all, as much as she might wish it. Once the game was over, she would go home: back being nothing and nobody. She had finally found a place she belonged and she couldn't stay. It wasn't fair.

Something her real father often said came back to her. He always asked it when she complained about how her sisters treated her. She would run to him for sympathy. He would listen closely and give good advice when she needed it. In the end, though, when it all came down to that age old whinge about fairness, he would smile sadly and say, 'Why do you expect life to be fair, Jade?'

He was right.

Life wasn't fair or unfair – it just was. As he often

said, it was how she reacted to things that made life good or bad.

Resolutely, Jade turned to her Elven father. She touched him on the arm to get his attention. Again those indigo eyes bored into her, dark with secret knowledge.

"You are troubled, daughter." It was a statement, not a question.

"I have friends who need my help, my lord." Her throat tightened on the words. "I'm on a difficult Quest and they need me. I don't want to leave but I have to. We must return Truda to her father in two days or it will mean the coming of Ragnarok. They need my help."

"Why do they need you? They are close. Can they not complete this quest without you?"

Jade shrugged. "It is more than just this quest. There are three more to complete after this. I can't abandon them. I'm a Spellweaver." She grimaced, remembering her recent mistakes. "Not a very good one, though. I need my herbs and the forests for strength. Without them I'm not very effective – but I'm all they've got."

Arawn smiled slightly and sent her a knowing, sidelong look. "Your mother thought the same thing about herself. She was wrong, too. You underestimate yourself. You are capable of more than you realise."

Before Jade could ask what he meant, Arawn bowed his head to her. "Nevertheless, I expected this. You will always be welcome here, daughter, but I understand the nature of duty."

He stood with fluid grace and clapped his hands once. The music and chatter stopped. All heads turned toward the dais.

"Good my people." Arawn spread his hands wide, and then swept one toward Jade. "My daughter is on a Quest. As your Lord, I ask you to spread the word to all our kindred to render her any and all assistance possible. Perhaps," he smiled faintly down at her, "she may return safely to us one day."

Jade stared at him, worried. When he sat again, she leaned over.

"You can't ask your people to help me, sir! We're fighting a warlock – Feng Zhudai. He hates the faery folk and will do anything to stop me. His people have weapons of iron that will be fatal to the Fair People."

Arawn seemed indifferent. "We have helped the Bretons, the Svear and many others against invaders before. This will be no different."

"But it will," she pleaded, laying a daring hand on his shimmering sleeve. "Please. All we…I need is to get Truda to Asgard and back to her father, Thor. Then you must promise me you won't let your people risk themselves for us…me."

All at once, the King's eyes were cold again. He drew his hand out from beneath hers. "You presume too much, daughter." He held her abashed gaze for a moment longer before softening. "Jade, you are young. You undervalue yourself and overvalue me." He touched her cheek, his fingers cool. "In memory of your mother, whom I loved, go with what help I can give you. Don't argue." He held up a warning finger when she opened her mouth. "We will arrange quick passage for you to Asgard."

Jade was beset by mixed emotions: joy that he refused to abandon her; fear that she might never see him again; profound sadness that she had to leave.

Arawn saw and smiled gently. "Don't distress yourself, child. Be strong. We will see each other again, I promise." He drew her to her feet. "Take the godling child. It is time for you to sleep. Asgard can wait one more night."

*****

"Where the heck are they?" Phoenix paced the room again, stopping first by the locked door to listen then by the dark window to stare out.

Jade and Truda had been gone for hours. He, Marcus and Brynn had been politely locked into their suite of rooms, fed and ignored. It was frustrating, to say the least.

Irritated, he spun to confront the ever-patient Marcus. The Roman lay comfortably on an ornate couch, his feet propped up on the arm, head resting on an embroidered cushion. Brynn had exhausted all the possibilities for escape and theft early on. The Elves, possibly aware of their youthful guests' abilities, had made their locks unpickable and stripped the rooms of anything small and valuable. After complaining bitterly about their lack of consideration for an underpaid thief, he was now similarly sprawled on another couch nearby, twiddling tunes on his new bronze whistle.

"How can you be so calm?" Phoenix demanded.

Marcus shrugged. "There's nothing else to do." He sent Phoenix an ironic look. "Pacing and ranting haven't helped, have they?"

Phoenix blinked at him in surprise. Marcus seemed to be loosening up a little. It was as if their ordeal together with the trolls had triggered a new level of trust between them. He still wasn't exactly talkative but flashes of humour and emotion showed through his guarded exterior now. Before Phoenix could utter a witty retort, which he admittedly hadn't yet thought of, the door creaked open and Jade walked in with Truda close behind.

Marcus uncoiled from the couch frowning at them.

"There you are!" Phoenix strode over to the pair. "What's going on? Did you find out anything? Can we get to Asgard from here? Will the king help us?" He stopped when he saw the distress on Jade's face. What had happened?

Truda skipped over to Brynn and began telling him all about the wonders she'd seen in the king's hall. Phoenix and Marcus ignored her but Brynn was eager to hear everything, so the child was content to chatter to him.

Jade sank onto the couch Marcus had just left. "A lot. Yes. Yes and yes," she sighed.

"Huh?" It took Phoenix a moment to realise she was answering his questions in the order he'd asked them. "The king will help us get to Asgard? Awesome!"

"Yeah," Jade sighed, "awesome."

Marcus moved to crouch before her, his frown deepening. "What's wrong? Did they hurt you?"

Jade dropped her head forward, so her face was hidden by a fall of white-blonde hair. She shook her head. A tear fell onto her tightly-clasped hands. Marcus covered them with his own as Phoenix stood by, feeling stupid and awkward. Why was she crying? Surely she should be happy that they were getting closer to the end of Level Two? She was the one who was so keen to get home. Girls!

Turning away, he wandered toward Brynn and Truda. The child goddess still chattered on about all the Faery folk she seen; what they'd said and done. Marcus sat next to Jade, his arm around her shoulder. Phoenix tried to suppress a spurt of annoyance. Couldn't the Roman see she was just being girly? All emotional and over-reactive – just trying to get attention. Overhearing Jade's name in Truda's talk, he listened more closely, while still keeping half-an eye on the others.

One sentence caught his attention and he whipped about to face Truda and Brynn.

"Jade is the king's daughter!? She's a real princess?" He almost choked on the word.

Truda stared at him with those innocent, wide blue eyes and nodded.

"Oh man!" Phoenix threw up his hands in exasperation. Fear and anger sleeted through him. This would be just what she wanted. She'd jump at the chance to stay here in safety. Anyone with half a brain would chose security over the life of fear and death they were currently living. She'd stay and he'd be on his own - again. Stalking over to the couch, he stood before Jade with his hands on his hips.

"So you really are a princess, huh?" He shook his head. "I bet you're pretty happy about that. Well," he pointed one finger accusingly at her, "let me tell you something, Jade. I-"

"No!" Jade jumped up, her face blotchy with tears. She poked him in the chest with one long finger. "Let me tell you something. You have no idea what I just gave up so you can play this stupid game." Tears flowed down her cheeks. She dashed them away. "All you care about is swinging that sword around and being all macho. Well, now you can keep doing it, so I hope you're happy!"

Snatching up her skirt-train, she spun away and ran to her bedroom door. It slammed behind her.

CHAPTER EIGHTEEN

The four remaining companions stood in a frozen tableau of shock for several moments. Finally, Phoenix looked around in bewilderment.

"What did she mean?"

Marcus groaned and sat down on the couch, holding his head. Brynn cast Phoenix a reproachful glance and turned away. Truda sighed and rolled her eyes at him.

"Arawn offered to let her stay here," the child said. "I think she really likes it here."

"I knew it!" Phoenix growled, anger burning in his guts again. "As soon as I heard she was Arawn's daughter. I knew she'd quit and-"

"She said 'no'," Truda interrupted scornfully. "She turned him down."

He blinked at her, anger derailed. "Really? Why?"

"I think you know the answer to that." Marcus' deep voice cut through Phoenix's ranting. He tapped his chest significantly, reminding him of the linked amulets, another world; the real world.

"Oh." Phoenix slumped onto a chair, deflated.

Truda huffed at him, yawned, excused herself and went into her own bedroom. Brynn and Marcus continued to sit, watching Phoenix as he struggled with his thoughts. He glanced up at Jade's closed door. He'd overreacted to the news of her noble status. He felt like an idiot now but he'd just been so angry with her: angry that she'd been so freaked out and unreliable recently; angry that she'd let him down; angry that she'd gone and died and scared the living spit out of him.

It had felt just like when his father died. Being so reliant on someone else was frightening. He didn't want to need her alive. Control of his own life again: that's what he wanted. That was why he'd started this game in the first place. If you needed people you were vulnerable; it hurt when they left.

When he'd heard Truda say Jade was a real princess, with a father and a family here, something in him snapped. He just knew that she was going to abandon him; that she would to quit the game she was so scared of and stay here, safe. He'd lashed out, unthinking, impulsive, reactive as usual.

Phoenix groaned aloud. He'd screwed up. He dropped his head into his hands, rubbing tired eyes with the heels of his palms.

"I really did it this time, didn't I?"

Marcus snorted. "I'd say you've got some serious apologising to do, yes."

"She doesn't really act like a princess, y'know," Brynn said meekly.

Phoenix sighed and looked at the boy. "I know. I just..." He waved a hand to indicate the confusion of feelings he was struggling with. "I'm an only child." He smiled wanly. "I'm not used to having siblings and I think of Jade like a sister. She's always thinking the worst will happen and arguing with me instead of following my lead. It's annoying." It was a weak excuse but the welter of thoughts in his head was too hard to explain. He didn't want to do something dumb like burst into tears about his father's death.

Marcus smiled ironically at him. "There's part of your problem. You see her as competing with you for leadership."

"Don't be ridiculous. I don't see her as competition," Phoenix scoffed. "She doesn't even want to be here. She just wants to go home."

Marcus shrugged and inspected his dagger.

Phoenix stared uneasily at the Roman. "She keeps letting me...us down!   She's losing the plot and she disagrees with me all the time."

Marcus raised an eyebrow at him but remained silent.

"But there can only be one leader," Phoenix finally growled.

"Get up," Marcus commanded. Phoenix did and the Roman boy took his hand in a handshake held at hip height. "Now," he said, "the object of this game is to score points." He tightened his grip on Phoenix's hand until it almost hurt. "If your hand touches your hip, you score a point. If mine touches my hip, I score a point. Brynn, you count to twenty for us to keep time. Ready?"

Phoenix nodded, tensing his arm to pull against Marcus's strength. It would be a pretty even match. Brynn leaned on his elbows over the back of a chair to watch.

"Go!"

Phoenix pulled hard, straining to haul their clasped hands to touch his right hip. Marcus' muscles bulged, his face contorted as they battled for supremacy. Slowly but surely, Phoenix dragged Marcus' hand toward himself. He was going to win.

".....nineteen, twenty!" Brynn shouted, laughing at their pained expressions as the pair released hands and shook blood back into them.

"OK," Phoenix said, irritated. "What was that supposed to prove? We're evenly matched. Nobody scored anything."

"Try again," Marcus suggested.

Phoenix sighed and gripped his friends' hand. On 'Go' he once more yanked as hard as he could. This time, Marcus gave no resistance and Phoenix's hand touched his own hip easily. Shocked, he didn't react quickly enough to stop Marcus from pulling back to score his own point. When he did think to pull, Marcus simply let him score another point.

A blinding light went on in Phoenix's head. He stared at Marcus for a moment then down at their hands. He relaxed. Marcus pulled; then Phoenix pulled back in turn. Hands blurred as they both racked up points faster than could be counted.

"....nineteen, twenty!" Brynn giggled again, this time at the look of stunned amazement in Phoenix's eyes.

Marcus sat down again and put his feet up, raising one dark eyebrow at Phoenix.

"I get it, I get it," Phoenix said humbly. "Co-operation means we both score points. Competition means we both lose. Oh man!" He sank onto the couch.

"You have to learn to co-operate with Jade," Marcus murmured. "This isn't a game, Phoenix. It's not just about points and winning. You need all of us to survive but Jade especially. She needs you, too. This is about friendship. If you fight with her or belittle her, we all lose. You help her go a little easier on herself; help her to feel good about herself - and we all win."

By the time dawn sent its pale fingers into his window, Phoenix had pretty much given up on sleep and lay on the bed, staring up at the smooth, white ceiling. The ideas Marcus had started kept him awake, thinking. In many ways, the concept Marcus was trying to teach him was the spirit of Aikido and the essence of the YinYang symbol he and Jade both wore – balance and harmony. Resisting your opponent - or friend, in this case - lead to conflict. Harmonising with and understanding your partner lead to power and control - self-control. He shook his head and could imagine his sensei doing the same. Why had it taken him so long to understand something so basic?

Something inside him had changed during the night. He wasn't sure exactly what but he knew that Jade's emotional ups and downs wouldn't bother him anymore. Well, not much. OK, not *as* much. He couldn't keep expecting her to change to suit him. She was who she was. If he really was the leader then it was his job to work out how they could get along and work together. Marcus was right. If one of them didn't pull their head in and learn to co-operate, they would all die. Several times for Jade and himself.

Idly, Phoenix fingered the tear-drop shaped amulet around his neck. He still had a major apology to make. Overreacting like that had been way out of line He nodded with decision, happy to have a plan of action in place. He'd speak with her first chance he got.

Yawning, he scrubbed a hand over his face. In the mean time, the bathroom was calling. Thank goodness the Elves had discovered indoor plumbing. Having a bath last night had been utter bliss; sitting on a real toilet had been heaven. He'd never really appreciated the value of nice, soft, double-ply toilet paper before now.

Grinning at his whimsy, Phoenix rubbed gritty eyes and swung his legs off the bed.

An hour later, he was no closer to apologising to Jade or to finding out how to work with her. They'd been served breakfast and Phoenix was now not sure what he would miss most about Alfheim – the food or the plumbing. He'd joined the other three in the living area of their rooms, but Jade had requested her food in her room. He'd tried knocking but she wouldn't answer. Brynn and Marcus could get no response either.

She'd emerged only when the king had summoned them all. In the presence of an Elvish escort, it was impossible to talk about anything more than how they'd slept. Wan and tired-looking, Jade had met his gaze only briefly before turning away. Concerned, Phoenix followed the others to the king's audience chamber.

There was barely time to take in the wonders of the huge, tapestry-hung hall before a bizarre sight claimed their attention. All five of their horses were in the luxurious space; eyes rolling and hooves clattering loudly on the white stone floor. They seemed nervous in the presence of the Elves holding their bridles. One of the animals dropped a large, steaming pile of something unpleasant on the floor.

"Oh, great!" Phoenix muttered, embarrassed.

Brynn and Truda clutched at each other, giggling at the sight. Marcus hurried to the Elves, bowed and took charge of two of the horses. Phoenix moved to do the same. The last thing he needed was the king of the Elves angry because a horse had fouled his palace.

He was so busy calming the horses, he didn't notice Arawn and Aurfanon enter. They came in quietly, with no fuss. When Phoenix looked up, he saw Jade nodding solemnly and listening to the king. What was he saying? Feeling slightly panicked, he handed the reins over to Brynn, who looked alarmed at having control of three large, nervous horses.

Hurrying over to the royal party, Phoenix managed a sketchy bow. Aurfanon smiled faintly but Arawn merely looked at him with those cool, unreadably-dark eyes. Jade inspected her own hands.

"Your majesties," Phoenix said. "Thank you for your hospitality." He nodded toward Jade. "I can never repay you for your help with the troll and in bringing Jade back to us. We..." he stopped and glanced at her, catching her eye as she finally looked up, "I need her. She's a vital part of our company and," he paused to take a deep breath, "a much valued friend." Her green eyes widened.

"It is good to know that you rate my daughter so highly, mortal," the king said quietly. "I entrust you with her care and, believe me, I shall know if you break my trust," he warned.

Phoenix swallowed, knowing what he had to do. Why was doing the right thing so hard sometimes?

"We'll do our best to look after her my lord but," he glanced at Jade again, "I understand you've offered her a place here. I'd like both of you to know that, if she truly wants to stay, we won't stop her." Jade gasped but Phoenix hurried on, not wanting her to get the wrong idea. "I'd like you to come with us," he assured her, "but if you really don't want to go back then I won't make you. I'll find some way to win or I'll find a way to make a home here, too." He looked away, feeling awkward. "I don't want you to be unhappy. So you choose. Plus...I'm sorry for the things I said last night. I was way out of line," he added.

For a long moment there was silence, except for the snortings and clatterings of the horses. Jade stared at Phoenix for ages, her eyes now swimming in tears. Then she sniffed and managed a watery smile.

"Thanks Phoenix." Her voice broke and she gripped his hands for a moment. "I'm sorry, too. It's been so scary and I feel safe in Alfheim."

His heart sank. She was going to stay. He'd really hoped that she'd come with them. As much as he didn't like the idea of having to depend on her, he was pretty sure he'd never get home without her. Well, he'd just have to give it a shot. Sighing, he let go of her hands and stepped back.

"Right then," he said firmly. "Good luck. I'll try and come back to see you if I don't make it home."

Jade blinked at him, confused. "What?"

"You're staying here, aren't you?"

"Idiot," she grinned up at him and punched him on the arm, hard, "as if you'd make it through another three levels without me."

"Ow!" Phoenix rubbed his arm and smiled back, hugely relieved.

"Well, children," Aurfanon's soft voice broke in on their reunion of spirit. "Now that's all settled, we should see you on your way to Asgard. Through here." She moved toward one of the massive tapestries that hung from ceiling to floor on one wall.

Its bright colours depicted a whole world of mountains, plains, forests, castles and people in what seemed to be a series of detailed stories. Phoenix looked closer, blinking and squinting. He stepped even nearer, until his nose almost touched the fabric. The figures on the tapestry seemed to move. A quick look around the room showed seven other similar, enormous tapestries. They all showed scenes of other worlds, on which figures moved and lived.

"Oh! This one's Asgard." Truda's excited exclamation drew his eyes to her pointing finger. "I can see Pa with Grandpa Odinn! I wonder why Pa's in Gladsheim?"

Sure enough, inside a massive hall in the middle of a huge plain, sat a small, hooded figure on a throne. As they watched, a second figure paced back and forward in front of the throne, apparently talking to half a dozen people who stood around him.

"Gladsheim?" Jade asked. "Gods-home?"

"Gladsheim's here," Truda pointed again, "the hall in the middle of the Plain of Idavoll. The gods all meet here to talk, but I live here, in Bilskirnir." She pointed to a great castle in a valley at the foot of a ring of mountains. "See, there's Ma and Modi and Magni in the kitchen." Truda giggled. "Ma's getting mad at them 'cause they're snitching food again." She inspected Gladsheim again. "There's Uncle Loki – I wonder who that funny-looking man he's with is?"

Phoenix wasn't listening to her any longer. The import of this wall-hanging dawned on him. He turned to stare at Aurfanon and Arawn.

"This is how we're getting to Asgard? You're going to magic us into this tapestry somehow?"

Arawn bowed slightly. "This is the fastest way. You simply walk into the hanging and arrive on the Plain of Idavoll, right outside Gladsheim, since that seems to be where Thor is at the moment. You will have your opportunity to return Truda to her father immediately but," he smiled faintly, "do try not to annoy Thor. He does have a rather quick temper."

"Thanks for the warning." Phoenix couldn't help the sarcasm that crept in to his reply.

Their chances of not annoying Thor were zero and none – unless they could find a way for him to be happy about losing his hammer.

As Jade said her final farewells to Arawn and Aurfanon, Phoenix muttered in an aside to Marcus. "At least it looks like we'll get Truda home in time to prevent the end of the world but how the heck are we supposed to steal that stupid hammer from Thor when he's in the middle of a roomful of gods?"

Marcus sent him a sly look and a small smile. "I'm sure, together, we'll think of something suitably dramatic. Shall we go?"

Phoenix bowed mockingly and waved a hand at the tapestry. "After you, I insist."

Marcus took a tighter grip on his horses' reins and, with a solemn salute to the Elves, he stepped into the tapestry. His broad-shouldered figure shimmered weirdly purple-blue for an instant before disappearing. A second later, his horses vanished similarly.

Brynn gasped and pointed. "Look! There he is!"

Phoenix peered closer at his friend's embroidered figure. It stood on the grass outside Gladsheim, looking rather lonely and very small. He seemed to be having trouble controlling the horses.

"Well, let's not keep the gods waiting then," Phoenix said, with more resolution than he felt.

Grasping Truda's wrist with one hand and two sets of reins by the other, he nodded his thanks to Arawn and stepped forward with eyes firmly closed.

CHAPTER NINETEEN

There was a brief, unpleasant sensation of being tightly squeezed, twisted and somehow turned inside-out. When it was over, Phoenix stood with Truda, Marcus and four freaked-out horses in the middle of a wide, flat prairie. A cool wind whistled around them, making the short, dry grass-stalks ripple and swish. It smelled of dust and a hint of snow from distant mountains. There were no trees anywhere but white-topped, purplish mountain peaks clawed the sky on all sides. A few seconds later, Jade appeared out of thin air, followed by her wild-eyed horse and an equally unsettled Brynn.

"OK, that was weird," Phoenix commented. Looking up, he waved madly at the sky.

"What are you doing?" Truda giggled. "You look really silly."

"I feel silly but I'm waving to Arawn and Aurfanon." He grinned.

The others laughed and did the same.

Eventually, they turned around to look for Gladsheim. Truda clapped her hands and did a little dance step of joy. Her companions stared in shock. The building was massive. It looked as though a giant, white marble Lego block had been dropped in the middle of the Plain of Idavoll. There were just a few, small windows high up and one, large double-door at the end. The door stood over thirty feet high and glinted gold in the morning sunlight.

"Why is it so big?" Jade breathed.

"Oh, lots of the gods are giants or half-giants or quarter-giants." Truda's blithe reply made Phoenix's stomach sink. "Grandma Jörð is a giantess. Uncle Loki's a shapeshifter as well as a giant. Lots of them are. C'mon! Pa'll be so happy to see me!" She skipped ahead, waving them anxiously on.

"At least that explains why she's so tall, but will Thor be happy to see us?" Jade muttered to Phoenix.

"Why shouldn't he? We're returning his daughter to him."

"Dunno." She shrugged seeming uneasy as she stared up at the massive building. "I've just got a bad feeling about this. It's been too simple."

He snorted. "I don't think fighting off wolves, traipsing through freezing snow, outwitting two trolls, getting killed and persuading the Light-elves to help us could be called 'simple'."

"I don't know." She sighed. "It just doesn't seem hard enough for the second level of the game. Where's Zhudai this time? We haven't seen anything of him or his henchmen."

Phoenix thought about it. "You did put that spell on Marcus to hide him, so Zhudai probably can't find us." He gripped her shoulder. "Don't worry too much about Zhudai. We need to concentrate on stealing the Hammer of Thor, remember?" He glanced over at Brynn. "At least we have our very own thief to help with that."

Brynn grinned and saluted him with two jaunty fingers. His step had a cocky bounce in it.

Jade nodded then frowned. "Oh, I forgot to tell you something."

"What?"

"While I was...umm...dead, I ended up in that grey limbo place again and heard someone explaining all the stuff we have to do on the next three levels. I think it was the same old woman we met there in Albion but I'm not sure. The voice sounded similar, at least."

"Brilliant!" Phoenix heaved a sigh of relief. "I was

getting worried about that. All I could remember was that the next one is something about Egypt."

"But I'm not sure it was her and we still don't even know who she is or why she's helping," Jade shook her head, worried. "What if it was Zhudai trying to put us on the wrong track?"

"Good point," he conceded. "What did she say we had to do next? If it was Zhudai, he'd be sure to feed us wrong information."

"The voice said we have to use the Hammer of Thor to destroy a tekhen in Egypt. I think 'tekhen' is the Egyptian word for an obelisk. Destroying it will release Anuket, the goddess of fertility of the Nile valley."

"Yeah," Phoenix cocked his head, thinking hard, "that sounds right from what I remember reading, which means it probably wasn't Zhudai in your dream."

"She also said we have to do it before the death of the moon," Jade continued, her expression anxious. "But I don't know what that means!"

He shrugged. "Neither do I but we can't do much about it here anyway. Let's solve that one once we actually make it to Egypt."

"If we make it," Jade muttered.

There was a depressed pause as they all considered the scope of the task still facing them in this level, let alone the unknowns in the next.

"What's a 'tekhen'?" Brynn asked.

With her hands Jade outlined the shape of a tall, pointed column in the air. "It's kind of...you know... a tall, skinny stone pillar with a point on the top and decorations all over the sides."

"Right..." Brynn cocked his head, looking bemused.

It occurred to Phoenix that, if you'd never even seen a picture of an obelisk, it might be hard to imagine one.

They walked for a few moments in silence, trying to keep the horses moving. All they seemed to want to do was crop the grass. Phoenix stopped and struggled out of his too-warm fur coat. The others followed suit. Jade jammed the clothes into the Hyllion Bagia. There wasn't much they could do about the fur-lined trousers they all wore, so they simply continued in sweaty silence.

Phoenix only truly realised how vast Gladsheim was by the length of time it took them to get there. Its size made it seem closer than it really was. Finally, it loomed overhead, blocking the morning sun and casting a threatening shadow over the grassland.

Brynn scouted around one end of the building and found tether points and a watering trough for the animals. The horses taken care of, four of the companions crept toward the golden front door. Truda, comfortable on home ground, ran straight past them before anyone could stop her. To their horror, she raced to the door and banged on it with her small fist, yelling at the top of her lungs.

"PA! PA! Open the door, I'm here! It's nearly my birthday and I'm home!"

"Oh man," Jade groaned. "There went any idea of sneaking in to case the place."

"Well," Marcus said philosophically, "maybe an open approach is best. After all, Thor should be grateful that we're returning his long-lost daughter."

"And how long will that last, once we've stolen his hammer?" Phoenix asked.

"Shhhh," Jade admonished. "Truda doesn't know about that, remember?"

"Maybe we could just ask for it?" Brynn whispered. "I mean, I'm good but I'm not sure I'm that good."

"Hard to imagine a god voluntarily giving up his best weapon to a bunch of strange mortals, daughter or not," Jade replied, her tone scornful.

"Still," Marcus was thoughtful, "it might be worth a try."

Phoenix didn't get to reply to that because the great

entrance creaked ponderously outward at that point. Truda scampered back from the opening then rushed forward with a squeal of delight.

They all looked up, expecting a giant to step out, then down again when Truda threw herself into the arms of a normal-sized man.

"Ullr!"

The blond man stared down at the girl in astonishment for a moment then lifted her up in a bone-crushing hug. "Stepsister! How did you come here? Where have you been these months?" He glanced up and sighted Truda's companions. Frowning he put her down and pushed her to one side. With the smooth action of a seasoned warrior, he unslung a massive bow from across his broad shoulders and nocked an arrow.

Marcus responded with the same move and Brynn followed suit with a deft twist of his sling. Jade hefted her quarterstaff in the guard position and Phoenix laid a hand on the hilt of Blódbál.

"Who are these mortals, sister?" Ullr demanded, not taking his ice-blue eyes off Marcus. Truda laid a hand on his leather-clad arm.

"They brought me home, step-brother. Please don't hurt them. They brought me back in time to stop Ragnarok."

The god looked narrowly at all four companions. "Very well. Thor will wish to speak with them. Inside, all of you." He gestured with the tip of his arrow.

Jade put a warning hand on Marcus' shoulder and the Roman boy lowered his bow. At Phoenix's nod, Brynn stopped swinging his sling but kept it to hand. Truda, clearly considering the emergency over, dashed through the open door. The others followed more slowly, Ullr behind them with his bow still ready.

"I still think this is a bad idea," Jade murmured to Phoenix.

"Got a better one?" he asked.

She shook her head and stepped into the cool dimness within.

Instead of one, massive hall, the entrance to Gladsheim was a fairly small chamber with several doors leading off it. Truda skipped ahead, her footsteps echoing on the marble floor. She headed straight out of the antechamber, through an ornate archway. The others followed and found themselves in a truly great hall.

Phoenix had little time to take in the wonders of it. Their entrance stirred up a storm of voices all clamouring for information and attention. Truda ran, full tilt, to hurl herself into the enormous arms of her father, Thor. The God of Thunder picked his daughter up like she was a precious doll. He held her at arm's length for several seconds, staring at her smiling face. Then he wrapped her in a gentle hug, his rugged, red-bearded face showing astonished delight and disbelief. There was a babble of talk as half a dozen gods of all sizes crowded around, hugging and petting the little redheaded goddess.

Finally, one deep, powerful voice cut through the noise.

"Silence!"

An expectant hush fell and the crowd parted as a stooped, bearded man stepped down from a throne at the end of the hall. He wore a simple tunic and breeches, with a long, brown hooded cloak. His beard and loose hair were white, his left eyelid was closed and sunken over a missing eye. In one hand he held a javelin. Over his head flew two ravens and by his side paced two silver-coated wolves. He looked harmless enough but power emanated almost visibly from him.

Jade gasped. Phoenix frowned, wondering who it was: obviously someone important.

"Grandpa!" Squealed Truda, launching herself at the newcomer.

His lined face softened for a moment as the old man hugged his granddaughter then hardened again as he put her aside.

"What are these mortals who dare to enter Gladsheim uninvited?"

Phoenix stepped forward and bowed. He was getting better at it now. "My lord..." Panic seized him as he realised he had no idea what to call him.

"Odinn," Jade hissed, "king of the gods."

"Odinn," he finished. "We are simply returning Tr...Thrudr to her home."

There was a quick babble of talk from the other gods before they were silenced by a wave of Odinn's gnarled hand.

"It is a miracle she is come back in time to forestall the coming of Ragnarok but by what right did you abduct her in the first place, mortal?" he growled.

Taken aback by the accusation, Phoenix stared in astonishment. "No, no, sir! We didn't take her. It was..."

"That's them! Seize them!" A triumphant shout interrupted him. From the back of the group, a tall, dark-haired man pushed through. He too wore simple clothes but in grey cloth with a dark grey cloak buckled over one shoulder. His eyes gleamed with cunning and secret knowledge. Thor and the other gods murmured amongst themselves, looking back and forth between the newcomer, Odinn and Phoenix.

"Loki!" Odinn's sharp tone brought everyone back under control again.

Phoenix felt Jade, Brynn and Marcus press closer as the gods moved to encircle them. This really didn't feel like a win-win situation.

"I thought Truda said Loki was a giant," Phoenix whispered out of the corner of his mouth.

"And a shapeshifter," Jade murmured back, "and the God of mischief and chaos."

"Fabulous."

"Look at his eyes!" she hissed.

Phoenix did. They were a familiar, hard, rain-grey. The wolf's eyes. Loki was a shapeshifter, indeed. The question was: why had he lead the wolfpack against them and what was he up to now?

Loki came closer to the companions, a wicked smile lifting his lips. He circled them, moving with the grace of a dancer.

"My king, these are the mortals who abducted your granddaughter. They thought to hold her to ransom by threatening us with the coming of the End. Thwarted in that," he spun to face the gods, throwing up his arms, "they come in the guise of her saviours, trying to pretend they rescued and returned her; but I know their true purpose here." He grinned evilly at the companions before schooling his handsome face once more into an expression of righteous wrath. "What they wanted as ransom they now seek instead to steal - Mjölnir, the Hammer of Thor!"

A great shout went up from the assembled gods. Thor yelled, holding his hammer high and shaking it in defiance at the four friends. Surrounded by her angry family, Truda pushed vainly, trying to get through, her shrill young voice lost in the din.

Swords slithered from sheaths; staves and clubs were lifted in menace; and ominous roll of thunder echoed outside as the sky darkened with Thor's wrath.

"This was so not the plan," Phoenix groaned.

"It is now," Marcus replied, drawing his sword.

"Actually, I'm pretty sure we didn't have a plan," Brynn muttered.

"Shut up and try not to kill anyone," Phoenix said.

Marcus sent him a swift, ironic look. "Will they be doing the same?"

"Brynn, get to Truda if you can," Jade urged the boy. "Maybe she can stop this by telling them the truth."

He nodded and began peering through the thick bodies around them, looking for a way out.

Phoenix laid a hand on Blódbál and its song flowered in his head. "Damn," he shook it, trying to think clearly. "Stupid sword. Where are the Avengers when you need to oppose someone in Asgard."

"Who?" It was Jade's strident question.

Phoenix shrugged and quirked a grin at her."Y'know - Iron Man, the Hulk, Captain America - the Avengers."

She sent him a half-annoyed, half-frightened glare. "I don't think..."

Then there was no time to look or think. With a hoarse cry, ten gods threw themselves into battle. Phoenix drew Blódbál. The sound of blade sliding against scabbard was like a song in his veins. It urged him on; fired him with the desire to whet the blade on the bones and blood of gods.

Grinning fiercely, he blocked a sword-thrust with ease. Blódbál sang louder in his head, masking everything but the lust for battle. Fear vanished, replaced by exultation and excitement. Phoenix cut down toward a leg and was rewarded with a grunt of pain. The blade came back red. Shifting, he unslung his shield and blocked another blow even as he sliced to his right.

There was a shout behind him. He turned to catch a club on his blade before it smacked into the unprotected side of Marcus' head. Marcus called his thanks. Phoenix laughed. This was easy. He could see everything, anticipate anything. To his left, Jade blocked another club then swiftly retaliated, slamming the end of her staff into a vulnerable groin. Her opponent doubled over in breathless pain, staggering away, retching.

Brynn vanished, hopefully to find Truda.

Phoenix sidestepped a javelin thrust, grabbed the wood and yanked hard. The owner fell forward and Jade clubbed him over the back of the head. A thrown dagger ricocheted off Phoenix's shield. Blódbál twitched in his hands, begging to be used but Phoenix was wary of it. If possible, he didn't really want to kill. Having gods angry with you was a bad idea. They were already quite irritated enough.

Where were Truda and Brynn?

"Sleep!" Jade's desperate Command spell washed over the fighting gods.

Two of them shook their heads and blinked, their weapons lowered. She whacked them both upside the head and they collapsed, insensible. The other gods seemed unaffected by her magic and waded back into the fray.

There were only four fighters left. Odinn stood back, observing. Loki had disappeared. Thor, towering over his brethren, shoved to the front, Mjölnir held high over his shaggy head. Thunder rolled, shaking the building. Dark clouds seemed to gather inside, beneath the white ceiling. Lightning flickered and the air tasted of electricity.

Phoenix jabbed with Blódbál, trying to distract Thor with a blow to the legs but his thrust was parried by Ullr's sword. Straining, Phoenix pushed the blond god aside and tried again for Thor's legs. Thunder growled louder, directly overhead.

Jade screamed a word Phoenix didn't catch. The world exploded. A vast noise lashed at them; a blinding flash of light edged with purple-blue and tasting of hot iron. Then there was silence and the now-familiar blackness of unconsciousness.

*****

Baiyu clutched at his head, reeling with the fresh stab of death. No! Too many. They were losing too many lives. They would never make it. Why had this happened? They should have been safely in Asgard, welcomed and feted by the Gods. What treachery was this?

He was too weak to send his mind out of his body to seek help again. Too weak to even reach out for help closer at hand. Only time would reveal if they had survived.

CHAPTER TWENTY

Jade opened her eyes. Blackness pressed against her eyeballs. She turned her head - and regretted it. Somewhere in her brain, fireworks of pain went off. Keeping still, she tried to work out where she was by touch. Cold stone seemed to be her bed. Why was that? Why was she lying on the ground? Why was it so dark?

Memory returned with another spectacular display of shooting stars. They had been holding their own in a battle with the Gods of Asgard. Then Thor had summoned a thunderstorm – inside the building! With it, he'd blasted them all into unconsciousness. Actually, it felt more like she'd been dead – again. This time the return wasn't nearly so gentle as last. Aurfanon had obviously helped heal her injuries in Alfheim. Now she felt bruised and battered all over. The nauseating smell of burnt hair caught in her nose.

Rolling onto one side, she eased into a sitting position. Pain made her gasp and swallow against the urge to throw up. Fumbling at her throat, Jade found her amulet. They hadn't taken it. Holding it tightly between two fingers, she reached deep within to find strength. There wasn't much but, without the aid of her herbs, she had nothing else.

"Heal," she whispered, willing her body to repair itself. Warmth spread through her fingers from the amulet. It seeped into her bones, flesh and skin like mud oozing between toes. Halfway through the process, she lost consciousness, drained by the effort.

She awoke again with no idea how much time had passed. It was still dark but her head was clear and the pain bearable. She felt all over her body. There didn't seem to be any major injuries, just bruising. In the process, she discovered she was still dressed in the same clothes but her weapons, bag and boots were all gone. Her feet were cold.

She progressed to finding out what was around. First she reached up, feeling for a roof. When she found there was no danger of smacking her head, she got shakily onto her hands and knees. With a hand outstretched, she crawled in what she hoped was a straight line.

"Phoenix?" she whispered, afraid to alert any guards. "Marcus? Brynn?"

She found three walls and no people before finally hearing a slight noise and a faint groan off to her left. She crawled cautiously over and felt fur, cloth and skin beneath her questing hands. A face came under her fingers. The mouth opened.

"Can you take your finger out of my nose, please?" Phoenix asked, his voice slightly nasal. Jade snatched her hand away and wiped it on her pants.

"You ok?"

He groaned again. "For a dead man, I feel amazingly well but if I'm alive, I feel awful. What happened?"

"Well, I'm pretty sure you didn't die this time," Jade said.

There was another noise nearby. She moved over and found Marcus. As her hands reached his chest, he grabbed her wrist in a painfully tight grip. She whimpered.

"It's me, Marcus, let go!"

He relaxed his grip but didn't release her hand as he sat up.

"Jade." He sounded relieved. "Are you alright?" His fingers touched her face gently. "Where's Phoenix and Brynn? I seem to be, quite surprisingly, alive."

"Phoenix and I are ok, but I haven't found Brynn." She shivered as he stroked her cheek once then let go of her hand.

The three scouted the rest of their cell until they were forced to admit Brynn was not imprisoned with them. They found a slop-bucket, a couple of dead rats and a door with what was probably a food-hatch in it, but no boy.

Now they sat together in the middle of the room, leaning up against each other's backs for comfort and warmth.

"So," Phoenix said with false cheerfulness, "three of us locked up in the dark again, huh? This is getting to be a habit."

Jade laughed weakly.

"What happened out there?" Marcus asked.

"Last I remember, Thor went nuts and summoned a storm into the place," Phoenix said seriously. "Then Jade yelled and everything went nova. I don't think I lost another life, though," he added, sounding surprised. "Jade?"

"Well," she paused, thinking it through, "I figured Thor would probably hit us with lightning but I couldn't shield all of us. Brynn slipped away, so I did what I could for you two with a shield spell."

There was a long silence as the two warriors digested her words.

"So you sacrificed your life to save us?" Marcus' tone was humble, with an inexplicable edge of anger.

"Well," Jade, tiredness catching up with her again, "you can't really call it sacrificing your life when you know you have a few to spare."

"Damn!" Phoenix's hand grabbed at her arm in the dark. "Don't get me wrong, Jade, I appreciate what you did, but now you've only got four more deaths before you run out and we've still got three levels to go."

"I know," Jade drooped, "but it was all I could think of. Besides," she attempted to cheer them up, "remember last time we were captured? Brynn brought the cavalry to rescue us."

"There aren't any Druids around this time."

"Maybe we could try putting the amulets together again? Maybe it will show us another sign or tell us what to do next."

She felt Phoenix shrug against her back. "Worth a try."

By touch, they brought the two halves together. Jade held her breath, waiting for a sign. Waiting...

After several dark, silent minutes, she accepted defeat, gave a heavy sigh and pulled her amulet away. "Looks like we're on our own."

"Quiet!" Marcus hushed them.

They scrambled to their feet, listening. Footsteps approached. An orangey-yellow light began to glow beneath the door. As one, they faced the door.

"Stand aside!" a rough voice yelled.

The three hastily stepped back. The door flew inward so it smacked into the stone wall, ensuring no-one lurked behind it. A tall, cloaked man stood, silhouetted against torchlight for a moment before he stepped inside. With him came three guards.

"Loki." Jade glared at the god.

He bowed, his slick, dark hair glinting in the torchlight.

"Indeed, but you have the advantage of me. I would like to tell my bloodbrother, Odinn, just who he will be passing judgement upon. You are...?"

"Don't tell him," Jade warned. "If you give your name to your enemy, you give him power over you."

Loki smiled ironically and bowed again. "Old magic. You are wise," he peered closer at her face, his eyes widening slightly, "and a Light-elf; no, a half-breed." His admiration turned to contempt. "Perhaps I should let Freyr deal with you."

She started. If he sent her to Alfheim, she could beg her father to intervene for Marcus and Phoenix. Loki's next words dashed her hopes. The god came closer, tapping one finger on his chin.

"No, I think not. Someone else has plans for you. Now tell me," he smiled charmingly, changing subjects before they had time to question him, "when you are brought before Odinn to answer for your crimes, what defence will you put forward?"

"What are we charged with?" Phoenix challenged.

Loki ticked points off his fingers. "Abduction of Thrudr; almost causing the end of the world; conspiring to steal Mjölnir; oh," he flashed them a grin, "and the murder of Hrothgar, king of the Svears – a close friend of Thor's I understand."

"What?" Phoenix started forward. Jade and Marcus leapt to restrain him. "We did not kill Hrothgar!"

Loki shrugged. "So you say but he is dead and here you stand, carrying Blódbál into battle. Damning evidence to my thinking. How will you defend yourselves?"

Phoenix opened his mouth but Jade pulled him back and faced Loki herself.

"Why does it matter?"

"I only wish to apprise Odinn of all the facts before he passes judgment," Loki replied suavely.

Jade drew herself up to her full height, looking down her nose at him in the haughtiest manner she could manage. "You are the master of lies, Loki. No matter what we say you'll twist it somehow. We'll tell Odinn ourselves. We have a witness."

Loki raised one thin eyebrow. "Do you mean..." He turned his back to them. There was a strange sound, like wind rushing; then a brief purple-blue glow. When he turned to face them again, they all gasped in shock.

Truda now stood where Loki had; her sweet, childish face twisted into an expression of evil delight. "Oh yes," she piped, batting blue eyes, "I'll be sure to tell Grandpa Odinn exactly how you took me and hid me away for months. Then, when the Romans chased you out of Albion, how you had to give up your plan to ransom me and you decided that pretending to rescue me would give you a chance to steal my pa's hammer instead." Truda/Loki smiled impishly then skipped out the door before turning to simper at them again. "By the way, I have the real Thrudr quite safe. All I need to do is string this little charade out for one more day. It will be her birthday tomorrow and if she doesn't perform her duties then the fun will really begin. Ragnarok. Yay!" She giggled as the guards slammed the door shut and left them in shadows again.

"That went well," Phoenix commented into the inky darkness.

Jade sniffed. "Such a typical bad-guy. Too much monologuing. Honestly." She blinked in the darkness. Blue spots danced in front of her eyes from the torchlight.

"I wonder what he meant when he said 'someone else has plans for you'," Marcus said.

"I wonder how we're going to defend ourselves when our chief witness is not who Odinn will think she is," Phoenix retorted.

"Maybe Brynn will bring Truda-" Marcus began.

"You heard what Loki said," Phoenix interrupted. "He has the real Truda locked up somewhere."

"I also heard Jade say Loki's the master of lies and the god of mischief and chaos," Marcus said reasonably. "He could be lying."

"I sure hope so." Phoenix grunted, sounds of rustling cloth betraying his restless movements. "Why's he doing this?"

"It must have something to do with Ragnarok," Jade mused bringing her knees up to her chin and wrapping her arms around them. "He wants her out of the way so it can happen. That's why he stole her in the first place and that's why he disguised himself as a wolf and tried to stop us from getting here. For some reason he either can't or won't kill her outright but he's doing everything he can to bring the world into chaos - Ragnarok - by preventing her from being here on time. Now that we *are* here, he's trying to stop Truda from doing her job."

"What sort of idiot deliberately engineers the end of the world?" Phoenix scoffed.

Jade sighed. "I don't know. It doesn't really make sense but it's the only explanation I can think of. He is the god of Chaos and Mischief, after all. Maybe it's just a big game to him. Like when he herded us toward the troll - he could have set the wolves on us but he must have thought it was more fun to get the troll to do it."

The friends were silent awhile until Phoenix groaned again. Cloth rustled and leather creaked as he moved. "Right. Enough lying about. Is there anything you can do to get us out of here, Jade?"

"What?" She'd been deep in thought. "No, sorry. I'm still not recovered from Thor's lightning. I used what strength I had to heal myself. I need my herbs to do anything more."

He grunted. "What about that book of spells Ásúlfr gave you?"

"I've only had time to read a few of them," she admitted regretfully. "There might be a few I could use but I still need to restore my own strength first. Sorry."

Phoenix sighed in the darkness. "Oh well, it was just wishful thinking. Guess it's probably my turn to get us out of trouble, anyway. Back to lying around for awhile then."

She couldn't think of anything to say to that. She wasn't sure if Phoenix was saying she hadn't done enough to save them now; or if he was obliquely complimenting her on her past efforts. She was too exhausted to try to think about it now, anyway. Lying down on the floor, she curled an arm under her head and closed her eyes.

Sleep eluded her. The last few days had been so

emotionally-charged that Jade actually welcomed the time to think. Dark-silence was a blissful change from constantly rushing around like lunatics. She wriggled to try and get more comfortable on the hard stone floor. Why did lying in a cold, dark, stone cell seem familiar? Just as she was, finally, drifting off, the door flew open and a guard growled at them.

"Odinn summons you to judgement, mortals. Get up."

"Oh man, already?" Phoenix grumbled. "I'd just got to sleep."

"The gods do not wait for mortals! If you don't appear, you'll be automatically found guilty. Get up!"

"Alright, alright!" He turned to give Marcus and Jade a hand up. "So much for 'innocent until proven guilty'."

"That's a legal idea pretty unique to what we call 'civilisation'," Jade said ironically. "In fact, if we'd lost the war against Napoleon we'd probably have the French system of 'guilty until proven innocent'. I'd say these feudal ancient Scandinavians are going to think the same way."

"You mean they assume we're guilty and we have to prove our innocence?" Phoenix sounded outraged at the idea.

She couldn't help laughing at his shocked expression as they preceded the guard out the door.

"'Fraid so," she said, trying to sound casual. In her chest, her heart felt like it was about to explode. She had no idea how to prevent a guilty verdict.

"Do we dare ask what the penalty is if we are found guilty?" Marcus asked.

The guard ahead must have heard, for he turned and sent them a knowing, unpleasant grin.

"Death." He sneered. "Not a warrior's death by blade, either. Valhalla is not for the likes of you. You'll die in the old way – garrotted and buried in the peat bogs as a sacrifice to Odinn and a warning to others who meddle in the gods' lives."

Jade drew a long, shuddering breath, trying to calm her racing blood. Phoenix was silent but his eyes were troubled.

He leaned over and murmured into her ear, "Now would be a good time to spring that plan I just know you're waiting to surprise me with."

Feeling helpless and thick-headed with exhaustion, she shook her head numbly. "I'm sorry, Phoenix, I can't think of anything."

"We will just have to tell the truth," Marcus said, raising his chin.

"Great." Phoenix threw up his hands. "The Truth against the Master of Lies and an assumption of guilt. I don't like our odds. Give me a sword and I'll show them where they can stick their truth."

CHAPTER TWENTY-ONE

Once again, the travellers found themselves in the great hall of Gladsheim. Dusty beams of afternoon sunlight poured in through the high windows, falling on a strange scene. The room had been converted into a sort of courtroom, with chairs and benches lining two sides. Odinn's throne was placed at one end and three stools stood forlornly out in the middle, facing the king of the Gods. This time, there were more than just a few gods in attendance – every seat was full. The entire Æsir and several of what Jade called the Vanir – other kinds of gods, evidently - were present for their trial.

Phoenix gazed at the assembled pantheon in awe. They were all shapes and sizes. Many were giants, thirty feet tall, or half- and quarter-giants. Not just gods, either; goddesses were in attendance, too. Both sexes were muscular, beautiful and barbaric-looking in iron-studded leather; cloaks and long, blond or red hair.

Loki was one of the exceptions. Dressed entirely in black leather, with his dark hair slicked back, he strode into the hall like he owned it. Finding a front-row seat, he raised an eyebrow at the current owner, who grumbled but moved away. Sitting gracefully, Loki sent Phoenix a cool smile and proceeded to inspect his fingernails with supreme disregard for his fellow deities.

Their guard prodded the three companions until they unwillingly sat on the stools provided. Several gods and goddesses muttered, frowning and pointing as the accused sat down.

"Silence!"

All three jumped as Thor's enormous voice boomed across the hall.

"All rise for Odinn, King of Asgard!" He growled, glaring at anyone who took too long to get up. There was a quick scraping of chairs as everyone stood.

Phoenix hastily hauled Jade to her feet when she didn't react swiftly enough. A rapid look at her face told him she was far from recovered. The circles beneath her green eyes were dark bruises and her expression almost vague. She blinked slowly, frowning again. For a moment he wondered if she'd somehow managed to find some more of that dratted lily plant. Then he dismissed the thought as unworthy. She was just exhausted from the effort of being killed twice within three days and protecting him and Marcus.

Odinn walked slowly into the room. Surveying the assembled beings with his one, bright blue eye, he eased himself onto the throne and leaned back.

"Begin," he said quietly. Somehow his voice carried to every ear.

Thor rose. He stood at least fifteen feet tall and had to be almost half that across the shoulders. The man – god – was enormous. In one massive, iron-gloved hand he gripped a war-hammer and on his head perched an iron helmet. Much of his face hid behind a reddish beard. When he moved, though, it was with surprising grace and silence. He moved like a warrior; a fierce animal restrained only by his intelligence. Frankly, he was scary.

"Father," he boomed, "these mortals dared to abduct my daughter and hold her hostage – putting our whole world in danger of the Chaos that is Ragnarok. They have also conspired to steal Mjölnir!" He brandished the hammer over his head and the crowd of deities muttered angrily.

"And..." he waved for quiet, "and they murdered my battle-companion and friend, Hrothgar, king of the Svear people. Here is Blódbál, the very sword I gave to Hrothgar in friendship." Thor hooked his hammer onto his belt and drew out the sword. It looked like a toothpick in his huge hands. He gazed sorrowfully down at it and then placed it on a table close beside Odinn's throne.

His great head snapped up and he glared at the three companions.

"For any one of these crimes, they should be sacrificed." Facing his father again, he drew himself up to his full, imposing height. "Pass judgment now, father, for there is no doubt of their guilt."

Odinn nodded slowly. Phoenix felt his heart leap into his mouth. Sliding his eyes sideways, he tried to see if there was any possible escape. Guards stood close by on all sides and the exits were similarly blocked. His heart sank.

The king of the gods opened his mouth.

"My lord." Jade stood up.

Phoenix gaped up at her. She looked fully alert and perfectly fine; in fact, better than fine. Her clothes and skin were inexplicably clean; her hair tidy and unsinged; her Elven features oddly accentuated. What the...? She must have drawn the dregs of her energy to cast an illusion spell on herself.

For a moment, he was stunned at her sheer vanity. What did it matter how she looked? Then it dawned on him that she was right – snap judgments were made on how people looked. Even the gods had to be guilty of that. Right now, Jade looked like a true, noble Light-elf, not some half-dead homeless nobody.

"My lord, I humbly request you grant us the right to speak," Jade repeated as the gods' voices swelled in outrage.

"Who are you to make such a request, mortal?" Odinn asked coolly.

Jade dipped him a deep curtsy but kept her head high.

"I am Jade, daughter of Freyr, lord of the Ljósálfar."

The tumult that arose from her statement was deafening. Loki started half out of his chair, his eyes narrow and jaw clenched. Odinn waved her forward and nodded. Now Phoenix understood why Jade had refused to tell their names. Names did have power, even if it wasn't always magical. Did they have a hope now? Was Freyr an important enough name to drop here? Could he be called as a witness?

Phoenix dug his nails into his palms. He wanted to jump up and yell at them all; force them to believe. He gripped the chair seat hard, pinning himself down so he wouldn't wreck everything with his stupid impulsiveness.

Jade rode out the furore with queenly hauteur, ignoring the audience as she glided forward into the centre of the room. Phoenix admired her guts but he was afraid she might collapse in the middle. He had a feeling she was running on sheer adrenalin now.

"My lord," she drew a breath, obviously considering her words, "there is no evidence to support my lord Thor's accusations. Hrothgar himself, in gratitude for services rendered, gave Blódbál to my companion." She had to shout to make herself heard as the room again erupted into talk. "Hrothgar was killed by a troll, not us. Freyr and all of Hrothgar's village can attest to that. Thrudr is safely returned to you and will tell you herself that we did not abduct her."

Beside him, Marcus stiffened and gripped Phoenix's arm tightly. He sat rigidly upright, staring at Loki.

"What is it?" Phoenix whispered.

"That man, sitting next to Loki." Marcus jerked his head.

Phoenix saw a sallow-skinned, slender man leaning in to speak with the god of mischief. With his face turned away, only the back of his dark head could be seen. He wore a close-fitting black cap with decorated tassels sticking out on either side and his long black hair braided into an intricate knot at the back. His floor-length robes of black were decorated with gold embroidery. He seemed strangely out of place amongst the fur-and-leather clad gods.

"What about him?"

"It's Zhudai!"

At that moment, every god and goddess in the room leapt to their feet, shouting denials and angry comments. Phoenix looked up to see Jade standing in a beam of sunlight, pointing dramatically at Loki's calm, smiling figure. Obviously she'd just named him as Truda's kidnapper and it wasn't being well-received. Jade seemed to be doing what she could, so Phoenix turned his attention back to Marcus. She'd probably sweet talk them better than he would anyway. Where the heck was Brynn when they needed a silver tongue?

"Are you absolutely sure?"

Marcus sent him a look of complete, unshakeable certainty. Phoenix held up a hand in acknowledgement. The deities resumed their seats and Phoenix could now see their arch-enemy again whispering into Loki's ear.

"Damn. That changes things – for the worse, I might add."

"Agreed. There's no telling what Zhudai is saying to Loki."

"And no doubting who's running the show now," Phoenix muttered.

Marcus sent him a quick, confused look. "How could Zhudai be controlling a god?"

"You'll just have to trust me on this," Phoenix said, "he is – somehow."

"What can we do?"

Phoenix gritted his teeth. "As much as I hate to say it, I think we have to wait. Jade seems to be at least giving Odinn something to think about. The best we can hope for is some luck - maybe Brynn will turn up with Truda at just the right time."

Marcus bowed his head slightly, his eyes hard. "I prefer to make my own luck. Just get me close to Zhudai and I will find a way to kill him and end this right now." His fingers flexed as though gripping an invisible dagger.

Phoenix grabbed his hand. "Don't be stupid. We're in a room full of people with divine powers and Zhudai himself is an arch-wizard. You don't stand a chance."

The Roman met his gaze, his face stony. "This counsel from you?" He relaxed a little and nodded. "Very well. Let's hope you're right then and the real Truda shows up. Otherwise," he glanced at the impassive face of Odinn, "I don't think we're getting out of here alive. Look."

Phoenix turned back to the trial. As he watched, Loki nodded in response to some question from Odinn, rose and left the room. Possibly only Phoenix and Marcus caught the significant look that passed between the god and the Chinese villain. Zhudai closed his eyes. His lips moved briefly and his hands shifted in a slight, graceful gesture – as though he formed the outline of something in the air in front of him.

"What's he doing?"

Marcus didn't reply. His eyes were slitted in hatred.

They found out when Truda entered the room – with Loki striding beside her. If Loki was there, it had to be the real Truda but why was she with him? Phoenix started to rise. A guard pushed him roughly back down. Jade cast an anxious look back at them but Phoenix could only shrug his own disbelief. She bit her lip, frowning at Truda and Loki. Then she tilted her head to one side, staring harder. As Phoenix watched, Jade's eyes narrowed and her jaw firmed. Something magical was going on if he read the signs right, but what?

Odinn greeted his granddaughter with a gentle smile and a request to tell him exactly what had happened over the last few months. Phoenix and Marcus listened with increasing horror as the girl described an entirely fictitious abduction, months of imprisonment in Albion and a harrowing trip back to Svealand.

"Then," Truda's lip trembled and a tear slid down her cheek as she pointed to Phoenix and Marcus, "those two found Grendel, the troll, had died in the sunlight and they pretended they had done it, so Hrothgar would be nice to them. That's why Hrothgar gave them Blódbál. Then they left the village so Grendel's mother could come along and kill Hrothgar as they'd planned together."

Phoenix wished he could strangle the kid – or give her the Oscar for best actress. After all they'd done for her she was betraying them! Frowning, he remembered the Binding spell Jade had put on the companions back in England. She'd said that if any of the group betrayed them, they would all get a sharp pain in the hand and the vine she'd used to 'bind' them would reappear. So where was it?

Sick realisation hit. Truda hadn't been part of their group when Jade had done the Binding ceremony. She wasn't constrained by that particular magic. There was nothing to stop her deceiving them.

Had she been working with Loki and Zhudai all along? Was this all some elaborate trap? Phoenix's head spun as he tried to wrap his brain around all the 'what ifs' and 'but thens' of the situation. It just didn't make sense.

"My lord!" Jade shouted over the hubbub that followed Truda's testimony.

Truda now sat quietly beside her father, looking the picture of injured innocence. Loki sat next to Zhudai, neither speaking nor moving. Odinn frowned at Jade but waved the audience quiet again. Phoenix wondered what on earth she could do after that little performance. As far as he could tell, they were so toast it was a wonder they hadn't already been sliced up.

"That is not Thrudr." Jade pointed at Truda.

This time, Odinn quelled the uproar before it even started.

"Explain yourself, mortal," the king of the gods growled.

Thor laid a protective hand on Truda's head.

Jade drew a deep breath. "If I can prove I speak the truth, will you listen? If you bring me two small items, I promise you will see what is real and who is lying."

Odinn hesitated, obviously annoyed.

"Please," she begged. "This girl is not who you think she is."

Phoenix held his breath. So did the entire room. Odinn glanced narrowly back and forth between Truda, Jade and Thor. Thor shrugged slightly. Odinn nodded.

"Very well. What do you need?"

"Just one small seed and a handful of wet soil." Jade's lips drew back in a fierce, glittering smile.

Truda gasped. Phoenix and Marcus exchanged puzzled looks. What on earth did she need a seed for?

After a flurry of discussion and argument, a guard brought a bucket of soil and some sort of seed and dropped it into Jade's hand. She gestured toward Truda, who shook her head and shrank back against her father.

"Come, daughter," Thor prompted. "You are well protected here. There is nothing to fear from this mortal. Let her fail her little experiment and we can get on with sacrificing them." He pushed her in the small of the back and she stumbled out into the room.

Jade knelt on the floor. She tipped dirt out and poked a finger into the top of the pile. Understanding lit up Phoenix's brain. Marcus nudged him and pointed toward Zhudai and Loki. While Loki still sat like a statue, Zhudai frowned, clearly unsure what was going on.

Jade dropped the seed into the hole and patted it closed. She stood up, glaring at Truda.

"Make it grow."

The assembled gods gasped as enlightenment hit. Truda was a goddess of spring growth. If this girl was Truda then she should be able to make the seed grow into a plant.

Phoenix looked again at Zhudai. His face was a mask of fury. His lips moved as he stared fiercely at the small pile of dirt. Phoenix blinked in surprise. Loki had, just for a second, flickered like a bad special effect in a movie. It happened again. What the...?

Jade grabbed another handful of dirt. In one smooth move, she threw it at Loki and Zhudai. Zhudai flung up his hands to shield his face. Loki simply sat there, unresponsive. The dirt flew straight through his body, falling to splatter on the people behind and the floor around. Still, he didn't move.

There was stunned silence as the assembled gods tried to work out what was happening.

"That is an illusion cast by him," Jade yelled, pointing at Loki and Zhudai. "This girl is the true Loki, Shapeshifter and Master of Deceit. They are your enemy, not us!"

With a cry of frustration, Truda/Loki morphed mindbendingly back into his familiar shape. The illusion Loki dissolved. Zhudai stood and tried to slide out through the confused crowd. He came up against the huge, hard body of Thor and stopped dead. Loki snatched Jade into his arms. H spun her about, a long, wicked-looking blade to her throat.

Phoenix grinned. Time to move. Jade had done her part, now it was time for his.

CHAPTER TWENTY-TWO

Leaping to his feet, Phoenix sprinted the length of the hall with Marcus pounding only a few steps behind.

"Stop!" Loki shouted, "or I'll kill her!" He pressed his knife into Jade's throat. A scarlet trickle slid down, showing bright against her white skin.

Phoenix skidded to a halt only metres away. He looked at Jade. She stared back, green eyes wide. She'd already lost two lives in this level and couldn't afford to lose any more. He had to save her without letting her die again. An idea hit. These were war-gods. Surely...

"My lord Odinn," he yelled, not taking his eyes off Loki. "I ask for the right to justice by combat! We have proved ourselves innocent of the charges falsely laid by Loki and his advisor but he has wronged us and I will be avenged." That ought to be suitably dramatic for a hall full of Norse gods. Phoenix grinned nastily at the astonished look in Loki's eyes.

"Granted!" Odinn roared, thumping the end of his javelin into the floor.

The pantheon of gods sat back down, breathlessly awaiting a battle.

Loki shoved Jade aside. She stumbled, falling into the arms of a guard. Loki held out his hand. A guard slapped a sword into it. He sheathed his knife and dropped into a fighter's crouch, circling left toward Phoenix.

Phoenix glanced about for help. Surely someone would hand him a sword, too? Marcus and Jade both struggled in the grip of guards. No-one rushed to his aid. Great. Bare hands against a sword. What the hell was he thinking? Oh well, he squared his shoulders, at least with his aikido training, he had some chance. Hopefully. He really didn't want to lose another life. It hurt too much.

Loki glided closer. Phoenix watched closely, trying to judge how he would attack. These people favoured broadswords, which meant slower, sweeping attacks. That might work in his favour.

Sure enough, Loki came at him with a war-cry, committing himself to a two-handed, overhead strike. Perfect. Phoenix allowed his aikido reflexes to take over. Instead of stepping away or dodging, he stepped toward Loki. Swiftly, he slipped inside and under Loki's descending arms. He put his back hard up against Loki's gut, grabbed an arm and dropped. The god sailed overhead as Phoenix fell to his knees and let go.

There was a moment of shocked silence as Loki crashed heavily on his back and slid across the stone floor.

Phoenix jumped up, measuring the distance between himself and Blódbál, lying near Odinn's throne. Too far. Loki rose, shaking his head. He rotated his shoulders and neck. Damn. People weren't supposed to get up so fast after being thrown like that. Well, Loki wasn't exactly 'people' in the ordinary sense of the word. This called for something more drastic.

The god came at him again, more warily this time. He'd learned his lesson and now began jabbing at Phoenix almost like a fencer. A broadsword wasn't the ideal weapon for this technique and even a god's arm would tire after awhile, hopefully. He just had to stay out of reach until it did.

So they danced around the room, with Phoenix spinning, twisting and trying to manoeuvre closer to where Blódbál lay, just out of reach. Twice the tip of Loki's sword caught in his clothes, tearing them and scoring across his stomach. Both times the crowd gasped. Blood dripped and Loki's grin became triumphant.

At last, the opening Phoenix waited for appeared. Loki overreached himself just a fraction. Stepping aside and turning fast, he grabbed Loki's sword-hand and helped him overbalance just a little more. Then, with a quick twist of his hips, Phoenix folded Loki's wrist back and threw him in a move known as kotagaeshi.

The god fell heavily, hopefully with a painfully dislocated shoulder or wrist. Phoenix held on to the hand and yanked the sword free. Putting his foot on Loki's neck and the tip of the sword there too, Phoenix grinned down at the god.

"Yield."

"No!" Loki snarled.

From under his clothes he pulled a dagger and jammed it to the hilt into Phoenix's calf.

Someone screamed. Several people yelled in anger.

Pain lanced through his leg and Phoenix staggered back, dropping the sword as he overbalanced. Loki sprang lithely to his feet and snatched the blade up again. He stalked closer, bloody dagger in one hand, broadsword in the other, murder in his grey eyes. No dislocation then. Man, these guys were tough!

Phoenix steadied himself and tried to put weight on his foot. The leg refused and the pain blinded him. Loki's blade had severed the hamstring. He forced himself to stand straight and smile. Loki frowned, glancing at the blood pooling now on the floor beneath Phoenix's foot. His frown vanished into a gloating gleam. He advanced. Phoenix stood his ground – he had no choice.

"Phoenix, catch!"

A shrill, familiar voice pierced the fog of pain. Brynn! The Breton boy held something – Blódbál! He threw it. The blade arced through the air. With a roar, Loki launched himself at Phoenix.

Too late. Phoenix snatched the hilt and parried Loki's blow at the last second. Strength, power and exultation flowed through his blood from the sword. It warmed his body like a hot drink on a cold day. Vigour pulsed back into his limbs. Tentatively, he put weight on his injured leg, surprised to find he could. The injury was either gone or irrelevant, he wasn't sure which.

Heady and glutted with power, Phoenix crossed swords with Loki in a flurry of blows too quick to analyse. Blódbál sang in his heart, called to his mind, enticed him toward victory. Phoenix let the sword take over, flicking it in to slice Loki's skin once, twice, three times. The blood that spattered the floor was now a god's life-offering.

This was too easy. Phoenix grinned madly, quite enjoying the bout now. He couldn't lose with Blódbál in his hands. Loki snarled, his face contorting, shifting, morphing into the familiar black wolf that had harried them through the woods. Razor fangs snapped at Phoenix's left arm. Latching on they sliced through to the bone. Phoenix screamed in pain.

In desperation, he twisted and hacked awkwardly at the wolf. Loki released his arm and skittered away, his claws rattling across the marble. He shifted back to his human form. Picking up his sword he strode casually over to where Phoenix knelt on the blood-slippery floor.

Phoenix sucked a deep, ragged breath. Heaving to his feet, he set himself for the next attack. Arrogant in his belief of victory, Loki smiled, baring reddened human teeth in a barbaric, frightening display. The god swung his sword in a furious flurry of strikes that Phoenix barely managed to deflect. Even with the sword's magic, his body weakened through loss of blood. He had to end this and fast.

At last he saw an opening. Turning aside, he sliced across Loki's arm. Black leather parted and red showed. Loki dropped his sword from useless fingers. Phoenix lunged, stopping the point of his blade just short of Loki's exposed throat.

"Yield," he repeated, panting.

Loki glared. "Never!"

His eyes rolled up as his body twisted in a logic-defying, purple-blue shimmer. Startled, Phoenix backed away. Loki grew…and grew. Too late, he remembered that Loki's true form was of a giant. Blódbál's song faded as cold logic replaced battle fever.

Jade, Brynn, Truda and Marcus appeared by his side, all staring up at Loki's towering shape. At a gesture, Loki's sword leapt back into his hand – and grew to match his size. He now wielded a blade fully twelve foot long.

"Run!" Phoenix advised the others.

They turned – and faced a tired, one-eyed old man.

Odinn looked at them with an expression of weary regret in that single eye then switched his gaze to the looming darkness of the god of mischief. He thumped the end of his spear on the floor once. The sound echoed hollowly around the great chamber.

"Enough," he said quietly but his voice blanked out all other noise.

The world stopped. A strange, muffled silence fell on Gladsheim. Loki paused in mid-strike, his booted feet clumping only faintly on the stone floor. Everyone watched their king. No-one spoke.

Odinn waved a hand. Most of the gods and goddesses left the room with regretful, backward looks. Shortly, only Thor, Truda, Loki and the four companions remained with the king of the Norse gods.

Odinn sighed and limped slowly back to his throne.

"Loki, why must you continually stir up trouble in Midgard and Asgard?" Odinn's face showed paternal regret – like a father who's child has been brought before the principal once too often. "It was you, who stole my granddaughter and hid her in Albion, wasn't it? And also you who set the wolves on these mortals and the trolls on Hrothgar's people? Why do you wish for Ragnarok?"

Loki sneered and slouched over to sit at his ease in a chair nearby. Phoenix did a double-take. The god had reverted to human size. His body and clothes were unmarked, whole. Phoenix wished his were the same. He kept Blódbál to hand, just for its pain-numbing effect and wondered if he'd pass out soon.

"What can I say, my king?" Loki shrugged. "I'm the God of Chaos. Ragnarok is the ultimate Chaos; a chance to start afresh with a better world and a better ruler. Besides, Thor annoyed me. I wanted to teach him a lesson."

Phoenix started to limp forward but Jade and Marcus grabbed his arms and held him.

"Let them sort it out," Jade whispered, tearing at her shirt and winding strips around his dripping arm and leg.

Truda, however, was under no such restrictions. She stomped past them to stand before Loki with her hands on her hips. She wagged a finger at him.

"You're a bad, bad man, Uncle Loki. First you stole me from my bed then you made the nice Druids keep me and they all got killed by the Romans. You got poor Hrothgar killed and then, when I finally got home you put my friends and me in prison. You're not my friend any more, you hear me! I hate you!" Overwrought the god-child stamped her foot then burst into tears and threw herself into her father's arms, sobbing.

Loki raised one dark eyebrow. "I'm devastated, I assure you."

Thor stepped forward, his face thunderous. "I've had enough, too Loki. You're my father's blood-brother and we've put up with a lot from you but taking out your anger at me on a child and mortals is beyond acceptable. You're no longer welcome in my home." He picked Truda up and held her against his huge chest, patting her fiery hair soothingly.

Loki yawned. "Again, I'm distraught. Not to be allowed to babysit those hell-children of yours ever again.

Oh me, oh my, how will I cope?"

"Perhaps this will not bother you either, my brother," Odinn's soft voice cut in. "You are henceforth banished from Asgard and Midgard for a full millennium and a day. You may not come to any place of the Norse gods or man for that time or until Ragnarok does descend upon us – whichever is first."

Loki turned an insolent look on his king and bowed his head. "Very well, old man, the petty politics of Asgard bores me to tears anyway. Just remember, though, if Ragnarok does come first, don't look for me to fight alongside the Æsir in that final battle for the end of the worlds. You are no kin of mine any longer!" With that scornful, ringing declaration, the god of mischief and deceit turned on his heel and walked away.

"Wait!" Jade's clear voice spoiled his masterful exit. "What happened to that man – Zhudai? What was he doing here?"

Loki stopped, glancing back over his shoulder. Everyone looked around, only now noticing Zhudai was, indeed, missing. Marcus swore imaginatively. Phoenix breathed a sigh of relief. He was so not ready to face the ultimate badguy yet, even with his new sword.

The God of Chaos raised his brows in cool hauteur. "I have no idea. He came a few days ago with a warning that you were on your way to return Truda and a charming plan for how to make her homecoming more fun. Oh, the wolves, Grendel and setting Grendel's mother on the village were all his ideas, too. I would have let the wolves eat you. He wanted you two alive." He pointed at Jade and Phoenix. "I don't care who he is, where he is or where he came from. He can rot with the rest of you mortals." He gave them a stiff, shallow bow and left the hall without looking back.

EPILOGUE

"Do you believe him?" Jade asked the others.

It was the next morning and Truda was off with Thor, celebrating her birthday by bringing Spring to Midgard. Ragnarok had been averted. The companions sat comfortably around a long table in Truda's home, Bilskirnir. After Loki's departure Odinn had wearily dismissed the charges against them, healed Phoenix's wounds and sent them all to Bilskirnir with a careless wave of his hand. There, Thor's wife, Sif, fussed over Truda and then over all of them. They slept in wonderful beds, bathed luxuriously, and ate until they were stuffed and sleepy. Sif even managed to trim Jade's singed hair neatly, although it was a lot shorter now.

"Who?" Phoenix asked, yawning.

Brynn attempted to slice an apple in half in mid-air with his hand-me-down sword. Phoenix and Marcus had been teaching him swordplay while Jade replenished her strength and her herb supply in Sifs garden. Unfortunately, the only real result was Sif's annoyance at the number of bruised apples lying around.

"Loki," Jade sighed, sorting herbs without really paying attention. "Do you believe that he only just met Zhudai and doesn't care where he is?"

Marcus looked up intently. Nearby, Brynn picked up the bruised apple and tossed it in the air again.

"No idea." Phoenix shrugged. "Anyway, it's not really important now. We still have to complete this level, remember?"

"I know but it doesn't seem right to just steal the

hammer after all this." She shook her head, frowning at the bunch of aconite in her hand.

"WHAT?" Thor's booming voice made them all jump guiltily.

Phoenix's hand dropped to his sword. Jade gasped as Thor shouldered his way into the room and bore down on them. Truda was right behind him, hurt and anger clouding her big blue eyes. Thor thumped a massive fist on the table, making the herbs bounce.

"You *are* trying to steal Mjölnir, just as Loki said? Guards!"

"No, no!" Jade jumped up and ran to the thunder god. "No," she pleaded, feeling sick that he and Truda thought they'd go through with it, now. "Please listen to us. Truda, please?"

Thor hesitated, looking down at his daughter. Truda poked out her bottom lip then nodded reluctantly. Thor waved the guards away and the two sat down.

Feeling like she was once again on trial, Jade paced the floor. She outlined their first two quests, prudently leaving out bits that related to coming from another world. Phoenix nodded at her encouragingly, so she hoped he was in agreement with her. There'd been no time to consult, after all.

"So you see," she spread her hands, "we can't continue without your hammer. With the hammer, we're supposed to go to Egypt and release the goddess Anuket. She's trapped in a tekhen there. That's all we need it for. Then we can go on to the next quest, and the next and finally we can kill Zhudai, the one who's behind all of this." Jade finished, looking hopefully at Thor. "We'd return it straight away, I promise," she added in a small voice.

There was a long silence as Thor glared at all four. They each met his eye as bravely as they could. He drummed his thick fingers on the wooden table and stared at his daughter for a long moment. Then he slapped the palm of his hand on the table, startling them once more.

"By Odinn's eyepatch, I'll do it!" Thor grinned, his bushy red beard quivering and his blue eyes glittering with anticipation. "It sounds like you'll only need it for a week or so. With Loki gone things should be pretty peaceful for awhile. I can live without Mjölnir for that long." He looked down at Truda again, stroking her bright hair. "Besides, I do owe you a favour for bringing my daughter safely home. Without her, Midgard would have been locked in winter and thousands of gods and mortals alike would have died in the ensuing battle. Anyway, Hrothgar would only have given my gift-sword to a true hero. Here."

He got up and unhooked Mjölnir from his belt. Striding over to Marcus, who was nearest, he held the short-handled hammer out.

Standing, Marcus hesitantly reached out and grasped the handle. Thor let go. Marcus yelped as the hammer smashed to the ground, cracking the granite floor. Thor laughed uproariously at his own joke. Still chuckling, he unbuckled his belt and stripped off his iron gloves.

"Sorry. Couldn't resist. You'll need Megingjörð – the belt - and my gloves. They give you the strength to lift the hammer, boy." Thor explained, still laughing as Marcus strained to lift the weapon.

The belt and gloves shrank, becoming a perfect fit when Marcus pulled them on. He wiggled his fingers, raising his eyebrows at the flexibility of the iron. Reaching down, he yanked at the hammer, staggering back as it lifted easily now. Brynn giggled.

Marcus turned to Phoenix. "You should carry it."

Phoenix shook his head and patted Blódbál. "Not a chance. I'm sticking with my little friend, here."

"Jade?" Marcus held the hammer out toward her.

She backed away, hands behind her. "Iron gloves? I don't think so. It's all yours."

Marcus glanced at Brynn who grinned cheekily and shook his head. "You're the warrior. I'm just a thief, remember? I can barely handle a normal sword, let alone a magic hammer. Besides," he shrugged, "whoever heard of a thief giving things back at the end?"

Sighing, the Roman nodded, accepting the burden. Thor patted him on the shoulder and led him to one side, explaining how to handle the weapon.

Jade drew the others to Truda. "I guess it's time for us to say 'good-bye'," she said sadly. She'd had become quite fond of the girl. It had been nice to have another female along.

Truda threw her arms around here and squeezed tightly. "You'll take care of Brynn for me? He picked the lock to let me out of jail, y'know."

Jade smiled and tweaked one red braid. "Of course we will but he has a habit of taking care of us, really. We'd be lost without him."

Brynn came up, blushing furiously. Truda hugged him and gave him a kiss on the cheek. He flushed even more. Phoenix rescued him by tapping Truda on the shoulder. The girl looked at him doubtfully for a moment before wrapping her arms around his stomach and hugging him, too.

"Thanks for bringing me home in time to balance out the seasons again like I'm s'posed to. You take care of yourself, ok?" She frowned up at him like a little mother.

"You take care of yourself too, brat," he said. "This must be what it's like to be an older brother, huh? It's not so bad. You're alright kid." He gave her an awkward, one-armed hug.

Truda sniffed and nodded. Without looking back, she ran to Marcus, gave him a flying hug and dashed out the door, bawling.

Thor looked after her with an indulgent smile then came back with Marcus to join them. He rubbed his hands together and grinned broadly.

"Right then, off to Ægyptus is it?"

They nodded, looking at each other doubtfully.

"Stupid place, that." Thor turned away, waving at them to follow. "Full of arrogant gods with the heads of animals and the brains of them, too. It's the heat: makes them idiots." He snorted and shook his shaggy, red head. "Now when you're done, all you need to do is make some small sacrifice to me, call my name and I'll know you're ready to give Mjölnir back. In the mean time," he shook a warning finger at Marcus, "look after it. I'd hate for that thing to fall into the wrong hands."

They followed him for some time, through the twisting stone corridors of Bilskirnir. Finally, Thor led them outside. Three servants waited, holding their horses and all the gear. Jade blinked. She'd forgotten about the horses.

Thor smiled. "Ready then?"

"Umm," Jade began. "How do we get there?"

Thor chuckled and pointed toward a stone gateway in his garden. It looked remarkably like the three-stone doorway they'd stepped through in Stonehenge. Extremely like, in fact.

Phoenix eyed it then looked around. "Another Spring Equinox ceremony, I suppose?" He sighed, his shoulders twitching, probably at the thought of more Roman arrows.

Thor waved a hand dismissively. "Nah. Those Druids have no idea. You don't need a ceremony to use their portal," he winked, "just timing. It only opens at the Equinoxes. Stupid mortals. This portal, however, links up with Midgard anytime and anywhere you want. Just say where you want to go, walk through and there you are." He walked up, laid a thick-fingered hand on it and said "Ægyptus" in a clear voice. Then he nodded with satisfaction as the liquid-looking surface shimmered into existence. "I know the Elves use those tapestries of theirs but this has so much more dramatic flair, don't you think?

Makes a good garden ornament, too."

The group was silent a moment.

"You mean that whole Spring Ceremony thing back in Albion was a waste of time and people!?" Jade couldn't help the surge of anger and grief that welled up in her heart at the thought of the sacrificed druids and destruction of Stonehenge.

"And we didn't have to ride up that bloody rainbow bridge to Alfheim?" Phoenix chimed in.

Thor shook his head, laughing. "You rode over Bifrost? Hah! I'd say Freyr just wanted to scare you. Well, there you go then." The god nodded genially at the stone doorway.

The four companions exchanged grim glances. Thor's scornful laughter at the Druids brought home, once more, the precarious nature of their quest. They were at the whim of the gods, whatever magic forces pushed them on and an archvillain who wanted them dead. As soon as they stepped through the portal, it all started again – but harder.

Jade caught Brynn's eye then Marcus'. "Are you sure you two want to do this? You can back out now and use this thing to go back to your homes, if you want."

For a second, Brynn's young face showed a flash of longing and fear. Then he squared his thin shoulders and shook his head. Marcus stepped forward and laid a hand on the boy's shoulder.

"We're with you," he said firmly.

"Let's go then." Phoenix grabbed the reins of the nearest horse.

He waved thanks to Thor and marched purposefully toward the glistening doorway. Brynn, Marcus and Jade followed quickly, leading their mounts.

Thor watched a moment until first they, and then the shimmering surface vanished then shook his head and walked away. "What fools mortals are."

.....

Nearby, a lean man in severe black robes emerged from the deep shadows of an oak tree. He gazed at the empty stones for a long time then smiled a particularly mirthless, unpleasant smile. Zhudai touched the grey granite and murmured softly. When the glistening portal appeared, he sent a last, contemptuous look at Thor's castle...and vanished through the stones.

THE END

APPENDIX

Roman weights:
One Libra = ¾ of a pound or 336 grams, so Marcus is saying Phoenix feels like he weighs 300 libra approx = 100kg. The Libra is also the basis for the modern abbreviation for 'pound' – lb. The Roman'uncia' is one modern 'ounce' or 28 grams.

Mjolnir is pronounced "Muhyollnear." It is Thor's hammer in all the tales of the Nordic gods. Even Thor cannot wield it without the gloves and belt, though.

Tacitus actually wrote about Svealand in 98AD, although he never actually travelled in all the Germanic countries he wrote about.

The foreign-language words used are a mixture of Old Norse and modern Swedish, which are closely related. There are few written records of the Proto-Norse language used in Sweden in 80AD, but Old Norse would be close. The Proto-Norse (ElderFurthark) runic alphabet (below), are actually versions of Roman lettering. They are angular because they were either chopped into wood or chiselled into stone. They came into use around about 100AD, representing the sounds of a language that was much older than these new symbols for it.

All of the gods, worlds and places named in this book are from stories told by the ancient Norse/Swedish/Danish people. There are many more, not named here, and all have fascinating stories.

Trolltiven is a real place. It is part of Tiveden, a Swedish forest, famous for its scenery and notorious for its wilderness and dangers. It has a history of being used by thieves as a hideout.

"Thursvidur" means "ogre forest", but it's not a real place.

Geatsland was, in 80AD, an area in the south of Sweden. 500 years later, it was the homeland of Beowulf, the hero of the famous Nordic saga mentioned in this story. Beowulf travelled to Denmark in the story and defeated the troll Grendel there.

Arawn is a Celtic word – the traditional folk tale name in Celic/British lands for the king of the Faery & the leader of the Wild Hunt. The Scandinavian leader of the Wild Hunt and King of the Light Elves was named **Freyr**.

Nymphaea alba, also known as the **European White Waterlily**, is an aquatic flowering plant. The red variety comes from lake *Fagertärn* (Fair tarn) in the forest of Tiveden, Sweden. It contains the active alkaloids nupharine and nymphaeine, and is a sedative. Although roots and stalks are used in traditional herbal medicine along with the flower, the petals and other flower parts are the most potent.

A taste of things to come…..

Book Three: The Tekhen of Anuket

CHAPTER ONE

Phoenix stepped through the portal into hot, still darkness. As an afterthought he drew his sword, Blódbál, and held it ready. Peering into the gloom he listened for movement. Nothing. This unknown place was heavy with ancient, silent shadows; its air dusty and dead.

As his eyes adjusted to the glimmer of light given off by the portal, Phoenix could dimly see a large, rectangular room of some sort. Regularly spaced stone columns supported a stone roof.

He edged forward with his sword out, the other hand still holding firmly onto his horse's reins. The stallion whuffled, pushing at him with its nose. Hooves clattered on a stone floor.

What was it with the darkness thing? Everywhere they went, he, Jade and their companions seemed to end up in some lightless hole – usually a prison. Didn't anyone build with windows in the year 80AD? Or were the programmers of this benighted computer game just plain nasty?

After consideration, he favoured the latter idea. The guys who wrote the game in which he and Jade were trapped, probably quite enjoyed dreaming up the unpleasant little nuisances he'd experienced so far: giant trolls, armies of Roman soldiers, evil sorcerers and power-mad gods. So what was in store for his troupe now? They were in Egypt, so surely it would be mummies, or Sphinxes, or maybe a horde of bad-tempered, stampeding camels.

"Ow!" Jade's pained outcry told him the others were right on his heels.

He tugged his horse forward to make space for them. More hooves echoed. Brynn and Marcus stepped through. Marcus' bow was ready, an arrow nocked. Brynn drew his new sword and glared into the gloom.

Abruptly, the faint light vanished as the gateway between Asgard and Egypt popped out of existence with a slight *schlorp*ing sound. Come what may, they'd arrived on Level Three.

"Everyone ok?" Phoenix called over the stompings and nickerings. One by one, the others assured him they were all ok.

"So," he aimed for cheerful, "on to the second question. Anyone know where we are?"

There was a small silence then Brynn's cocky voice piped up. "Ægyptus?"

"Thanks for that. Helpful," Phoenix said sarcastically.

He heard a fleshy thump. Brynn squawked and Phoenix grinned, guessing Marcus had whacked the boy on the arm.

"Hang on," Jade said.

Phoenix gripped her staff reflexively as she thrust it into his hand. Seconds later, a greenish light appeared in her cupped hands. She'd cast a light-spell. Next she murmured a few words over the glowing ball and blew on it. To Phoenix's surprise, it wafted out of her hands and began to drift around the room.

"Nice trick," he admired, handing the staff back.

Jade grinned. "Courtesy of that spell-book Ásúlfr gave me back in Sweden." She sent another off in a different direction, then a third. Soon the room was eerily lit by what looked like a dozen giant firefly-backsides.

She exclaimed in soft delight and hurried over to the nearest wall. Phoenix passed the horses' reins to Brynn and joined her. What was so fascinating. As far as he could see, it was just a wall covered in pretty pictures.

"They're hieroglyphs," she breathed, brushing the tips of her fingers over the jewel-coloured images.

Brynn and Marcus came over, peering at the wall.

"Did you tie the horses?" Phoenix asked Brynn.

"Nope. Where would they go?" The Breton boy raised an eyebrow at him.

"Good point." Phoenix glanced around the room.

There were definitely no windows and, more concerning, no doors. Even the dimension-gate entrance they had come through was now merely a three-stone door-frame set into solid wall.

"Maybe we shouldn't waste time on the walls, Jade." He laid a hand on her shoulder. "Maybe we should be looking for a way out of here."

"I suppose." She didn't turn away.

Phoenix waited a second then gestured to the other two. There didn't seem to be any immediate danger. It wouldn't hurt to let her stay while they looked for a way out. He and Jade had had their differences in the past but Phoenix was determined to be a true leader now and earn her respect and co-operation. Ordering her to come away from the hieroglyphs would be a poor way to start.

"Could you at least lend us some of the lights?" He prodded her gently in the ribs. All of the light-balls danced around her head, illuminating the wall.

Jade nodded, tucked a stray strand of shoulder-length, white-blond hair behind a pointed ear and waved a hand absently at the hovering lights. Three of them drifted down to bob just over the boys' heads.

"Right," Phoenix peered into the gloomiest corners,

"there has to be an exit. Let's split up and find it – but don't get lost. We don't know how big this place is." The other two nodded and walked away, green lights dancing around their heads. Phoenix headed in the opposite direction.

As it turned out, they were in no danger of getting lost. The room was fairly small and flanked by two rooms that were even smaller. Brynn found what had to be the original door but it had been built in with large, firmly-mortared limestone blocks. There was no exit.

Finally, the three gathered around a central stone altar.

"Unless there's some sort of secret entrance, I can't see a way out of here," Phoenix admitted. "Ideas?"

"We could look for a secret entrance," Brynn offered, grinning.

Phoenix raised his eyes to the ceiling but nodded. "It was a joke. Any *other* ideas?"

Marcus glanced over his shoulder. "Let's ask Jade."

All three turned to look at her. Their half-elven companion still stared at the hieroglyphs covering the walls. Her mouth moved silently and her eyes were almost crossed with intense concentration.

"I've got it!" She turned and beckoned them, excitement making her green eyes glitter.

Relieved, Phoenix jogged over. Trust Jade to come up with a decent plan to get them out of trouble.

"So?"

She pointed at a set of pictures encircled by an oval. To Phoenix it looked like a hook and a shovel followed by a flying saucer and a small chicken. Outside the oval was a hamburger bun, a sailing boat and something that looked like a complicated showerhead. Perplexed, he raised his eyebrows at Jade.

She grinned at him. "See? It says we're in the offering chapel of Snefru's Shining Pyramid. The game programmers are obviously fans of the Stargate Sci-fi TV series. Any minute now it will be aliens landing on the pyramid."

Phoenix, Brynn and Marcus all stared at her with looks of blank astonishment for a moment before blinking again at the pictures. Phoenix decided to ignore the Stargate comment, as he'd never watched the show and had no idea what connection it had to their current problems. He examined the hieroglyphs again. He even tilted his head and closed one eye, hoping that would help. It still looked like a chicken and a complicated shower device.

"I'll take your word for it," he conceded. "Does it say how to get *out* of the chapel of Snefru's Shining pyramid by any chance?"

"What? No, it's all about what a great Pharaoh Snefru was and how he's going to get to the afterlife." She blinked at him. "Can't you read it?"

All three of the boys shook their heads.

"Huh." She pulled down her mouth. "I thought that language spell Ásúlfr cast back in Olshammar would work the same on all of us but I guess I'm the only one who can understand *and* read other languages. Weird."

"Very weird." Phoenix tried to curb his rising impatience. "But will it help us get *out* of here?" He reached out and grabbed her shoulder as she turned back to the hieroglyphs. "Jade! Focus! We're bricked up in this place and I'll bet horses use lots of oxygen. We need to get out of here!"

She looked around the room, frowning.

"Oh," he added as an afterthought, "and please tell me that bit about aliens was just a joke?"

Her expression cleared to a smile. "I'm pretty sure they wouldn't write something like that into the plot. There was no mention in the game manual, was there?"

Phoenix thought hard then shook his head, relieved. "Ultimate badguy to kill, Yu Dragon to master; plus five levels of evil henchmen, Gods, Elves, magic and monsters, yes; but no aliens, thank goodness."

"OK, so we just need to get out of here and get on our way to releasing the goddess Anuket from her prison then," Jade summed up. "And remember, we were told we have to release Anuket before the 'death of the moon'. I still don't know what that means, though."

"Then we have to start by getting out." He shrugged. They all stared around again, seeking inspiration.

"Secret passage?" She raised her brows at them.

"Already thought of it," Phoenix replied. Brynn snorted a laugh.

"But did anyone actually look for one?"

The three boys exchanged sheepish glances.

"Obviously not." Jade sighed, shaking her head. "Let's go then."

For a good ten minutes, the companions prowled around the temple, poking, pushing, twisting and prodding any likely-looking carving and stone they could find. The room got hotter and stuffier. Various bits of fur clothing from their time in Sweden and Asgard ended up on the altar, stripped as sweat began to drip. The horses' heads drooped and their breathing became laboured.

The group gathered again. Jade shoved their furs into the Hyllion Bagia and retrieved cooler clothing from within its endless, black depths. They all changed. It helped a bit but there was no ignoring the shortness of breath that now bothered all of them. They were running out of air.

"Why is the back wall so slanty?" Brynn wiped sweat from his face.

Jade tilted her head and eyed the wall. "I guess the temple is right up against the pyramid."

"What *is* a pyramid, anyway?" Brynn seemed aggrieved he didn't know.

Phoenix stared at the boy. It was hard to remember that Brynn came from a small village in early Roman Britain. He was so smart Phoenix often forgot they came from vastly different backgrounds. How *could* a peasant boy from 80AD know about other cultures? He couldn't exactly watch a documentary.

"The people of Ægyptus call them *mer*." Marcus' quiet comment intruded on his thoughts.

"They do?" Phoenix switched his gaze to him, amazed.

Normally Jade was the walking encyclopaedia. Marcus hardly said a word.

The Roman boy nodded. "Pyramid is the word the Greeks gave them. Mer are the tombs of dead kings – the *paros*, they call them."

"Pharaohs. Hey!" Jade's green eyes were wide. "How do you know so much?"

Phoenix sent her a narrow look. Was she jealous of Marcus' knowledge? She was pretty sensitive about being the smartest in the group.

"I came to Ægyptus with my uncle." Marcus shrugged. "He took me on a trading mission and we stayed in Alexandria for several months. My uncle thought I found the place and the people too fascinating and sent me home again. Rome owns Egypt but we are not well-liked here and he was worried I would get myself killed wandering around the streets on my own."

Phoenix stared at Marcus for several seconds, wondering what had prompted that long a speech.

Sweat dribbled into his eyes, reminding him of their situation.

"OK." He slapped his hands flat on the altar. "So we know the back wall is part of the pyramid – mer, I mean," he corrected himself. "Does that help us? Would there be a secret passage there?"

Jade shook her head. "Even if there was, it would only lead deeper into the pyramid, not to the outside. I have no idea when Snefru's Shining pyramid was built but the air in there would probably be bad if the tomb hasn't been robbed."

Brynn's eyes lit up. "Robbed? As in treasure?" He sent a covetous look at the sloping back wall. "Couldn't we just try? We've hardly found any treasure at all so far."

Phoenix laughed at the little thief and laid his sword on the altar. "C'mon, a magic sword is pretty good treasure, so is a magic bag full of Roman denarii and the Horn of Aurfanon that we used to summon help against the troll in Svealand."

The boy made a face. "I want some gold to take home with me, thanks. We can only use that horn twice more, anyway, remember?"

"Don't forget what our true mission is," Marcus reminded him, frowning.

Brynn waved him away. "I know, I know. We're out to kill Feng Zhudai, the big badguy. But hey, can't a guy dream of more than just revenge?" He blinked innocent brown eyes up at the Roman.

Marcus sent him a sceptical look.

"C'mon, you lot," Phoenix urged. "We've got to stay on track. We need to find a way out. Look." He pointed at the horses. One of them slipped to her knees and lay half on her side on the stone floor, panting.

Jade ran to the mare's side and muttered in her ear. One by one, she went to all five horses and spoke to them in low tones. One by one, the animals' breathing calmed and their eyes closed. She came back to the altar, looking a worried and guilty.

"I should have put them to sleep earlier. It would have saved oxygen and caused them less stress."

"It's a good idea, whenever," he assured her. He was rewarded with a quick, grateful look. "Back to the problem at hand. How do we get out?"

Marcus ran a hand through his short, dark hair. Brynn chewed on his bottom lip, eyes darting around the room. Jade tilted her head to one side and tapped one finger on her teeth. Her eyes widened. Phoenix looked at her, waiting.

"If you were at home, Phoenix," she mused, "how would you deal with this?"

It took him a second to understand what she meant then enlightenment hit and he smiled. Of course! If he were back in his bedroom in the real world, he'd be playing this as a computer game. It would be a simple matter to...

"I'd shoot my way out!" he exclaimed. "Blow up the entrance."

"What with?" Marcus frowned, iron-gloved hands spread. "We have only my bow, and my arrows won't penetrate rock."

"Oh." Phoenix sagged. Another idea bloomed. Iron gloves! He pointed at Marcus' belt. "Thor's hammer! That's it. You can use Mjölnir to smash the blocked up doorway and get us out. Go on! Do it now!" Stepping around the altar, he gripped Marcus's arm and shook it.

####

You'll have to get the next book to see what happens after that....

Discover other titles by Aiki Flinthart at:
http://aikiflinthart.weebly.com/

The 80AD series
(YA Adventure/Fantasy)

80AD Book 1: *The Jewel of Asgard*
80AD Book 2: *The Hammer of Thor*
80AD Book 3: *The Tekhen of Anuket*
80AD Book 4: *The Sudarshana*
80AD Book 5: *The Yu Dragon*

The Kalima Chronicles
(YA Adventure/Fantasy)

IRON (Book 1)

ABOUT THE AUTHOR

Aiki Flinthart lives in Australia. In between running a business and being with her husband of many years, she pursues writing, archery, knife-throwing, martial arts, art, music, bellydancing and watches too much television. After many years of writing for her own amusement, she finally decided to write for others' – and discovered it was even more fun.

Discover other titles by Aiki Flinthart at:
http://aikiflinthart.weebly.com/

Connect with Aiki on Facebook